Bloody work

Pulling their K-Bar knives, Brannigan and Mike moved slowly towards the two fighters who were guarding the hostages, appreciative of the noise from all the shooting some hundred meters away. They stopped a scant two paces from the guards, then Brannigan nodded the order to attack. Both SEALs struck simultaneously with the viciousness of cobras, driving the blades of the weapons under the back of the rib cages and up into vital areas where organs and arteries were located. The knives were violently twisted to enlarge the wounds. Brannigan and Mike kept their hands over the victims' mouths, working the knives until the mujahideen went limp. At that point the dead men were lowered gently to the ground to avoid unnecessary noise.

"Damn!" Mike whispered. "The son of a bitch vomited."

"It's a messy job no matter which way you cut it." Brannigan said. "No pun intended."

SEALS

JACK TERRAL

JOVE BOOKS, NEW YORK

THE BERKLEY PUBLISHING GROUP
Published by the Penguin Group
Penguin Group (USA) Inc.
375 Hudson Street, New York, New York 10014, USA
Penguin Group (Canada), 90 Eglinton Avenue East, Suite 700, Toronto, Ontario M4P 2Y3, Canada
(a division of Pearson Penguin Canada Inc.)
Penguin Books Ltd., 80 Strand, London WC2R 0RL, England
Penguin Group Ireland, 25 St. Stephen's Green, Dublin 2, Ireland (a division of Penguin Books Ltd.)
Penguin Group (Australia), 250 Camberwell Road, Camberwell, Victoria 3124, Australia
(a division of Pearson Australia Group Pty. Ltd.)
Penguin Books India Pvt. Ltd., 11 Community Centre, Panchsheel Park, New Delhi—110 017, India
Penguin Group (NZ), Cnr. Airbone and Rosedale Roads, Albany, Auckland 1310, New Zealand
(a division of Pearson New Zealand Ltd.)
Penguin Books (South Africa) (Pty.) Ltd., 24 Sturdee Avenue, Rosebank, Johannesburg 2196, South
Africa

Penguin Books Ltd., Registered Offices: 80 Strand, London WC2R 0RL, England.

This is a work of fiction. Names, characters, places, and incidents either are the product of the
author's imagination or are used fictitiously, and any resemblance to actual persons, living or dead,
business establishments, events, or locales is entirely coincidental. The publisher does not have any
control over and does not assume any responsibility for author or third-party websites or their
content.

SEALS

A Jove Book / published by arrangement with the author.

PRINTING HISTORY
Jove mass market edition / December 2005

Copyright © 2005 by The Berkley Publishing Group.
Cover design by Larry Rostant.
Text design by Kristin del Rosario.

ISBN: 0-515-14041-4

JOVE®
Jove Books are published by The Berkley Publishing Group,
a division of Penguin Group (USA) Inc.,
375 Hudson Street, New York, New York 10014.
JOVE is a registered trademark of Penguin Group (USA) Inc.
The "J" design is a trademark belonging to Penguin Group (USA) Inc.

PRINTED IN THE UNITED STATES OF AMERICA

10   9   8   7   6   5   4   3   2   1

To D. B. Burns
The World's Best Cousin

Special Acknowledgment to
Patrick E. Andrews

NOTE: Enlisted personnel in this book are identified by their ranks (petty officer third class, chief petty officer, master chief petty officer, etc.) rather than their ratings (boatswain's mate, yeoman, hospital corpsman, etc.) for clarification of status and position within the chain of command.

TABLE OF ORGANIZATION
BRANNIGAN'S BRIGANDS

FIRST SQUAD

William "Wild Bill" Brannigan
Lieutenant
Platoon Commander, First Squad
and Alpha Fire Team Leader

ALPHA FIRE TEAM, FIRST SQUAD

PO2C Mikael "Mike" Assad
(Recon/Scout)

PO2C Francisco "Frank" Gomez
(Radio Operator)

PO2C David "Dave" Leibowitz
(Recon/Scout)

BRAVO FIRE TEAM, FIRST SQUAD

SCPO Buford Dawkins
(Team Leader)

PO1C Mike "Connie" Concord
(Weapons/Fire Support)

PO2C Guttorm "Gutsy" Olson

PO3C Chadwick "Chad" Murchison

SECOND SQUAD

James "Jim" Cruiser
Lieutenant (J.G.)
Platoon Executive Officer, Second Squad
and Charlie Fire Team Leader

CHARLIE FIRE TEAM, SECOND SQUAD

PO2C Michael "Milly" Mills

PO2C Josef "Joe" Miskoski
(Demolitions)

PO3C Kevin Albee

DELTA FIRE TEAM, SECOND SQUAD

CPO Matthew "Matt" Gunnarson
(Team Leader)

PO1C Adam Clifford

PO2C Bruno Puglisi
(Weapons/Fire Support)

PO3C James Bradley
(Hospital Corpsman)

When you're wounded
an' left on Afghanistan's plains,
An' the women come out to cut up what remains,
Jest roll to your rifle and blow out your brains,
An' go to your Gawd like a soldier.

—Rudyard Kipling, *Barracks Room Ballads*

PROLOGUE

THE stranger walking through the bazaar showed obvious signs of having endured a difficult, strength-sapping ordeal. His clothing was dusty and sweat-caked as would be expected from a traveler who had made a long foot journey. His eyes, red with fatigue, looked out from under his bushy eyebrows in a dazed sort of way, and his thick black beard was unkempt and in bad need of a trim. What casual observers couldn't perceive was that deep inside the man's psyche, his waning strength and alertness functioned more out of stark fear than physical vigor. He struggled to keep moving in spite of the exhaustion that threatened to drop him to his knees.

A couple of thieves skulking in the marketplace caught sight of the limping man. They tried to determine if the fellow might be worth robbing. After a few moments of observation, they changed their minds about any attempts to overpower him, even though he seemed an easy mark. The

Kalashnikov assault rifle and bandoleer of ammunition across his chest gave evidence that his lifestyle was not a particularly peaceful one. An old Pashtun proverb taught that an exhausted man with a weapon was like a wounded tiger with teeth. Both could summon spiritual rage to fight off enemies.

The man seemed to know where he was going as he painfully shuffled through the crowd and lines of kiosks in the bazaar. He reached a narrow alleyway, and turned down it to walk past a blacksmith's stall before reaching a gun merchant's shop. He went inside and nodded to the clerk, who was cleaning a Heckler & Koch assault rifle in preparation for display.

The gun cleaner, a teenage boy, politely stood up. "*Asalaam aleikum,* sir. How may I serve you?"

"I wish to speak to Ilyas," the man said in a raspy voice.

The name he spoke caught the boy's interest. This was one of those special customers that came around now and then, and only the boss could speak to them. "I shall inform him, sir." He went through a curtained door and entered an interior room. His employer, Nader Abiska, sat in his favorite chair, sipping a hot cup of *sur chai* tea with milk. The boy approached him closely and whispered in his ear. "A man has come making inquiries about Ilyas."

Abiska pulled the Beretta automatic from his shoulder holster and went to the curtain to peer out. He could see the disheveled man leaning against the counter. The shop owner opened the curtain. "Come in."

The boy went out as the stranger entered. "Sit down," Abiska invited him.

"*Shukhria*—thanks," the man said gratefully, settling down onto the cushion of a wicker chair. "I am Ishaq."

"We thought you were dead," Abiska said.

"I damn near was."

"You are compromised, *la*?"

"True," Ishaq said wearily. "But I am still useful. I must get out of here."

"That can be arranged," Abiska said. "But first I suggest you take a few days to recover from whatever hardships you have endured so recently. You are obviously exhausted."

Ishaq shook his head. "There is no time to be wasted. I must get back."

CHAPTER 1

THE platoon was new, having been activated less than a month previously from veteran personnel drawn out of the ranks of SEAL Teams One, Three and Five. Most of the men knew each other well from having served together at various times in the past. They also had participated in many drinking sessions at the Fouled Anchor Tavern in Coronado, thus it didn't take them long to form into a cohesive unit. Within a short time they began referring to themselves as Brannigan's Brigands after their commanding officer Lieutenant William "Wild Bill" Brannigan.

They were a typically dedicated SEAL unit who had endured the near unendurable to earn their way into that elite branch of the United States Navy. Consequently, they performed their duties with exceptionally high morale, esprit de corps and a special élan. Among the other platoons, Brannigan's Brigands were noted to possess that little extra something special that occurs when the right chemistry develops among congruous people. The men even had unique T-shirts made up from a design a couple of the more artistic in the group had dreamed up. It consisted of the unit's name around the image of a leering buccaneer wearing a pirate hat. But instead of the usual skull-and-crossbones emblem on the headgear, it bore the eagle-and-trident insignia of the SEALs.

The platoon consisted of sixteen men divided into two squads of eight men each as per SOP. The squads were further broken down into pairs of four-man fire teams. The commanding officer led the First Squad and its Alpha Fire Team, while a senior chief petty officer honchoed the Bravo Fire Team. The platoon's executive officer commanded the Second Squad and bossed Charlie Fire Team, while a chief petty officer led the Deltas.

The Brigands' camaraderie went beyond duty hours. They spent most of their liberties in the company of other platoon members. Their favorite watering hole was the Fouled Anchor, owned by Salty Donovan, a leathery SEAL veteran who ran the establishment with his wife Dixie. Salty spent thirty years in the Navy, from 1967 to 1997, serving in Vietnam, Somalia, and the Gulf War. He had earned a chestful of decorations, including the Navy Cross, and stories of his exploits were still part of the SEAL legend.

It was a toss-up whether Salty or Dixie was in charge of the tavern. She was the feminine version of her husband, i.e., muscular, with an Irish temper. They were both in their fifties, and as an evening of boozing progressed, Dixie let Salty come out from behind the bar and sit with his old buddies or the young guys still on active duty, to knock back what seemed to be endless rounds of brew. Though he drank his share of the pitchers and more, Salty was most certainly not a tub of beer guts. Even after a long session of drinking, he would still be out early the next morning double-timing down Silver Strand Boulevard—AKA State Highway 75— all the way past the state beach before reversing direction for the return run. That was a distance of ten miles, and Salty arrived back home invigorated and ready to take on the world for the rest of the day.

Dixie, on the other hand, didn't exercise at all. But she didn't smoke or drink except for an occasional glass of wine and had inherited a robust natural health from her Irish ancestors. She and Salty didn't have any kids, and lavished their affections on the youngsters who patronized the tavern. Sometimes, when the testosterone and beer mixed a little too well, Dixie would break up the fights with kind words, a motherly smile and a hard grip around the muscular necks of the combatants. They always settled down to shake hands and let bygones be bygones. Dixie did not allow grudges.

And on occasions when reports came back of young SEALs giving their lives for their country in training accidents or combat, both Salty and Dixie wept with the deep grief of parents losing a child.

PLATOON HUT
4 AUGUST
0530 HOURS LOCAL

SENIOR Chief Petty Officer Buford Dawkins stood in front of the twelve men who were arranged in a reveille formation of two ranks of six. Buford, an Alabaman, was the senior enlisted man of the platoon, while his buddy Chief Petty Officer Matt Gunnarson ranked just under him. At that particular moment, Gunnarson stood off to the side, aloof and in somewhat of a bad mood. Neither of the two platoon officers was present, which meant that everyone was at Dawkins's mercy.

A bit of confusion was evident at this early morning formation. Everyone was dressed for the normally scheduled run. The platoon T-shirts, shorts and boots made up the prescribed uniform. The footgear was the skipper's idea. Wild Bill Brannigan considered jogging shoes candy-ass. If a

SEAL fought in boots, the Skipper reasoned, he should damn well run in them too.

The two chief petty officers, however, were not garbed for physical activity. They wore the normal BDUs. Senior Chief Dawkins gazed at his charges, the grin on his face making a blatant display of devious humor. "I see we have a dozen smiling faces this morning. That pleases me. Did y'all have a good time last night? Did you see your little honeys and get some sweet loving and affection from 'em?" He looked into the second rank, at Petty Officer Second Class Bruno Puglisi. "What about you, Bruno, ol' buddy? Score some poontang, did you?"

"I did awright, Chief," Puglisi said. "I always do awright, you know that."

"Well, I'm glad you did all right," Dawkins said. "In fact, I hope all y'all did just fine with the ladies. And I use that term loosely where y'all are concerned since I seen some of the sorry wimmen you guys attract. But, looks aside, it's my fondest wish that y'all got yourselves laid, re-laid and par-laid."

Joe Miskoski, holding the right guide's position, snickered. "That's real nice of you, Senior Chief. You ain't always this concerned about our love lives."

"I'm nice this morning, because I got some bad news for ever'body," Dawkins said. "If you didn't get any loving last night, that's too damn bad 'cause you sure as hell ain't gonna get another chance for romance for a good long while." He winked over at Gunnarson. "Tell 'em why, Chief."

"Because as of this very minute the platoon is on alert," Gunnarson said morosely. "We're all going into Isolation."

The men were caught between elation and disappointment. They were glad to be going on active ops since it would be the first for them as a platoon, but some of them had been working hard establishing some very satisfactory and shallow relationships with cuties in both Coronado and San Diego. Their activities with the female of the species had been progressing nicely.

"Is that why you aren't dressed for PT?" James Bradley asked, thinking of the pretty San Diego State University coed he was currently romancing.

"That's it," Dawkins answered. "Me and Chief Gunnarson was hauled out of our racks at oh-two-thirty for notification of the alert. Unfortunately it took so long to brief us, I wasn't able to arrange early chow for you this morning. It looks like you'll have to wait for box lunches to be brought into Isolation at noon."

"How about you, Chief?" Joe Miskoski asked. "Did you get early chow?"

"If you don't get to eat, then I don't eat," Dawkins answered. "I just hate having a guilty conscience. It was the same for Chief Gunnarson."

The men weren't surprised that the two had purposely skipped a meal because none of the others in the platoon would have breakfast that morning. This was typical in the SEALs, where bad luck, danger and food were shared equally in times of feast and famine, regardless of rank or position.

"Okay, now," Dawkins continued. "When I fall you out, go into the platoon hut and grab your alert bags. You can change into the uniforms you got in 'em when we get to Isolation. Albee! Murchison! You two get the Skipper's and Lieutenant Cruiser's. All right! Fall *out*!"

The men went inside to grab the parachute kit bags where their field gear, extra clothing, boots and other items needed for operations were packed. Once alerted, all they had to do was grab the bags and they were ready to go. In less than three-quarters of a minute they were back outside in formation with the baggage.

"So let's get ourselves into the middle of this exciting happening, shall we?" Dawkins said. "Atten-*hut*! Right, face! For'd, *harch*!"

The platoon marched out of the garrison toward the barbed wire and sentries in the Isolation area.

SENIOR Chief Petty Officer Buford Dawkins called the room to attention at the moment the door opened. The thirteen SEALs slid out from the desk chairs and braced. The first officer through the door was the Skipper, Lieutenant Wild Bill Brannigan. He was followed by his 2IC Lieutenant (J.G.) Jim Cruiser. Commander Thomas Carey, the team N3 officer, and a swarthy, bearded man in a civilian suit followed. Lieutenant Commander Ernest Berringer, the N2, brought up the rear.

"Take your seats, guys," Brannigan said. He was a tall, muscular man with light brown hair and bright blue eyes. His features had been coarsened by continued exposure to sun, sea and wind. The result was the rugged handsomeness that fascinated women, yet made them a bit uneasy. He grinned at his subordinates. "Good morning and welcome to the SEALs' favorite place in the world—Isolation. This is an auspicious occasion since it is the first time since our activation, and believe me, I'm as surprised to be here this morning as you are." He gestured toward the others who had followed him into the building. "Everyone knows our N2 and 3, and we have another guest. The gentleman with them is Ishaq. He is our asset for this mission, but circumstances preclude him from accompanying the platoon into the OA. He is here to supply us with all the useful information he can."

The SEALs knew that anyone introduced with only one name would be from that deep, dark world of clandestine operations where secrets, double-dealing and deadly encounters abounded.

"Therefore," Brannigan continued, "without further ado, I shall turn this session over to Commander Carey."

Carey went to the podium. "Although I know all of you, I'm pleased to meet you as Brannigan's Brigands. You already have a good reputation in the team. I hope you guys are rested and eager, because there's a hell of a job for you to do. First of all, the mission statement: You are to infiltrate into northeast Afghanistan and retrieve a defector." He paused a moment, adding, "That sounds simple enough, but let's get into the specifics."

Jim Cruiser chuckled. "Is this going to be one of those good news/bad news situations, sir?"

Carey shook his head. "This is bad news and *worst* news, Jim. I know everyone in the SEALs has become uneasy about the new tactical and strategical situations that have grown out of Nine-Eleven. We're used to quick hit-and-run raids in coastal areas. We always like to keep one foot in the water, but now we have to make deep penetrations into outlaw country and stay there awhile. On this particular operation, however, you have an estimated time limit of ten days. After that, consider it a lost cause."

"Just how far into Afghanistan are we going to penetrate, sir?" Brannigan asked.

"Approximately six hundred miles," Carey replied. "I say 'approximately' because we don't have any accurate maps of the location. Even Queen Victoria's troops in the heyday of the British Empire were unable to fight their way that far through the native tribes. I should mention you'll have roughly two hundred miles of Pakistan to fly over before you reach the Afghan border." He paused to let that bit of unpleasant information sink in. "You'll go from here to Station Bravo in Bahrain. From there you'll launch the operation to the OA, where you'll meet a guy at a certain location. Unfortunately, it was impossible to arrange a definite time for this linkup. But once you've gotten your hands on him, you can go into your exfiltration mode and bring him back with you. Questions? None at the moment? I'll be available for any that might pop up."

That ended the N3's briefing. There wasn't much to it, only a mission statement with some explanation hitting the basic intentions and goals. The execution portion of the OPLAN would be worked out by the Brigands among themselves.

They would have to relate that information to Carey in a session termed the briefback.

The next speaker was the N2 Berringer. He was a heavily muscled young man who was balding perceptively and prematurely. He spoke in a businesslike manner, delivering his introduction with military precision. "Your OA is in a territory tightly controlled by a local warlord who is decidedly unfriendly to infidels from the west. If those outsiders happen to be American, he goes ballistic. Anybody falling into his hands can expect an unpleasant, lingering death. In the overall strategic and tactical situation in Afghanistan, it is most important—I say again—*most* important to either win over or neutralize the warlords. The basic objective of the permanent removal of the Taliban along with the destruction of Al-Qaeda depends on controlling the warlords. The successful completion of your mission will be one step closer to reaching that goal. Now I'll turn the floor over to our asset Ishaq who will take over this intelligence briefing. He will be able to handle any questions that you may have."

The SEALs noticed that the man appeared haggard and tired as he walked to the podium. Although he was obviously a Middle-Easterner, when he spoke, he did so in a clipped, upper-class English accent:

"Good morning, gentleman. I have recently returned from your OA and I am quite familiar with that particular territory. As Commander Carey said, the area where you will make the linkup is uncharted, but I have prepared some hand-drawn maps for you that should prove at least a bit helpful."

Mike Assad raised his hand. "Are they to scale, sir?"

"I'm afraid I was only as accurate as my drawing hand and estimates permit," Ishaq said apologetically. "The terrain in which you shall be operating is in the highlands. There exist two prominent mountain ridges running north and south. They eventually break off into other ranges that have rugged foothills marked by deep ravines. A rather long and wide valley also dominates the area. However, none of this will affect you."

"Are you speaking of steep terrain?" Dave Leibowitz asked.

"Not so much that men in excellent physical condition would have trouble ascending the hills," Ishaq answered. "You'll need no mountain-climbing gear. There are also flat arable sections in the OA where the local farmers raise wheat, barley and the inevitable opium poppies."

Brannigan looked up from his note-taking. "Who's running the show in that particular spot?"

"The area is tightly controlled by a rather nasty chap who goes by the name of Ayyuub Durtami. He is the warlord and absolute ruler, collecting taxes, forcing young men into his fighting band, and in general has qualified as the poster lad for cruelty and despotism." He smiled. "I'm afraid that is about all I learned of him during my ninety-day stay in his fiefdom."

"How many men are in his private army?" Chief Matt Gunnarson asked.

"There is no exact count since he's continually adding mujahideen to his roster while chopping off the heads of the poor blokes who displease him," Ishaq said. "But I can confidently tell you that you can expect him to be able to muster somewhere between two hundred and three hundred able-bodied fighters." He showed a sympathetic smile. "I see there are sixteen of you chaps."

"We'll each have to whack around eighteen to twenty of the rat bastards," Bruno Puglisi remarked. "No problem."

"Right," Ishaq said. "Warlord Durtami operates out of a fortified compound that is surrounded by a mud-brick wall some twelve feet high and a yard thick. It is approximately seventy-five yards on each of four sides. He has firing positions all along the perimeter and machine gun posts in sandbagged towers at each corner. At least a third of these firing positions are manned twenty-four hours a day."

"What sort of weapons can he deploy?" Petty Officer First Class Connie Concord asked.

"The AK-47 is his basic issue," Ishaq answered. "He's short of RPGs since most of those have been snapped up for the nasty blokes in Iraq. He has a brother-in-law by the name of Hassan Khamami. Khamami as a warlord makes Durtami look like a juvenile delinquent. He has an extremely large fighting force and controls a vast area of land. I recommend you avoid him if at all possible."

"We'll sure as hell try," Brannigan said. "Who is this defector we'll be linking up with?"

"His name is Omar Kariska," Ishaq replied. "The meeting place is a bombed-out village marked on the map. The challenge will be to mention a number between one and nine in the Pashto language. The password is to reply in a number that adds up to ten when applied to the challenge."

Brannigan frowned. "None of us speak Pashto."

"I have written out the pronunciation of the necessary numerals," Ishaq said. "You will have to memorize them."

As Ishaq continued to deliver his description of the enemy, the N2 passed out copies of the hand-drawn maps along with satellite images of the OA. When the asset finished his presentation, the SEALs felt somewhat better informed, but the lack of precise information was acute enough that it was hard to come up with meaningful questions.

Brannigan summed it up by saying, "In other words, this will be a typical mission where we will have to make up the rules as the game progresses."

"Correct," Berringer interjected. "And the penalties for erroneous reasoning or guesses can easily result in things going terribly wrong."

Commander Carey took over the proceedings. "Okay, men. That's all we've got for you. It's pretty sketchy, so you're going to be carrying quite a load when it comes to forming your OPLAN. Are there any questions?"

"A pretty basic one, sir," Brannigan said, standing up. "It may not be our business or only need-to-know information, but I'm curious as to the long-range benefits of bringing this Kariska guy out of the OA."

Berringer fielded that question. "Simply stated: he has a hell of a lot of valuable information."

"This is a cog in the wheel that is turning Afghanistan into a secular democracy," Carey explained further. "The latest intelligence, most of it garnered by Mr. Ishaq, is that the warlords are doing their damnedest to stop all efforts to democratize Afghanistan. If they succeed, we can expect decades of war in the Middle East. It will become a base of operation for every Islamic terrorist group that exists. That is all, gentlemen. We wish you a good day and will see you for the briefback."

The three visitors trooped out of the Isolation area, and Brannigan took the floor, checking his notebook. "Okay. Here're your assignments." The men listened carefully to the pre-mission jobs that were so important.

Petty Officers Second Class Mike Assad and Dave Leibowitz were assigned to work out the route from the DZ or LZ to the meeting place with the defector. The two, who served as scouts and recon, were known as the "Odd Couple" among the other members of the platoon because Mike was an Arab-American and Dave Jewish. But despite that mix that could have been volatile, they were the best of buddies. They had a lot in common. Both had been disappointments to their families for their lack of interest in religion, making money or getting an advanced education. Each disliked Palestinian terrorists and Israeli settlers, who moved into disputed areas with equal intensity. Assad and Leibowitz were dedicated SEALs and Americans who liked taking direct actions to solve problems.

The responsibilities for medical matters were handed over to Petty Officer Third Class James Bradley. This quiet African-American had graduated from the premed course at Boston University, but had decided against pursuing his MD degree out of deep patriotism. He enlisted in the Navy and volunteered for the SEALs to fight against terrorism. His background made him a natural to score a hospital corpsmen's rating, and he planned on taking advantage of the NCP later on to become a Navy doctor.

Bruno Puglisi, a petty officer second class from South

Philadelphia, came from a mob family. With most of his male relatives either whacked or jailed, he decided the best place for him to find a macho lifestyle was in the Navy SEALs. He had a special affinity for hand-fired weaponry—particularly the automatic variety—and he was assigned to the maintenance, repair and issue of all firearms used in the platoon. Additionally, Puglisi was the platoon sniper. At other times he was one-half of the fire support element, working with Petty Officer First Class Connie Concord, who grew up in rural Arkansas, spent a boyhood hunting and was an expert with shotguns and the M-203 grenade launcher.

Demolitions were the bailiwick of Joe Miskoski, a petty officer second class who had attended the Army's Special Warfare Center Demolition Course. He had become a virtual artist with C4 plastic explosive, claymore mines, detonation cord, satchel charges and limpet mines.

All the communications in the Brigands was in the capable hands of Petty Officer Second Class Frank Gomez, who not only operated radios but was expert in keeping them in good working order.

The two chief petty officers Dawkins and Gunnarson were tasked with choosing the right equipment and gear for whatever jobs the platoon drew.

When all the assignments had been made, Lieutenant Brannigan finished his discourse with a final announcement. "Lieutenant Cruiser and I will work out the infiltration and exfiltration. The rest of you stand by for other tasks that will be popping up from time to time. There's going to be a lot of fetching and carrying. That's it, guys. Turn to!"

There was a scuffling of desks and boots on the deck as they left the area to attend to their assigned duties.

CHAPTER 2

THE desks were arranged in a semicircle, and a table with two chairs had been placed to the direct front of the room. Commander Tom Carey and Lieutenant Commander Ernest Berringer occupied these. They had maps and notebooks opened, and were poised to get into the proceedings of the debriefing. A blown-up photograph of the OA taken from satellite imagery was mounted on the wall. There was a large urn of the Navy's version of coffee sitting on an ammo box, and every man in the room had a steaming cup of the invigorating brew sitting in front of him.

"Have you all learned to count from one to ten in Pashto?" Berringer asked. When everyone nodded affirmatively, he said, "I haven't learned them but I wrote them down." He looked over at Dave Leibowitz. *"Salor!"*

Dave instantly replied, *"Shpag!"*

"Right!" Berringer said. "Four and six make ten."

"Now that we've gone through basic Pashto arithmetic,"

Carey said, "let's get on with the briefing. We're both ready, guys. Shoot."

Lieutenant Bill Brannigan sat off to one side, relaxed and at ease while his 2IC Jim Cruiser took the floor. Cruiser used his laser beam pointer to indicate a spot on the satellite photograph. "We will be making a HALO infiltration and will land on this DZ. The jump will be executed at the twilight hour of eighteen-forty-five. You will note then there are two mountain ridges between that area and"—he shifted the red dot of light—"there! That is where the warlord's compound is located."

Carey leaned forward to get a better look. "That must be some five miles, Lieutenant. Why so far from the DZ?"

"Security of the jump, sir," Cruiser explained. "We'll exit the aircraft at twelve thousand feet AGL and open at thirty-five hundred. That will give us minimum exposure just before we descend out of view below the mountaintops." He moved the laser again. "Here is where we'll set up a base camp on the western ridge. The idea is to go to the contact point over here across the two mountains. We have dubbed the ridge nearest the DZ as West Ridge. The one nearest the contact point is called East Ridge." Another laser shift to the bombed-out village. "Our contact party will link up with the defector here and head directly back to the base camp. After calling in the aircraft for exfiltration, we will meet it there on the DZ that then becomes an LZ."

"Can a C-130 land there?" the intelligence officer, Berringer, asked.

"Yes, sir," Cruiser answered. "I checked with Mr. Ishaq and he assured me it was a suitable location. The terrain is firm and flat."

"Will there be any special platoon equipment?" Carey inquired.

"No, sir," Cruiser said. "There's no need for that. Everyone will be capable of carrying the necessary gear of their specialty to accomplish the mission."

When the 2IC finished his presentation, Petty Officer

Second Class Mike Assad took the floor. "The only recon Petty Officer Leibowitz and I could do was obviously a map reconnaissance, sir," he explained. "We combined that with questions to Mr. Ishaq to figure out the best course. Our contact party will follow this route." He now began employing his own laser beam. "There is an easy way down from the base camp on West Ridge to the first valley floor. There seems to be plenty of cover. The problem is crossing that valley, because it has only sparse, skimpy brush. We're going to have to adopt a heavy-security mode as we go across. A single skirmish line would be best, since it would be the fastest way. And if we are attacked from the direction of the compound, all our firepower will be going directly to our front. From that point on we go into fire-and-maneuver as the situation dictates."

"What about that second ridge line, Petty Officer?" Carey asked. "I'm speaking of the one you people are calling East Ridge. That's an open, exposed top and the side leading down to the flat lands where the contact point is located hasn't got as much as a blade of grass on it."

"Our guys can move along here below the ridge line on the far side from the contact point," Mike said. "We found a place right here that looks down on the village where the defector is supposed to show up. There's excellent concealment in the rocks here where we can provide covering fire for the contact party if necessary. There shouldn't be more than three or four guys going down for the meet, so that leaves fourteen of us to back 'em up."

"Looks good to me," Carey remarked, writing in his notebook.

James Bradley took Mike's place. With no reason to put on a dog-and-pony show, he stood empty-handed in front of the two officers. "Sir, I'm the platoon hospital corpsman. I'm going to supply each man an emergency medical kit that will fit in a pocket of his assault vest. This will be a basic 'help yourself' setup with a battle dressing and an Ace bandage. There will also be some codeine and morphine, along with sedatives, stimulants and a couple of sets of pills for constipation and diarrhea. I'll be bringing along my own field surgical kit for major trauma. That will include extra battle dressings, painkillers, lactate solution and catheter kits, among other items. All this is standard."

"It sounds like you've got everything covered in your health care program," Carey remarked.

"Yes, sir," James said. "And I do make house calls and my fees are reasonable."

Chuckles rippled across the room and Berringer said, "And no insurance forms to fill out either, I bet."

Weapons and fire support were next on the agenda. Petty Officer First Class Connie Concord was the senior man in that effort, but he was never fond of public speaking, so he delegated the function to his only subordinate, Petty Officer Second Class Bruno Puglisi, who loved an audience. Puglisi, like Bradley, had no use for the satellite map. He cut straight to the chase. "All the guys is gonna be packing SIG Sauer nine-millimeter auto pistols in drop holsters. They'll also be bringing along two extra fifteen-round magazines in addition to the one in the weapon. That's forty-five friggin' rounds, y'know? Plenty, believe me. If some dumb bastard gets himself into a position where he's gotta use his pistol and shoot up that many bullets, he's either the worst shot this side o' Jersey or the unluckiest guy that ever survived Hell Week."

"Well said, Puglisi," Carey remarked.

"Right, sir. Ever'body except Petty Officer Concord and me is gonna go on the mission with CAR-15s and five extra thirty-round magazines. Me and him is gonna have M-16 rifles along with M-203 grenade launchers. We'll take along plenty of HE, star shells and smoke rounds for signaling on the LZ."

"What about machine gun fire support?" Carey asked.

"We won't need it, sir," Puglisi said. "Between the M-16s and the CAR-15s we'll be able to put out all the firepower we need. An M-60 machine gun and all that ammo it needs is too frigging heavy. Another thing to take into consideration is that we'd have to pull a guy out of one of the fire teams as a bullet toter."

"If the lieutenant has faith in your choice, then it's fine with us, Puglisi," Carey said. "Next!"

"I'm in charge of commo," Petty Officer Second Class Frank Gomez announced to the N2 and N3. "Everybody is going to get a LASH radio headset for intra-platoon use. The guys can speak in whispers and the throat mike will pick it up and transmit it like normal speech. That'll come in handy if the bad guys are nearby. As for me, since I'll be communicating with the aircraft for the pickup, I'm bringing along an AN/PSC-5 Shadowfire radio. The nearly twenty pounds of weight is worth putting up with in case there is a need for long-range commo. I'm planning on leaving it at the base camp when we move out to pick up the defector."

"It seems you have that aspect of the operation well thought out, Petty Officer," Berringer said. He looked over the other men. "What about demolitions?"

Petty Officer Joe Miskoski got to his feet. "No boom-boom, sir. On this trip I'm gonna be strictly a grunt."

"Now let's hear about your other gear," Berringer said.

This was the signal for Chief Petty Officer Matt Gunnarson to give his pitch. "Me and Senior Chief Dawkins worked out the basic load that will affect ever'body. First line equipment is what the guys will wear. It'll be the usual BDU, and we recommend an emergency compass, matches, a good Swiss Army knife, a couple of Powerbars and some condoms. The rubbers won't be for loving since there ain't gonna be much of a chance to meet any friendly ladies out there. But they'll be real handy for waterproofing and dust-proofing stuff."

Carey interrupted. "You say you *recommend* those items?"

"When me and the senior chief *recommend* a piece of equipment, every swinging dick better damn well have it on him."

"Understood, Chief," Carey stated.

Chief Gunnarson continued. "The platoon also needs to take along field jackets since it can get really cool in the highlands of Afghanistan, even in August."

"Sounds satisfactory for a short mission like this," Carey said. "Are you contemplating combat vests or LBEs?"

"Vests, sir," Gunnarson answered. "That's where we'll stick our second line equipment. That stuff consists of a day's worth of MREs, the medical kit Petty Officer Bradley is handing out, a two-quart canteen, a couple o' frag grenades, binoculars, a GPS and water purification tablets."

"I take it that the guys will be able to bring along some items of their own choice," Carey remarked.

"Right, sir," Gunnarson said. "They're the ones that'll hump the stuff, so I'm sure there won't be any unnecessary items. The rucksacks will be for the third line equipment. That'll be the basic load of MREs, entrenching tool, poncho, poncho liner, foam mattress, extra socks, water bladder, an extra BDU, night vision goggles and those other goodies I just mentioned. That's it, sir."

"What about sleeping bags?" Berringer asked.

"We won't need 'em, sir," Gunnarson answered. "The mission shouldn't go on that long."

"Don't forget contingencies, Chief," Carey cautioned him.

"If there's a delay, we can make envelope rolls out of the ponchos and liners to sleep in. If we keep our clothes on and we put them foam mattresses between us and the ground, we'll all sleep toasty warm."

Carey smiled at the tough SEAL using a term like "toasty warm." He glanced over at Bill Brannigan. "It seems you're well prepared for the operational part of the mission. Now it's my turn. Here's your itinerary. You'll fly from North Island via C-130 on a easterly flight with the necessary refueling stops. You'll make station time aboard the aircraft at eighteen hundred hours this evening. The minute the landing gear goes up, you're between commands. Your ETA at Station Bravo in Bahrain will be oh-six-hundred local on 7 August.

At that point, the Army S-3 of the area's SOCOM will take you under his wing." He picked up his papers and put them in his briefcase. "Now, this just in. I saved it for the last to avoid interrupting the debriefing. Be prepared to extend your mission if so ordered. The situation is very unstable at the moment."

"It won't change much," Brannigan said. "We might have to make a couple of adjustments. No sweat. The problem will be resupply if we need it. That's out of our hands."

"That will be handled by SOCOM in the area," Berringer interjected.

"They damn well better handle it perfectly or we'll be in deep shit," Brannigan commented dryly.

"In a situation like that you'll have to hope for the best," Carey said. "If there're no more comments or questions, I say good luck and God bless."

After the two staff officers exited Isolation, Senior Chief Buford Dawkins went into his senior enlisted man's mode. "All right! Equipment inspection in one half hour! Turn to it, gentlemen!"

WARLORD DURTAMI'S COMPOUND
AFGHANISTAN
1830 HOURS LOCAL

THE bucolic fort was well organized, with a dozen mud buildings behind a high, thick defensive wall. The largest structure was Durtami's residence, and there was also a small village of huts where the mujahideen lived with their families. Some portable storage containers and a vehicle park with pickup trucks, motor-rickshaws and motorbikes made up the remainder of the layout.

The narrow streets were laid out in a zigzag pattern to create sudden ninety-degree turns, then a short distance before the street veered back in the original direction. There was excellent reasoning behind the asymmetrical arrangement.

Such streets could be easily defended, while attackers, unable to see ahead any great distance, would have to slow down at each intersection, where gunmen would be waiting to ambush them.

Everyone living within the walls was armed to the teeth. Even ten- to twelve-year-old boys toted AK-47s, eagerly waiting to reach the age to become mujahideen and fight the many enemies of their community. Not far away was a village where the farmers who cultivated opium poppies lived. This was the area's main source of income.

Warlord Durtami and his people called themselves Pashtuns, though outsiders had named them Pathans sometime nearly two hundred years before. The Pashtuns spoke their own language called Pashto and had a long warrior tradition that went back eons. This male-dominated society governed itself with a set of laws and rules they called *Pashtunwali.* This code of conduct had four main elements:

Melmastia—a requirement for showing hospitality to strangers. Many times Warlord Durtami ignored this stipulation. All strangers were potential enemies to this schizophrenic megalomaniac.

Badal—an obligation to avenge any insult, mistreatment or injustice. Durtami twisted this one to suit his personal needs. The fact that he started all the trouble he faced meant little to him. This, like *melmastia,* was more for strangers than his own people.

Nanwatai—a requirement to submit completely to anyone who is victorious over you. The loser must beg forgiveness and admit fault, while the victor is expected to be magnanimous. This was the situation in which Durtami enthusiastically practiced *badal* when outsiders were concerned.

Nang involved sexual matters. A man must defend the honor of his family's women to the death. A lingering glance, unwarranted conversation, flirting or having sex with a woman meant death to the couple involved. The warlord was devout in the observance of this most important law. Sexual matters were the main reasons behind the bloodiest intracommunity conflicts, and no quarter was given or expected in these situations. It was one-sided where men were concerned, however. A raped woman was punished as harshly as her rapist.

The territory that Durtami controlled was part of Afghanistan the British had occupied while spending many long years fighting his Pashtun ancestors in the nineteenth century. This fierce resistance was the biggest problem Queen Victoria's soldiers faced. In desperation, they constructed a long string of forts to contain these native rebels, but this did little to bring the situation under control. Eventually, things got so bad that the Pashtuns were given complete rule over their own territory with a promise that they would be left alone. This didn't make the warlike people all that happy, and over the decades there were times when they rebelled in fury; fighting skirmishes with the British troops on many occasions. As late as 1937 the Pashtuns attacked and massacred an entire British column in one memorable battle.

WARLORD Ayyub Durtami and his chief lieutenant, Ahmet Kharani, had just returned from inspecting the compound redoubts, and settled down at a table in the warlord's private quarters. The warlord was a thin, wiry man with a pointed beard. His eyes betrayed his devious and suspicious attitudes.

Within moments three prepubescent girls appeared carrying an urn of *khawa* green tea, small cups and a platter of deep-fried vegetables called *pakoras*. They were at an age where *nang* did not apply to them. The warlord and Kharani smiled and spoke to them openly in a friendly, paternal way as the service was set out. The young females smiled shyly, pleased by the pleasant attention.

After the girls left, Kharani took a sip of tea. "It appears that the attacks of the Taliban on the balloting centers in the cities will not stop any more planned elections."

Durtami shrugged. "I do not concern myself with such madness. Even if they hold a thousand more elections, my activities will never be governed by a crowd of idiot voters being given unlicensed liberties by the lackeys of infidels."

"We are too far away for such activities to seriously affect us," Kharani said, taking a piece of *pakora* and biting into it. "The only thing that worries me is the formation of a national army."

"Only fret about a *large* national army," Durtami counseled him. "Sparse patrol activity by a weak force will never harm us. They would be like fleas biting at our ankles."

"We do not want the poppy crops threatened, *Amir*," Kharani said.

"I will be able to provide all the necessary protection for the farmers," Durtami assured him.

A knock on the door sounded, and one of the sentries on duty outside opened it and peered into the room. "Hamid is here to see you, *Amir*."

"Send him in," Durtami ordered. He looked over at Kharani. "I hope he has been able to drag some useful information out of that cursed prisoner."

Hamid walked in, smiling broadly. He was a large, fat man, but the thick layer of flesh on his body covered solid muscle beneath, and he served as the warlord's jailer and inquisitor. "I have broken Kariska, *Amir*."

"*Der khey*—very good!" Durtami said. "I thought he would have died by now."

"He begs for death even as we speak," Hamid said. "Beatings meant nothing to him. It was fire that finally brought him to the point that he wished the torment to stop. Branding and hot coals loosen even the most stubborn of tongues."

"What information have you?" Kharani asked impatiently. He both disliked and feared the torturer.

"When the man Ishaq snuck away, he promised Kariska he could get people to come here and fetch him," Hamid said. "They were to meet him at the village that was attacked by the Soviet helicopters so many years ago."

"Why would Kariska help him sneak away from us?" Durtami asked. "We knew they were friends. That is why we chose to question Kariska after we noticed Ishaq's absence."

"Kariska promised to tell all he knew about the activities in this area," Hamid said. "It would serve the infidels well in working out a way to defeat us and destroy the poppy cultivation."

"That makes sense, *Amir*," Kharani said to his chief. "The infidels and their lackeys cannot fully control Afghanistan until the warlords are deprived of the money made from heroin."

"He said the people coming to get him would give him a number between one and nine," Hamid said. "Kariska would then say a number that added up to ten. That would prove he is the man they came for."

"They would have to keep it that simple for the stupid bumpkin," Durtami said with a laugh. "When is this meeting going to take place?"

"At any time," Hamid said, "between midnight and dawn. No particular day was picked."

Durtami smiled at Kharani. "From now on, put men out by that old village every night between midnight and dawn. They will stay there until the infidels try to make a contact."

"We shall begin tonight, *Amir*," Kharani said.

Durtami turned to Hamid. "You have done well. I will see that two goats are sent to your house."

"*Shukhria*—thank you, *Amir*!" Hamid exclaimed. "What shall I do with the prisoner Kariska?"

"He has had a rest now," Durtami said. "Go back and take him to death. Use that fire that he fears so much. Perhaps as he suffers under the torment he will ponder the terrible price of betrayal." He turned to Kharani. "Organize the group to go to the village. This is something that must be dealt with successfully."

"I will pick only the best fighters, *Amir*," Kharani promised.

CHAPTER 3

LIEUTENANT Bill Brannigan glumly sat in the web seat just aft of the entrance to the cockpit. His mood seemed bad enough that the rest of the platoon, including his 2IC and chief petty officers, avoided him. Any comments or questions directed to the CO were met with curt, near angry responses.

As their leader seethed in solitude, the other Brigands coped in their individual ways with the monotony of the long and unpressurized airplane ride. Most were sleeping, but the Odd Couple Mike Assad and Dave Leibowitz were deeply involved in a pinochle game while others read paperback books. A few simply stared at nothing, their eyes directed at, but not focused on, the bulkheads opposite them. The more pensive platoon members had their minds turned to girlfriends, families back home, plans for their next furlough and dozens of other matters important to servicemen on active duty.

Brannigan was in that gloomily pensive mood because of
a deep personal problem. The time spent in Isolation had
worsened this inner tension because he was unable to telephone his wife Lisa. Things had been getting worse between
the couple. She was an aviator in a Prowler EA-6B squadron
at NAS North Island, not far from the naval amphibious
base the SEALs called home. Brannigan had met Lisa at
the North Island Officers' Club three years earlier. He'd
gone there to cruise the local civilian women who hung
out in the place on Saturday nights. These ladies were also
cruising, looking to hook up with handsome officers. Normally Brannigan concentrated on them without giving ser-
vicewomen a second glance, but the beautiful lady wearing a
summer khaki uniform sporting aviator wings caught his
eye. He tried to ignore her initially, but finally had to make
his move. The attraction turned out to be mutual, and that
particular evening was the beginning of a year of steady
dating.

When they married, the union seemed destined for long
happiness. But after a little more than a year, a tension
evolved between them, and they went through several crises,
as did all families where both husband and wife served in
the armed forces. Long separations and conflict of career
interests were the main culprits behind the unpleasantness.
But the strife between the Brannigans had additional friction
because of his being a SEAL.

This was the root of their biggest problem: he couldn't
stand her pilot friends. Several times yearly he was required
to attend functions of her squadron's officers, and Brannigan
found it difficult to act civil, much less pleasant, in their
presence. He fully realized that they did an important and
useful job for the United States Navy, and they were damn
good at it. The aircraft they flew jammed enemy weapons
systems and communications and were the most powerful
electronic warfare airplanes in a CVBG. Lisa and her friends
also had to meet high standards in the training that qualified
them as aviators, but it was nothing like the muscle-cramping,

sleepless, bone-chilling, sometimes frightening and exhausting ordeal of BUD/S. As far as Wild Bill Brannigan was concerned, this was a case of *them* and *us*.

Part of the contempt he directed toward the aviators stemmed from the fact that even when they were out with the fleet in harm's way, they weren't in combat situations very long. Within a couple of hours they would be back aboard a carrier or in an officers' club at some air station. They had hot chow served on china; never had to wear dirty clothing; were always well rested unless they went out partying; and they slept between sheets with roofs over their heads to keep away foul weather.

Lieutenant Bill Brannigan simply could not relate to them.

He had nothing in common with their attitudes or life experiences. As a schoolboy, Brannigan had spent at least one or two sessions in detention every week. He was notorious for turning in his homework late or not at all, and he detested the classroom environment. From the way those Navy aviators spoke of their school days, they must have all been on the honor roll and the pets of the faculty. Only a strong desire to attend Annapolis and have a career in the Navy had straightened Brannigan out as a student in high school, but he never lost his dislike of book learning.

Another thing that irritated him about the pilots was the workaday problems they complained about. This suffering seemed to center around having to fly a few extra patrols now and then or putting up with some sassy aviation machinist's mate who wouldn't take any shit off them. At times when he mentioned something going on in the SEALs, they looked at Brannigan like he was crazy as hell for getting himself into such a gut-pounding branch of the Navy. Their glances of dismay seemed to say that only a Neanderthal would spend six impossibly grueling months qualifying to live a demanding life fraught with danger, hardships and incredible discomfort.

Candy asses!

Brannigan and Lisa had gone to a formal function at the NAS officers' club a week before. Maybe he did drink a little too much, and maybe he wasn't real sure what that one aviator had said that pissed him off, but it must have been insulting or he wouldn't have gotten so goddamn mad and thrown the guy across the hors d'oeuvre table. Shrimp, cheeses, puffy delicacies and other delectable goodies went flying against the wall amid gasps and cries of shock and admonishment.

Needless to say, there was one hell of a showdown when he and Lisa got home later that night. And things hadn't improved one iota since then. Maybe it was a good thing this mission popped up after all; it gave the couple some time apart that would provide a bit of a cooling off period.

Brannigan yawned, closed his eyes and drifted off into a restless nap amid the thunder of the four T56 turboprop engines.

STATION BRAVO, BAHRAIN
7 AUGUST

THE platoon had been involved in several tasks at the base, which took a couple of hours, before they were able to go to the rigger shed to chute up. When they first arrived on station, a young Army Special Forces lieutenant from SO-COM had met them and taken them over to the armory to draw ammunition. After the 9- and 5.56-millimeter rounds and HE, illumination and smoke grenades for the M-203s were issued, the platoon was taken to an empty tent to make the final preparations on their gear.

Station Bravo was a new and unfinished garrison, and the closest thing to permanent buildings were portable models that looked like oversized mobile or manufactured homes. These resembled the domiciles that blew away in hurricanes and tornados, but all the command, staff and logistics matters were conducted in the structures.

The billets were no more than fifteen-by-twenty tents, with canvas sides that could be rolled up to expose netting to keep out insects. During the summer, the grumpy inhabitants of these crude quarters baked from the suffocating heat, getting a little relief from floor fans placed at strategic locations. But at those times when cooling breezes wafted in from the Persian Gulf, it wasn't really all that bad.

After loading magazines and stowing grenades, the Brigands made final preparations of their gear. The two officers and chiefs had to attend a session with the flight crew for final coordination of the route and azimuth over the DZ. While this was going on, the rest of the platoon settled down in the tent to grab some z's and store up energy for the ordeal ahead.

RIGGER SHED
1200 HOURS LOCAL

THE jumpmaster briefing given by Senior Chief Petty Officer Buford Dawkins was alarmingly short. He knew nothing of the velocity or direction of winds across the DZ. At least the ASL altitude of that important plot of ground was known, from data supplied by fighter pilots who had flown support missions in the vicinity. That meant the wrist altimeters could be set accurately for the jump. Dawkins also was unaware of what the exact direction of flight would be, except that it might be sort of southerly to northerly or sort of northerly to southerly. One way or another it had to run either up or down along the edge of the terrain feature the SEALs had named West Ridge. The flight crew would determine which direction, and react accordingly.

At least the senior chief could be precise about his jumpmaster inspection. He formed the men up in two rows of seven, and he and Chief Petty Officer Matt Gunnarson made careful examinations of the men's equipment, parachutes and everything that was strapped and buckled onto their bodies.

The first items of attention were the weapons. The slings had to be routed over the left shoulder, under the main lift webbing and to the outside of the chest strap. The SEALs also had to inspect the weapons' tie-downs, making sure they were between the belly band extension and the jumper. From there the two chiefs' attention was directed to the way the harnesses fit, the seating of rip cords, no twists in risers and a few dozen other things that, if ignored, had the very real potential of changing a routine jump into a situation where injuries or even death were more probable than possible. When the two chiefs finished with the platoon, they checked out each other with just as much thoroughness.

"Okay, guys," Dawkins said when Gunnarson had finished with him. "We are now deeply imbedded into the domain of Mr. Murphy and his law."

"That's right," Gunnarson said in his gloomy style. "And that law says that if anything can go wrong, it prob'ly will, just as sure as shit stinks."

"But don't worry," Dawkins added. "If you clobber into the DZ in the morning, you still get paid for all day."

Brannigan stepped forward. "And with those cheerful statements ringing in your ears, I'll lead you out to the aircraft."

ON THE RUNWAY
1500 HOURS LOCAL

THE engines were wide open, trying hard to pull the aircraft through the pressure of the brakes that held the flying machine in check. When the correct amount of RPM was reached, the pilot released the mechanical, electrical and hydraulic restraints, and the massive C-130 leaped like an eager racehorse charging out of the starting gate. The sound was deafening and the fuselage shook like it would fly apart, until the sudden smoothness of the forward motion showed it was now airborne. The banging and squeaking of the landing gear being raised sounded next, as the airplane climbed upward into the dark sky.

The senior chief was the jumpmaster, and as such he was in charge of the back of the aircraft. Even Lieutenants Brannigan and Cruiser were required to obey his orders during the flight. Before takeoff, Dawkins ordered everyone to don helmets and strap them down. The wearing of this protective headgear was mandatory before the airplane left the ground. This was one of the riskiest parts of any flight, and in case the C-130 suddenly lost power and crashed into the earth, any unstrapped helmets would be like projectiles flying around the interior of the fuselage, inflicting injury and even death on anyone they slammed into.

When Dawkins figured the aircraft was climbing safely, he gave the word that everyone could remove his helmet and unfasten his seat belt. Most of the men simply undid the helmet straps and remained belted in. This was a good time to doze a bit. Psychologists explained this strange habit as being the subconscious mind's way of dealing with pre-jump jitters by retreating from reality into peaceful slumber.

The psychologists were 100 percent correct.

OVER AFGHANISTAN
1825 HOURS LOCAL

THE loadmaster came down from the cockpit to give the twenty-minute warning to the jumpmaster. Dawkins got up out of his web seat and went from man to man to make sure they were all awake. He also issued orders to put on helmets and strap them down. Now was the time for the jumpers to begin hooking their gear onto the parachute webbing. They worked in teams, helping each other through the process. After dozens of jumps, they were quick and efficient. When the job was done, they knelt down on the gear. This was a lot easier than trying to sit back down on the seats with rucksacks strapped to their asses.

1835 HOURS LOCAL

WHEN the ten-minute warning was issued, Dawkins went aft, then turned and held up both hands with his fingers spread to indicate the number ten. Then he checked the red jump and/or caution light to make sure it was functioning properly. The doors in the rear slowly opened as the loadmaster manipulated the controls.

OVER THE OA
1842 HOURS LOCAL

BUFORD raised his right arm up from his side to signal the command STAND UP. The men struggled to get to their feet. The next gesture the senior chief displayed was to take his right arm and touch his helmet, to let the jumpers know it was time to move to the rear and join him. Lieutenant Bill Brannigan took the lead, walking to the opened tail area with the others following. This was a platoon custom established during their first jumps as a unit; the skipper would always be the first out of the aircraft. He glanced down twelve thousand feet to the bare terrain of rural Afghanistan in the fading light of early evening.

1845 HOURS LOCAL

SENIOR Chief Petty Officer Buford Dawkins crossed his right arm over his chest and pointed out the aircraft to order GO! Brannigan went off the ramp and out into the dull illumination of twilight. He quickly stabilized and glanced downward, noting that he was facing off to the west side of the valley as he plummeted toward terra firma below. The skipper quickly pushed his right arm straight down to execute a turn. When he was lined up from south to north on the DZ, he went back to a stable position with his chin up and back arched.

Slightly above him and thinly spread out, the rest of the platoon watched their leader, also noting the terrain thousands of feet beneath them. At that point they had the sensation of lying motionless on a cushion of air. Brannigan checked the altimeter strapped to his wrist. At an altitude of thirty-five hundred feet AGL, he activated the rip cord.

The pilot chute immediately inflated, pulling out the deployment bag and suspension lines, and a second later the canopy cells inflated. Brannigan looked around, happily noting that there were a total of fifteen deployed parachutes above him. Now he turned his attention to the ground. He wanted to stay close to where he was descending without going farther up the valley, so he put on half brakes by pulling the toggles down to chest level. When he was some two hundred feet AGL he raised them for full flight. The next action was something that took a lot of practice. As soon as he was about ten feet above the ground, he gently eased into a full brake position. At just the right instant, the parachute stalled, and the skipper's boots gently hit the ground.

The rest of platoon was also in contact with DZ terrain within the next three to four seconds. Everyone dropped the harnesses and began rolling up the canopies, using the belly bands to hold them together. There was no time for burying the parachutes, and they were carried over to a rocky outcrop for concealment. They would be retrieved when the aircraft came to pick up the platoon and defector for exfiltration.

With that done, the platoon assembled into a column formation with each squad taking up one side. Mike Assad and Dave Leibowitz went to their customary point positions, and led the outfit toward West Ridge, where they planned on setting up the base camp.

2200 HOURS LOCAL

THE trek from the DZ up the rock-strewn side of the mountain was arduous even for the superbly conditioned

SEALs. The route was so steep in some cases that it was necessary to push up against the rucksack of the man in front, to aid him in the demanding climb. James Bradley was the Tail-End Charlie with no one behind him. Between his personal gear and the medical kit, he had a hard row to hoe in the ascent. Bruno Puglisi helped him when he could, by turning and taking his hand to give a helping tug.

When Assad and Leibowitz reached the summit, they moved forward to the other side, which looked down the mountain. Both were pleased that the area for the camp was an excellent defensive position. There was plenty of cover in the rocks, and the visibility on both sides of the mountain couldn't have been better. A small stream fed by a spring guaranteed plenty of water. This unexpected boon didn't mean all that much on a mission as short as this one, but it was a blessing nevertheless.

As the fire teams picked out their positions and fields of fire, Frank Gomez warmed up the Shadowfire radio. His shoulders ached from the extra twenty pounds of commo gear he had carried up the mountain. After the commo check, he spoke the code words. "Green Valley. Green Valley. Green Valley. Out."

Now SOCOM back at Station Bravo knew they were on the ground and ready to rock and roll.

WARLORD DURTAMI'S COMPOUND
8 AUGUST
0715 HOURS LOCAL

BASHAR Abzai led the ambush party up to the front gate of the compound. They had spent the night sitting in the ruins of the bombed-out village waiting to see if the infidels wishing to contact the now dead Omar Kariska would show up. It had been a boring, useless attempt, and he had trouble keeping his men alert. He was a senior mujahideen and was put in charge of small patrols from time to time.

The men broke off to go to their homes while Abzai continued over to Warlord Ayyub Durtami's residence. He nodded to the guards at the door, who looked at him inquisitively. "I am here to report to the warlord about last night's ambush."

The guards' eyes opened wide. "Was there a battle last night?"

"Nothing happened," Abzai said. "There was nobody to shoot at."

"Not much to report to the warlord," one remarked.

His buddy went inside and reappeared moments later, nodding his head to indicate the mujahideen had permission to enter. Abzai walked into the building apprehensively. He hoped the fierce warlord would not consider the mission a failure. The least a mujahideen could expect in that case was a brutal caning. He found Durtami in conference with his chief lieutenant, Ahmet Kharani.

Abzai bowed and spoke in a tone of deep reverence. *"Asalaam aleikum, Amir."*

"Pakhair—welcome," Durtami said. "You seem disappointed, Brother Abzai. Did no one appear at your ambush?"

"Alas no," Abzai replied. "We waited in great alertness all through the night, but not one stranger appeared at the old village."

"You must be patient," Kharani said, not wanting to let him know there was a chance that the effort might be only a waste of time. The fighters had to feel that everything they did was important, in order to keep up their ardor for battle.

"Au!" Durtami agreed. "When we apprehend the infidel dogs who twisted Kariska away from Islam, your hours of futility will be forgotten."

"Yes, *Amir,*" Abzai said. "Meanwhile I have discovered the village to be very defendable. I have also had the men construct some strong positions from some of the rubble that was scattered about."

"Excellent," Durtami said. "You are doing a fine job, Brother Abzai. I am now promoting you to the rank of *jak bresh*—sergeant."

Abzai's features broke into a wide grin. "*Sukhria*—thank you, *Amir*."

"You are dismissed," Durtami said. After the new sergeant left the room, the warlord turned to his chief lieutenant to resume their interrupted conversation. "Are you sure about the news of a government team coming to register the village of Herandbe for future elections?"

"Absolutely, *Amir*," Kharani said.

"May Allah curse them into Hades!" Durtami said. He took a deep, calming breath. "I think this will be a chance to get some hostages. A million afghanis will prove very beneficial to our activities."

"Of course, *Amir*."

"Very well! You know what to do," Durtami said.

"I will attend to it immediately, *Amir*."

"Show no mercy!"

"I shall obey, *Amir*," Kharani said. "Your wrath is my wrath."

CHAPTER 4

THE Odd Couple Mike Assad and Dave Leibowitz moved silently across the firm ground of the valley, staying alert with the pessimistic apprehension that keeps professional combat troops vigilant and alive. A thick layer of clouds blocked the moon, but the darkness did not affect the two SEALs using AN/PVS-21 night vision system goggles. They had taken forty-minutes to travel a little more than a kilometer and a half, stopping every fifty meters to squat, look and listen during the move through the alien environment that held such a strong potential for danger.

They had left the remainder of the platoon in a defensive position at the base of East Ridge. The two-man patrol's mission was pure reconnaissance, and they were to avoid contact with the enemy.

"Hold it!" Dave whispered over the LASH headset.

"Whatcha see?"

"I think that's the village over there at about eleven o'clock."

Mike looked in the indicated direction. "Yeah. Let's do a little observing before we move any closer."

The Odd Couple loosened the headsets and pulled them back to free their ears to listen for any sounds as they carefully scrutinized the rubble of the village and the area around it. A kicked rock, a voice, a cough, belch or fart would be a sure sign somebody was in the vicinity. After a couple of minutes they were positive nobody else was around. The two replaced the LASH headsets, then stood up and cautiously moved forward, holding their CAR-15s ready.

When they reached the ruins, it was obvious the place had been wrecked by rocketing from helicopter gunships. No mortar or artillery damage was apparent. "This prob'ly happened when the Russkis were fighting here," Dave opined.

"I hope the women and kids got away," Mike said. "But I doubt it."

"Guerrilla warfare is nasty on civilians, man."

"The Afghan War happened in the 1970s and 1980s," Mike said. "That means this place was blown up between twenty and thirty-five years ago. And since nobody came back to live here again, it means they were all killed."

"Yeah," Dave said. "Shit happens. C'mon! The skipper wants us to watch this place for at least a half hour."

They left the ruins, and went out to a spot in some scrub brush twenty meters away to settle down for a further period of observation.

2310 HOURS LOCAL

CHAD Murchison knelt beside the rocks peering out into the darkness that was molded into a green and white visibility by his night vision device. He was with his mates of Bravo Fire Team, anxiously scanning the countryside to

the direct front of their defensive position. Assad and Leibowitz were out there someplace in that wilderness scoping
out the location where the defector was to show up.

This was Chad's fourth mission and his first as a Brigand,
yet he still could not believe he was a SEAL. He was from
a wealthy Boston family replete with old money, an ancestry
that could be traced back to the Pilgrims, and money-making
generations in banking, stockbroking and other financial
professions. Chad, who had grown up as a privileged preppy,
was skinny and awkward as a kid. In all his years at the exclusive Starkweather Academy in New Hampshire, he never
made an athletic team or even participated in intramural
sports between dormitories. Nobody wanted the kid with
two left feet on his team. This lack of physical prowess and
strength left him with a serious inferiority complex in spite
of his brilliant academic record. He dropped out of his fresh-
man year at Yale to enlist in the Navy after his girlfriend
dumped him for a jock. An indoctrination lecture about the
SEALs during boot camp made him decide to try for masculine glory one more time. He volunteered for the elite unit,
ignoring the discouragement given him by his commanding
officer. Chad reported to Coronado with a determination he
had never felt before. He swore he would kill himself if he
didn't make this cut.

Despite his resoluteness, Chad barely made it through the
training, as he struggled more with his natural clumsiness
than with a lack of zeal or courage. In the end it was his
stubborn, bulldog attitude that finally won over the instructors. Here was a guy who wouldn't quit; who would keep
fighting and busting his balls until there wasn't a breath left
in his body.

Now he was seriously considering disregarding family
traditions by not returning home to finish school and begin a
banking career in the family firm. At this time in his life, the
idea of not being a SEAL or one of Brannigan's Brigands
was beneath consideration as far as Petty Officer Third Class

Chadwick Murchison was concerned. He scorned everything in his past life, including Penny Brubaker, the girl
who dumped him. It was like the guys in the platoon always said, "Turn the broads upside down and they all look
alike."

A movement to the front caught Chad's attention, and he
instantly recognized the figures of Dave Leibowitz and Mike
Assad approaching the position. He could tell by their actions they were in an easy mood, and he stood up so the Odd
Couple could see him. He nodded to them as they walked
up. "Anything interesting out there?"

Mike shook his head. "Just a village like they told us in
Isolation."

"The fucking terrain out there looks like the high desert
in California," Dave added. "Remember that training operation at Trona south of the China Lake Weapons Center?
Same thing exactly."

They went back to the area where Bill Brannigan had set
up his command post with Senior Chief Dawkins. Both
squatted down in front of the honchos while Dave gave the
report. "Nothing there, sir. I'd hate to have to attack the
place though. There's dozens of places in those knocked
down buildings for cover and concealment."

Dawkins took a bite of his PowerBar. "Did it look like
anybody had been there lately?"

"It's hard to pick up tracks on the hard ground," Dave
said. "But nobody's obviously lived there for a hell of a long
time."

"Deserted," Mike pronounced.

"Well, I hope that defector shows up sometime tonight,"
Brannigan said. "Okay, guys. Take a break. Send Lieutenant
Cruiser, Chief Gunnarson and Puglisi over here."

"Aye, sir," Dave said.

A couple of minutes later the three SEALs responded to
the firm invitation and joined the skipper and senior chief in

the bucolic headquarters. Brannigan shifted his seat on the rocks he had been warming with his buttocks. "Assad and Leibowitz say there's nothing at the site. I want you three to go over there and see if somebody shows up for a meet. Take off at oh-two-hundred and wait until oh-five-hundred. If nothing happens by then, we'll have to try again tomorrow night."

"What if more than one guy shows up?" Jim Cruiser asked.

"Don't make contact in that case," Brannigan said. "We'll try again. If there're two of 'em, the next time we'll take a chance. But not now."

"Gotcha, sir," Cruiser said. He checked his watch. "Hell! We've got time for a two-hour nap."

VILLAGE RUINS
9 AUGUST
0100 HOURS LOCAL

BASHAR Abzai led his group of ten mujahideen into the rubble to set up for another period of waiting and watching. During the hike to the site, which started late because he had so much trouble rounding up the men, he had begun to wonder if this was some useless situation that wasn't going to amount to much. They really didn't have a lot of solid information to go on except a confession tortured out of a frightened man. Abzai wasn't so sure about that method of interrogation. He'd seen it a lot in the past, and most prisoners would end up saying anything, if only to get the awful pain to stop. But just the same, he had brought along an old Russian flare pistol and a half dozen star shells in case there was some validity to the situation.

After he placed everybody into proper firing positions, he settled down in one of the higher piles of rubble so he could keep an eye on everything. As he sat there, Abzai began to think about his promotion to sergeant. That was the first time he had ever heard rank mentioned in the warlord's band. Most people were called by whatever their jobs happened to be at a particular time. There were patrol leaders, senior guards, snipers, bombers and all that. Warlord Durtami had made him a sergeant. Abzai wondered if that meant a raise in his share of the money that was divided among the mujahideen when they sold the poppy gum, or ransomed hostages.

He looked out over the terrain to their front. He couldn't see a blessed thing. The darkness was as deep and black as the inside of one of the caves up in the mountains. They would have to rely on sounds if they were to catch anybody. He suddenly remembered the flare pistol, and loaded it. At the first disturbance, he would fire it off so he and his men could at least see what was going on for fifteen seconds or so.

A sudden snort, followed by snoring, broke the silence of the night. Abzai angrily got to his feet and stumbled toward the sound. He found one of the men leaning back against an old hearth, sleeping.

"Wake up!" Abzai exclaimed angrily, kicking him hard.

"Ow!" the mujahideen said. He got to his feet. "I shall cut your throat for that!"

"And the warlord will cut yours!" Abzai sneered. "Are you forgetting I am a sergeant by his personal command?"

The fellow rubbed his sore leg. "I do not even know what a sergeant is."

"It is a rank of authority," Abzai said, "like in the army, understand, bumpkin? And if you fall asleep again, I shall turn you over to Hamid the Jailer. Is that what you want? He can give you pain that is a thousand times worse than what you feel now. Shall we go see Hamid when we get back in the morning?"

"Na," the man said, shaking his head. "I will not fall asleep again."

"See that you don't," Abzai said.

He went back up to his own position to continue the night's waiting.

SEAL CP
0155 HOURS LOCAL

LIEUTENANT Jim Cruiser led Chief Gunnarson and Puglisi over to where the skipper and Senior Chief Dawkins sat in the rocks. "We're ready to move out, sir."

"You're going to have to play it by ear," Brannigan cautioned him. "That defector may be one of those nervous nellies who'll shoot first and ask questions later."

"Unless he has a night vision capability, we'll have a distinct advantage over him," Cruiser pointed out. "See you later. If nothing happens, we should be back here by oh-five-thirty."

The three-man contact team moved through the defensive perimeter and down toward the valley.

VILLAGE RUINS
0230 HOURS LOCAL

AS soon as the bombed-out village was spotted via the night vision goggles, Cruiser ordered Chief Gunnarson and Puglisi to hit the ground. "Have you got anything in that M-203?" the lieutenant asked.

"HE, sir."

"Good," Cruiser said. "You two stay here. I'm going to move a little closer. If I receive fire, cut loose with that HE grenade. I'll pull back while the bad guys duck their heads."

"Aye, sir."

"Then we'll make a firing withdrawal for only a few seconds," Cruiser said. "When we stop shooting, we'll move directly down the valley to the south. They won't be able to see which way we've gone. Everybody understand?"

"Affirmative," Chief Gunnarson replied.

Cruiser moved slowly toward the village, glad he didn't have to worry about being a silhouette because of the mountain behind him. A movement in the shadows off to one side caught his eye. He waited. Then it moved again. He eased toward it for another ten meters before kneeling down. Suddenly the sounds of somebody urinating could be heard. It stopped, then the figure moved from right to left.

"*Pinze!*" Cruiser said loudly, uttering the number five in Pashto as per the challenge.

Instead of a password in reply, the area to the front exploded with gun flashes. Bullets split the air around the SEAL and he went all the way down to the ground. The belch of Puglisi's grenade launcher broke into the din, and within seconds a detonation and a scream were heard.

The lieutenant had his CAR-15 set for automatic bursts of three rounds, and he stayed low as he scrambled backward. He didn't want to fire, knowing that the muzzle flashes would betray his position. When he reached Gunnarson and Puglisi, they all leaped up and turned to rush southward to break contact.

Then the star shell suddenly detonated overhead, its flare floating down under a parachute.

The SEALs went to the ground, turning to face the enemy in the stark glare. The mujahideen were more warriors than soldiers. They shouted Islamic slogans, leaping from the ruins, running at the SEALs. Puglisi had reloaded his M-203, and he lobbed another HE grenade at the enemy. He then joined in the fusillades from Cruiser and Chief Gunnarson that were ripping into the charging Pashtuns. A half dozen of them jerked under the impact of the bullets before collapsing to the ground. The flare burned out and the gun flashes died off.

Cruiser led his two men down the valley rather than straight back west toward the mountains, the way the mujahideen expected them to go. The sounds of bullets zipping and crunching the ground to the north showed that the ruse was working.

Another flare opened up and the Pashtuns caught sight of the SEALs once again. They resumed their wild assault, blasting out inaccurate volleys while running at the Americans. The bullets of two CAR-15s and an M-16 whipped back and forth into the last four mujahideen, knocking them sprawling to the dirt.

The latest flare went out and the sudden silence was overwhelming.

"I think that was all of them," Gunnarson said.

Cruiser had started to reply when a third flare went off above them. But this time there was no more firing. The lieutenant looked toward the village. "Goddamn it! There's some son of a bitch up there with a flare pistol."

"I'll take care of him," Puglisi said. He turned back to his trusty M-203 and fired a trio of HE rounds up into the rubble. Three widely spaced explosions quickly followed the last one just as the flare went out.

The SEALs waited for another illumination device, but twenty minutes went by with nothing lighting up the darkness. Cruiser signaled for the others to follow as he moved off toward East Ridge and the rest of the platoon.

Up in the village, a very frightened Bashar Abzai cowered in the rubble, determined not to fire the flare pistol again.

0315 HOURS LOCAL

THE contact team's return to the platoon caught everybody's attention. As Chief Matt Gunnarson passed through the perimeter, he ordered a hundred percent alert, warning of the possibility of an attack by reinforcements. The SEALs observed fire team integrity in placement and formation as everyone did his best to find the most advantageous field of fire within the illumination of his night vision goggles. Meanwhile Lieutenant Jim Cruiser and Chief Petty Officer Gunnarson reported in to Brannigan and Senior Chief Buford Dawkins.

"Our boy wasn't there," the 2IC informed the skipper. "But a group of real pissed off mujahideen sure as hell was."

The main thing the Skipper was concerned with was the potential of more fighters suddenly appearing out of the east. "How'd the firefight go?" he asked Cruiser.

"There's no doubt we got them all," the 2IC reported. "I think there was ten, but Chief Gunnarson estimates maybe nine. Neither one of us is sure. There was somebody in the village shooting up flares until Puglisi kicked off some grenades from his M-203. There might have been one guy alone or a couple."

"If he survived and isn't wounded, he's probably already legging it for his home base," the senior chief said. "That means the warlord or whatever he is, will be sending out every swinging dick he commands to get us."

"Then we'll kill 'em, by God, Buford!" Gunnarson said.

"Or we'll kill as many as we can until they kill all of us," Brannigan countered. "Remember that asset at the briefing said there was two or three hundred of the bastards."

"Well," Cruiser remarked, "here we are one way or the other." He winked and grinned. "This sort of situation makes you wish we were still doing those short raids. Hell, normally we could hightail it back to the water for pickup by boat."

"The nearest water is about eight hundred miles from here, sir," Senior Chief Dawkins said. "That would take a lot of hightailing."

"It's not going to be easy to call in a pickup," Brannigan said. "If those mujahideen have Stingers, they'll knock down any aircraft that comes for us."

"They probably have plenty," Cruiser said. "The CIA gave those fucking things away like lollipops when the Afghans were fighting the Russians."

Brannigan took a deep breath. "Okay. Let's get everyone on their feet. We'll be better off at our base camp on West Ridge. I want to get across that valley between it and this mountain before daylight."

The senior chief turned to the fire teams on the perimeter. "All right, people. Off and on! We got a fast trek to make before the sun comes a-shining with the dawn."

The platoon reacted quickly, moving out of the rocks to form up.

CHAPTER 5

THE top of the mountain's crest was as bare bones as it had been for eons. The small creek, not more than two yards wide, meandered through boulders, rocky outcrops and scrub brush. James Bradley tested the stream with his potable water chemical analysis kit, and found it to be safe for human consumption. That was great news. It meant no one had to use the water purification tablets that created a sour taste.

The sixteen men of Lieutenant Bill Brannigan's platoon occupied this pristine location without giving the slightest visual evidence of their presence. The soil was firm, without dust, thus the SEALs moving from spot to spot as they took up security and firing positions left no boot prints. Vital sound and light discipline so necessary for concealment came as instinctively to these veterans as did breathing and swearing. The SEALs blended deeply into the environment, making them deadly as cobras.

Brannigan set up his CP within an area enclosed by a natural wall of rock. A roof of thorny brush was put on top to provide overhead cover, and the entrance was blocked from sight by more vegetation and stones. The skipper killed a half dozen scorpions during the first few hours of occupation, and the surviving poisonous insects seemed to have concluded that, as Shakespeare wrote, "the better part of valor is discretion." They became discreet to the point of disappearing from sight.

Now, on this second day of the operation, Lieutenant (JG) Jim Cruiser, Senior Chief Petty Officer Buford Dawkins and Chief Petty Officer Matt Gunnarson crowded into the CP to drink instant coffee and have an official confab with the Skipper. Brannigan took a sip of coffee, grinning at his senior subordinates. "I was just wondering how many times I'm destined to sit in the middle of harm's way in the company of you guys and your ugly mugs."

Dawkins emitted a country-boy chuckle. "We ain't in harm's way, sir. Hell! We're on Harm's Freeway."

"Actually, we're on Harm's Freeway going north in the southbound lanes," Cruiser added with a grin.

"It's more'n that. We're on Harm's Freeway going north in the southbound lanes with no off-ramps," Gunnarson interjected in uncharacteristic humor.

"In other words," Brannigan said, "we're up the proverbial shit creek without a paddle. We were supposed to spend ten days in-country, but that's no longer applicable. The fact we were attacked in lieu of meeting a defector pretty much brings this mission to a screeching halt."

"It's time for an expedient aerial exfiltration," Cruiser said.

Brannigan shook his head. "Those mujahideen must have Stingers. The bastards know we're here now, so they'll nail any aircraft that comes in the area and tries a landing. There's a big possibility that we're going to have to get out of here by ourselves. The country west of here is made up of foothills and ravines. It provides damn good cover and concealment, but would mean a long walk through unfriendly territory in both Afghanistan and Pakistan. One big downside is that Al-Qaeda is split up and scattered all through those areas. It would just be a matter of time before we attracted the sort of attention that leads to complete disaster. The situation would really have to deteriorate before I'd choose that particular option."

"We'll be needing a supply drop if we stay here much longer," Cruiser said. "Our chow and ammo won't last forever."

"A fast-flying aircraft could make a low drop while spewing out flares," Brannigan said. "That would keep the Stinger projectiles off it."

"But that would reveal our location to the mujahideen," Gunnarson protested.

"Hell, Chief!" Brannigan said. "It's like I said. They already know we're up here. There're only two frigging mountains in this goddamn OA. They've probably figured we're on this one by now. And if they haven't, they soon will."

"One way or the other we have to make a decision," Cruiser pointed out.

"Don't worry about that," Brannigan said. "All decisions will be made by SOCOM. That means they damn well might tell us we're on our own."

The sounds of approaching footsteps broke into the conversation, and they looked up to see the radio operator, Frank Gomez. He knelt down and handed a message to Brannigan. "It's from SOCOM, sir. It's in reply to the SITREP you sent out earlier."

"Now we're going to get the word," Brannigan said. He read the neatly printed missive that Gomez had decoded from the five-letter word groups. "Well! SOCOM seems a bit wishy-washy. This is an order to stand fast and go on the defensive. They need some data to send a resupply mission to us."

"In other words," Senior Chief Dawkins said, "nobody back in SOCOM has figured out how to pull us out of this shit."

"From what I read into this, it appears that they're con-centrating as much on getting us out as they are on giving us another mission," Brannigan said. "Something's going on and we're in the middle of it."

"You can't be sure of that," Cruiser commented.

"Why not?" Brannigan remarked. "They have definite plans to resupply us, and that means there's a task in the off-ing. It might not be anything more than a potential mission that could be called off later. Either way, I have no intention of us just sitting on our asses in these rocks and thorns to await their bidding. We'll do a little sneaking-and-peeking along with some combat patrols to keep that warlord son of a bitch off balance. I want to create an atmosphere that will strike fear in his evil heathen heart."

"It's as we concluded," Cruiser remarked. "We're going north in the southbound lanes. Even with resupply, we can't stay here forever."

VILLAGE OF HERANDBE
WARLORD DURTAMI'S FIEFDOM

THE small community of mud huts consisted of fifteen families, and was under the protection and patronage of Warlord Ayyub Durtami. These farmers worked their fields in a single valley of the high country, pooling their resources and energy for a more efficient operation. If they planted the usual crops—wheat, barley and corn—each family would earn the equivalent of approximately 150 American dollars per year. But they had something more profitable to harvest. These peasants cultivated the opium poppy plant from which heroine is made. The crop afforded the farmers 64,500 afghanis annually, which translated into 1500 American dol-lars per year for each family. It was not surprising that this tenfold advantage in cash encouraged them to cultivate and process the poppies.

Their broker for the sale of the product was the warlord, who paid them cash for the illicit crops. He took care of the transport and sales to the manufacturers that smuggled the narcotics to European and American markets.

The farmers got the juice from the unripe seeds of the plants, and air dried it until it formed into a thick gum. Further drying of this gum resulted in a powder for the final product that the warlord's men transported to receiving points. From there, the substance was taken to processing centers in Kabul and Kandahar.

The farmers loved this arrangement and were deeply grateful to the warlord for providing them with the opportunity to make so much money. It was easy, fast work, without the backbreaking struggle of plowing and harvesting grain crops. These cultivators considered opiates a blessing from Allah. And if the stuff trapped infidels into the hell of addiction, so much the better. That was what the nonbelievers of Western civilization deserved.

The only food the families grew was taken care of by the women and girls. The females worked their personal vegetable gardens, and from these small plots they were able to get more than enough for a decent sustenance. They also tended the animals that provided milk, cheese, poultry and meat. With the income from the poppies, they could afford to buy enough flour for bread. Life was good under these conditions, and used to endless grinding poverty, these people now lived in what they considered shameless luxury.

The villagers did more for the warlord than produce poppy products. They provided him and his mujahideen with intelligence and backup. Their latest support would be in dealing with some people coming from Kabul to register them for the next national elections. This was the reason that the warlord's second-in-command, Ahmet Kharani, and six chosen men waited concealed in the village for the government voter registrars to show up.

THE white Toyota van covered in dust was preceded by a small Russian UAZ sedan. The two vehicles pulled into the village, turning into the small community square. Three elderly farmers sat on benches by the well, looking impassively as the visitors came to a halt next to them.

Four heavily armed men stepped from the sedan, holding American M-16 rifles at the ready. They were obviously city fellows, a bit soft and dressed a little too fancy for the countryside. These bodyguards looked around at the mud huts, then one of them nodded to his companions in the van. The two young men in the vehicle got out and walked up to the old men at the well.

"Asalaam aleikum," one greeted politely. He was wearing slacks and a white dress shirt opened at the collar. "We wish to speak to your head man, if we may."

The farmers made no reply, but stood up and walked away from the well, toward the nearest hut. As soon as they entered and closed the doors, gunshots detonated from nearby buildings with a deafening rapidity. The four armed bodyguards were caught in a murderous crossfire that pummeled them to the ground, leaving them sprawled in the undignified positions of sudden violent death. The other two visitors looked up in terror as Kharani and a half dozen gunmen stepped into view from their hidden firing positions around the huts.

"Put your hands up!" Kharani growled.

As the frightened men obeyed, two of the mujahideen went forward and roughly searched them for weapons, punctuating the procedure with sharp kicks and punches. Kharani walked over to the van and looked inside. A briefcase lay between the seats, and he reached in and grabbed it. He unbuckled the flap and looked inside. It was crammed with illustrated pamphlets and printed posters for placing on walls. He walked over to the prisoners.

"What is this all about?" he asked.

The man who seemed to be the senior of the two spoke in a quaking voice. "They are information about how to vote. The people in this area missed the last election."

"And what exactly were you going to do with this information on how to vote?" Kharani asked. "The people here do not want to vote."

"Uh . . . uh, Allah protect me!" the man stammered.

Kharani swung his gaze to the younger man. "Answer my question!"

"To teach the people how to vote."

"I see," Kharani said. "It seems you are unwanted intruders within our land. We do not like people to bother our farmers."

The first man found his tongue and spoke rapidly in a beseeching tone of voice. "We are officials of the government! They will ransom us! Do you understand? You will be paid much money to give us our freedom."

"That is correct," the second agreed. "You should not kill us."

"Why not?" Kharani asked mockingly, though he knew that Warlord Durtami had every intention of obtaining money for their release.

"Please, sir! We both have families!" the older man said, beginning to weep. "We are Muslims! Followers of Islam."

Kharani turned to his men and barked short, terse orders. One man ran to the sedan and got in while another took the driver's seat in the van. The prisoners were pushed and bullied into the back of the vehicle while Kharani and the remainder of the men joined them.

The two vehicles sped from the village and out to the dirt road, turning in the direction of the warlord's compound. The three old farmers came out and gazed at the sight of the four corpses. The dead had to be taken care of properly, since they were Muslims. The Holy Koran forbade leaving the bodies of the faithful unburied to be eaten by jackals and vultures.

MUJAHIDEEN PATROL
EAST RIDGE
1400 HOURS LOCAL

THE patrol was made up of a half dozen of the youngest mujahideen in the compound. This was more of a training mission than an actual reconnaissance patrol, and they had been sent out on their own to see if they could find any sign of the infidel interlopers who had proven so deadly. The senior men of the warlord's band were certain the attackers had drawn off and concealed themselves on the other mountain. This little excursion would be good for the kids without putting them in any real danger.

The boys laughed and shouted threats to the enemy, waving their weapons above their heads as they pranced around on their way up the rocky slope. Several wore green headbands with white lettering in Arabic that read *"Maut-la-Kafir"*—"Death to Infidels," while others said *"Ash Tawil al Jihad"*—"Long Live the Holy War."

This was going to be a great day. They were away from the strictness of the instructors for a few hours and had even been given some rice and wheat cakes, with cold tea to wash it all down. With luck they might run into the skulking cowards who had been brazen enough to enter the domains of Warlord Durtami. What an honor for them if they found the infidels and killed them all.

The lead boy, a sixteen-year-old, sped up to race the others to the top of the mountain. "I shall be the first to glory!" he shouted as a challenge to his comrades. He had just begun to gain speed when a shot echoed from somewhere, sending a bullet that struck him just below his right eye. His face caved in as the back of his head blew out, spewing brains and blood in one instantaneous millisecond of horror. He fell back on his buttocks, appearing to sit down on a boulder, then rolled to the side.

An instant later, two more of the boys spun under the impact of body shots, slumping down to the rock-strewn terrain.

The last three snapped out of the shock of the moment as they quickly got behind the sparse concealment of some thorn bushes. Two of them fired back some useless, unaimed shots while their buddy squatted in terror.

It was suddenly quiet, the only sound being the moaning of a dying young mujahideen up a bit higher on the mountain. The two active survivors stood up and moved upward toward the summit, pumping out quick bursts from their AK-47s. The sound of the M-203's firing was masked by the noise of their own shooting, and the kids failed to note the HE grenade falling toward them. It struck a waist-high boulder and exploded, shredding them with shrapnel, as they buckled under the multiple impacts of white hot metal pellets.

The last rookie, panicked into insanity, leaped up and began running down the slope toward the valley floor. He didn't quite make four full strides before a 5.56-millimeter round hit him between the shoulder blades. He tumbled face-first onto a spread of small stones. The neophyte mujahideen raised his head just in time for one more bullet to split his skull.

Bravo Fire Team, led by Senior Chief Buford Dawkins, came out of their ambush site, gazing down at the destruction they had blasted into the small patrol. Chad Murchison shook his head at the stupidity of the dead fighters. "It appears that we ruined their whole day."

"Let's go see if there's anything useful on them dumb shits," the senior chief said.

They made their way down to the corpses and stopped, shocked at the youth of their victims. *"Uff da!"* Gutsy Olson said, falling back into a Norwegian-American expression. "I thought they was just nuts the way they were singing and yelling. It never dawned on me they was a bunch of idiot kids."

Connie Concord, holding his combination M-16 and M-203, rolled one over. "There ain't any sense in searching these guys, Senior Chief. Nobody is gonna give 'em anything important to tote around."

"You're right," Dawkins agreed. "The sound of our shooting irons is gonna attract attention. We better pull back."

"Well, the Skipper said he wants to keep the sons of bitches off balance," Concord said. "Mission accomplished for today."

The Bravos turned and followed their fire team leader back up the mountain.

WARLORD'S COMPOUND
1800 HOURS LOCAL

WARLORD Ayyub Durtami seethed in silence, ignoring his tea. Across the table from him Ahmet Kharani kept his eyes averted. This was a dangerous time. Even though he had brought back two valuable hostages that would net them a million afghanis, his chief was in a black mood. When Durtami finally spoke, his voice was low in a subdued fury.

"Just before you arrived, I was told that six of our youngest fighters were discovered slaughtered," the warlord said. "We heard the firing and I sent some men to investigate. It was a massacre."

"I was not aware of that," Kharani said.

"This was supposed to be a pleasant outing for the lads," Durtami said. "The instructors let them go up onto the mountain ridge to have some fun after weeks of hard training. They were obviously victims of some vicious treachery by an older, more experienced enemy."

"Are you going to punish the instructors?" Kharani asked. He knew the men were probably fearfully anticipating certain death for the mishap.

But Durtami shook his head. "We have done this a dozen times to reward youngsters who have been training hard. Today was a most unusual event."

Kharani was relieved by this uncharacteristic mercy. One of his cousins was among the instructor cadre of the warlord's small army.

"It is now obvious that numerous enemies have invaded my fiefdom," Durtami said. "Perhaps they are Americans."

"It is possible," Kharani said. "And I think they are here to stay awhile. There is only one place for them to remain out of sight. They must be skulking atop the far mountain from here."

"I agree. But they could be anyplace up there. The entire ridge is a natural fortress."

"What about your brother-in-law Hassan Khamami? Does he not number mortars in his arsenal?"

"*Au,*" Durtami replied affirmatively. "He has a large cache of weaponry. Some of his arsenal is new."

"Ask Khamami to help you, *Amir,*" Kharani suggested. "With mortars we could shell that mountain from one end to the other."

"My brother-in-law would want too much money," Durtami said.

"With the ransom money for the two hostages you would get enough to refill your war treasury very quickly," Kharani said.

Durtami looked over at his second-in-command and smiled. "You are most clever, Brother Ahmet. In fact, you are so intelligent that at times you make me nervous."

"I desire only to serve you with loyalty, *Amir,*" Kharani said, humbling himself. To be too assertive could lead to a summary execution as a serious potential threat to the warlord's leadership.

"Make arrangements to send a message to Khamami."

"I will take care of it, *Amir.*"

CHAPTER 6

IN the complicated environment of international diplomacy, there is a clandestine segment of most proceedings that only a few insiders know about. The talented people of these secret negotiations are known outwardly as undersecretaries, envoys or attachés in their various state departments or foreign offices. But whatever the official title, they perform their surreptitious tasks in two phases; the first is "preparation" and the second is "wrapping up." The former paves the way to concurrence and the latter assures that the deals and treaties thus parleyed to conclusion are put into effect.

These anonymous negotiators are polite and sophisticated but speak among themselves in an open, candid manner that only people with proverbial "thick hides" can tolerate. If some of their exchanges of ideas were made public, the citizens of their respective nations would be outraged by much of the give-and-take aspects of the haggling. Their conferences get down to the nitty-gritty. Threats are made, warnings issued, concessions granted and agreements struck that are either happily or rationally accepted.

The bottom line is that solid covenants are made.

One of the world's best and most effective of these diplomats was an African-American undersecretary of the United States State Department by the name of Carl Joplin. The tall, slim man with a gentle voice came from Baltimore, Maryland, and was the forty-year-old son of a father who was a retired janitor and a mother who was still employed as a licensed vocational nurse in a local hospital. The couple had worked hard all their lives to maintain a steadfast home life for their family, at times juggling their regular jobs with additional part-time employment when the bills piled up. When it came to their children, they deemphasized sports, pushing the value of education to the four offspring, and each youngster recognized and appreciated these high standards. All obtained college degrees with the full scholarships they earned through scholastic excellence. Carl, the youngest, continued his education, obtaining a PhD in political science at Maryland State University.

Joplin was a softspoken man with an unusual insight into other human beings. Even in the earliest stages of his career, he'd demonstrated an uncanny ability to negotiate, knowing just how to convince a stubborn foreign counterpart that going along with the United States' side of an issue was not only in his nation's best interest but would benefit him personally as well. Joplin flattered, cajoled and demanded, while seeming not to. Consequently, he ended up with a reputation of being able to score diplomatic coups when the need for getting the American point of view across was the most critical.

NOW, in the meeting room just off his personal office, Joplin sat across the table from Zaid Aburrani, a special envoy from Afghanistan. He and Aburrani had known each other for three years, and though they were not close friends, they each felt respect and even a bit of affection for the other. The main subject of their undercover meetings was the thorny issue of warlords in Aburrani's native country. The Afghan had come to Washington from Kabul to discuss what he termed a "sensitive" and "judicious" issue. As usual, neither man had an attending stenographer or maintained personal notes. They kept the gist of their conversational exchange in their heads.

Joplin settled back in his chair and smiled. "I was most pleased yesterday when they informed me of your coming, Zaid. I don't believe we've seen each other for at least six months or so."

"I am happy for this opportunity to visit you, Carl," Aburrani replied. "There is much satisfaction when problems are solved, and we have been most fortunate in that process."

"Ah!" Joplin said. "You said 'problems.' Does that mean there are some difficulties we must address today?"

"What else?" Aburrani replied with a laugh. "At least there is only one issue for this particular session. As you know we had excellent results in our first national elections. However, there are still a great many problems to solve. Some of the more isolated areas of Afghanistan still resist the process. It is one of those two steps forward, one step back situations." He laughed. "It is like you Americans say. 'The faster I go, the behinder I get.'"

"I know the feeling," Joplin said, smiling. "Tell me, Zaid, does the big issue here today involve the warlords?"

"I fear so," Aburrani said. "It pains me to have to bring up our old friend Ayyub Durtami again."

Joplin chuckled. "An old friend, is he? That is one man I would like to have out of my life."

"I am in complete accord with you," Aburrani said. "For the past month we have been sending teams out into the countryside to address the question of elections with our rural populations. They show videotapes, pass out literature and give little talks. When that is done, they register their audiences as voters, then move on to the next village on their route."

"Has this friend of ours interfered with that?"

"Indeed," the Afghan said sadly. "We sent a two-man team into his territory, and their bodyguards were ambushed. Our agents were taken prisoner and are now being held for ransom. I fear the problem has been dropped into my lap."

"You have my sympathy," Joplin said sincerely. "At best, relations and negotiations with warlords are illogical and confusing. They are erratic, impetuous fellows who tend to be quite dangerous. That's what makes it so difficult to control opium poppy production."

"That is not all the warlords' fault, Carl," Aburrani said. "The poor farmers are mired in poverty. They can make as much as ten times the income from poppies than from normal crops. And they can plant two crops a year."

"It sounds as if you are defending the growing of opium poppies, Zaid."

"Not at all, Carl," Aburrani said. "I detest the scourge of heroin as much as any civilized man."

"Well," Joplin said, "let's turn our conversation back to the warlords."

"I think I may have an advantage in this particular situation," Aburrani said. "That is why I have come to you. Our intelligence services tell us that apparently there is a special operations group in Durtami's fiefdom, and they have been rather rude to him."

Joplin laughed aloud. "Rude? I can only imagine what you mean by that understated remark."

Aburrani smiled. "It is estimated that Durtami's difficulties with the invaders have resulted in somewhere between a dozen to two dozen of his men killed. And it is presumed the attackers are American."

"As of this moment I am completely in the dark about anything going on in that part of Afghanistan," Joplin admitted. "What exactly do you wish me to do?"

"I must negotiate with Durtami for the release of the hostages," Aburrani explained. "I can only be successful by paying a hefty ransom for those poor fellows. That means that Durtami wins." He leaned forward, a look of pleading on his face. "But if there is an American special operations team over there, perhaps they could rescue the prisoners. That would embarrass the warlord and diminish his reputation."

"I can certainly see the advantage in that," Joplin said.

"I am scheduled to visit him on the fifteenth of this month," Aburrani said. "I will not give in to his demands. Consequently, I will return to Kabul without the hostages. Of course Durtami will look forward to my return, thinking he has put me in a position where I must pay even more ransom than he initially demanded. However, if the hostages are rescued by a raid in the meantime, it will show up his shortcomings to his men. It might even encourage one of them to try to take over the group. If that brings about infighting, then Durtami might be forced to look to the central government for support. And *voila!* as the French say, he becomes a good citizen and patriot."

"As I said, I am not sure if there is a special operations team in that area or not," Joplin said. "But the information you've been given indicates there is. I will visit my contacts in SOLS and see what can be arranged. I'll send the information to you by diplomatic courier."

Aburrani stood up and leaned across the table, offering his hand. "Thank you, Carl. I shall await your message."

Joplin got to his feet and shook hands with his guest.

**EAST RIDGE
11 AUGUST
1820 HOURS LOCAL**

BRAVO Fire Team, heavily camouflaged, lay among the rocks at the top of the mountain, looking down at the warlord's compound in the valley below. Senior Chief Petty Officer Buford Dawkins checked the copy of the layout sketch given them by the operative Ishaq back in Isolation, comparing it with what he now studied through his binoculars.

Connie Concord, loosely holding his M-16 and attached M-203, lay beside the fire team leader. He looked down at the crude fort. "There ain't been too many changes since Ishaq made them sketches, huh?"

"Nope," Dawkins said. "But I can see more vehicles now. Ishaq said they was maybe a couple of vans and four Toyota pickups along with some of the motorbikes and rickshaws. I see three vans and a little sedan now."

"All of them vans is white," Connie said. "You'd think the dumb bastards would have painted 'em a camouflage pattern by now."

"They prob'ly ain't got any paint," Dawkins said. He noted a change in the number of houses in the village inside the walls, and entered the information on the map. "I've been noticing the women down there. Them Muslims is terrible mean to their females."

"Yeah," Connie agreed. "They make 'em wear those burqas so other men can't look at 'em."

"Ragheads must be real jealous sumbitches," Dawkins said. "Their women can't do much with their lives."

Connie thought about his two young daughters Karen Sue and Lilly. Both were doing very well in school and could realistically look forward to good careers and independence as adult women. If they decided to be stay-at-home moms, they could do that too. He couldn't imagine living in a system that would reduce his little girls to growing up to be nothing more than birth-giving, obedient automatons for barbaric husbands. He glanced at the senior chief. "Do you think them ragheads will ever join the twenty-first century?"

"Well," Dawkins mused, "maybe the twenty-second or twenty-third."

As the two SEALs conversed softly, the other two members of the team—Gutsy Olson and Chad Murchison—were up twenty meters higher on the mountain, scanning the area to make sure no mujahideen patrols snuck up on them. The mission had been laid on the night before by the Skipper. His intuitive expectation that the platoon was going to have at least one more operation in this particular OA made him want to have Ishaq's map checked out and updated.

Besides the number and placement of the buildings, the Bravos had noted the times of watch changes, the different sentry posts and the comings and goings of the various members of the band. They also quickly spotted what appeared to be a couple of prisoners brought out of a large portable storage container, then taken to a hut that was an obvious head. This had happened about four times in the previous eighteen hours.

Senior Chief Buford looked over to the mountaintop, happily noting the sinking of the sun. As soon as it was dark, they would pull out and hump it back to the CP on West Ridge.

WARLORD'S COMPOUND
15 AUGUST
1700 HOURS LOCAL

ZAID Aburrani sat in the seat of the reconfigured British Westland Whirlwind helicopter as it approached the compound. He glanced out the view port and could see the people a thousand feet below as they came streaming out of their homes to greet his arrival. They had no idea who he was or the reason for his visit, but the fact that an outsider had arrived was something for the locals to get excited about.

The chopper eased into a hover and began descending. Within moments the wind from its prop wash began kicking up dust from the thin cover of dirt over the hard-packed ground. The children rushed toward the aircraft, taking no

notice of any potential danger from the landing gear, the rotors or the fact that the helicopter might lose power and crash.
Aburrani was always amazed by the kids' inability to recognize danger in any form. It seemed to be a racial characteris-
tic of the people not to consider the consequences of their
actions. Even experienced fighting men of the Pashtuns
many times let their emotions get the best of them in battle.
They would take rash actions that resulted in heavier casualties than were necessary. The biggest reason for this illogical
behavior was the fatalistic teachings of Islam that encouraged
accepting death as the inevitable consequence of Allah's will.

Aburrani was a seriously practicing Islamic, and he resented older Muslims enticing their youth to sacrifice themselves in a misdirected version of martyrdom. It was rather
disconcerting that these volunteer victims were unable to
understand the political side of their self-immolation.

As soon as the helicopter wheels hit the ground, the motor
was cut and the crew chief slid the fuselage door open. Aburrani, carrying his briefcase, stepped down to the ground, where
he was met by Ahmet Kharani, the warlord's chief officer.

"Asalaam aleikum," Kharani said in greeting.

"God be with you," Aburrani replied.

"Warlord Durtami awaits you, Brother Aburrani," Kharani said eagerly. "I shall take you to him without delay."

"Shukhria," Aburrani said, thanking him.

The two men hurried through the throng of gaping, grinning adults and the yelling children, toward the gate. It took
only another half minute to reach the warlord's residence.

Aburrani went through a realistic greeting ceremony with
the warlord when he entered his presence. This included
some brief inquiries into each other's health and well-being,
then the inevitable drinking of tea. Some samosas—pastry
filled with potatoes and chickpeas—were also offered. All in
all, three-quarters of an hour passed before they were able to
get down to the real reason behind the visit.

"And what may I do for you, Brother Aburrani?" Durtami
asked, as if he had absolutely no idea as to why the other

man would endure a helicopter flight all the way from Kabul to call on him.

"I wish to discuss the hostages," Aburrani answered. "Are they well?"

"Of course," Durtami said. "They were most polite and cooperative when they were brought to me. I have rewarded their good manners with excellent accommodations."

"I am pleased by your kindness and merciful goodness," Aburrani said, knowing that the unfortunate men were undoubtedly locked up in a storage container and probably getting no more than one scanty, miserable meal a day. "We, of course, are anxious to have them back among us. May I ask what tribute you seek for their safe return?"

"One million American dollars," Durtami said. "They appear to be most valuable assets to the government's causes."

Aburrani shrugged. "They are low-ranking officials."

"But they must be important if they are sent all the way here to visit the farm village in my fiefdom."

"They visit many villages, *Amir,* all over Afghanistan," Aburrani said.

"Seven hundred thousand American dollars."

Aburrani seemed thoughtful before he said, "Twenty-five thousand dollars."

"I cannot let them go for fifty thousand dollars."

Aburrani shook his head. "That is twenty-five thousand dollars for *both*."

"One hundred thousand dollars for *both*!" Durtami said. He waved his hand in a gesture of finality. "That is it. I have bargained down as far as I can possibly go."

"I will have to take your offer back to Kabul."

Durtami frowned. That could mean several weeks more of feeding the hostages. Then he smiled confidently for appearance' sake. "I am sure your superiors will see the logic and fairness of my offer. Please inform them that I have good use for the money. My fiefdom has been invaded by infidels. I estimate there are a thousand of them. Maybe many more. A good number of my men have been treacherously slain, and some innocent youths out tending a herd of goats on yon mountain were hideously tortured and slaughtered."

"I shudder at such wanton cruelty," Aburrani said.

"Then you see my predicament."

"Perhaps the unconditional release of the hostages would convince the government to do something about this invasion," Aburrani suggested.

"I have purchased some weapons from my brother-in-law Hassan Khamami," Durtami said. "They are new French mortars. I will need no outside help to deal with the infidels."

Aburrani knew that Khamami was a powerful warlord with four to five times the men Durtami had in his band. He had always thought that the day would come when the brother-in-law would add this fiefdom to his own. The envoy took a thoughtful sip of tea, then said, "Now I shall turn to another item of discussion. The opium poppy crops. How do they go?"

"The resin will be ready for shipment soon," the warlord said. "We have a good yield on this last crop of the year."

"That will please the cartel," Aburrani said.

Aburrani was deeply imbedded in the opium trade out of Afghanistan. He talked the talk with outsiders about eradicating poppy production, but walked the walk with the dealers. There was more than greed in his motive for being a part of this local illicit industry. It raised the standard of living of the farmers, for whom he had a great sympathy and understanding. These people needed every advantage they could obtain in order to ease their physical and spiritual misery. By raising the poppies and processing them, a farm family was able to purchase a good wood-burning stove, some furniture or even a motorbike. Communities could chip in and buy a communal truck, tractor or minibus to make their lives easier.

The Americans and Europeans provided the market for the crops, and if they didn't approve of heroin addiction, they should turn inwardly, into their own society, to get rid of it. Zaid Aburrani and scores of other Afghanistan leaders and officials were not going to sacrifice their people to assuage the hypocrisy of Western civilization. As long as there was a market, a product would be produced for it. Was that not the basic philosophy of the infidels and their capitalism?

"I must return to Kabul," Aburrani said, standing up. "I fear they will not meet your ransom demands."

"Tell them I need the money to put back in my treasury after purchasing the mortars," Durtami said. "It is the leaders like me that will guarantee Afghanistan for Afghans."

"I will tell them, *Amir*," Aburrani said with a slight bow. *"De khudey pea man."*

"Pa makha de kha."

CHAPTER 7

THE Special Operations Liaison Staff had an office in a little used area of the Pentagon. This small team had been organized to ease the efforts of coordination and communication between the various special operations branches of the nation's armed forces. Access to this small administrative group was severely limited. Only a select few military and political echelons knew of its existence.

The concept behind SOLS was not unlike the U.S. government's intention of placing intelligence matters into a more compact administrative body to expedite functions and exchange of information. The main purpose was to create a convenient method for the nation's sneakiest and hardest hitting components to communicate. Basically, they had to make sure the left hand knew what the right hand was doing among all special operations all over the world.

The officers assigned to SOLS performed duties that sounded much easier and simpler than what the jobs actually demanded. The hard part was to prevent misunderstandings and wrongful conclusions based on the available information. The officers chosen for this staff were all SOF veterans who had been injured in the line of duty. Rather than accept physical disability separations from the service, they chose to serve in administrative capacities while remaining on active duty.

The chief of this staff was Colonel John Turnbull, U.S. Army. This Delta Force veteran had broken his ankle on a parachute jump, and the fracture was deteriorating to the point that it eventually would have to be fused. That would leave him with less pain, but more crippled. The affected leg would be much shorter than the other.

Commander Timothy Jones, U.S. Navy, was a former SEAL with a hernia. Lieutenant Colonel Steve Lee, U.S. Air Force, had injured his back in a helicopter crash, while Major Scott Marchand, U.S. Marine Corps, had touched a live power line with his foot when coming in to make a PLF during a parachute jump at Tank Park DZ, Camp Pendleton, California. His right leg had been amputated just below the knee.

Their workdays went from very early in the morning to very late in the evening; and on one particularly screwed-up project that involved not only the military but politicians and diplomats, they worked for a straight thirty-six hours without a break, making sure that no inadvertent interference occurred during a multi-agency kidnapping and assassination in the same OA.

These four officers were ably served by only two administrative assistants, who were wise beyond their years. Both these young women were E-4s but in different branches of the service. Specialist Mary Kincaid was U.S. Army while Senior Airman Lucille Zinkowski was U.S. Air Force.

The day before, when an appointment was made for them to be visited by Carl Joplin of the State Department, the two young ladies cringed, knowing it was going to put their bosses in a bad mood. The undersecretary was well respected, but he generally didn't show up on their doorstep unless a situation seemed to be totally and irretrievably fucked up.

DR. Carl Joplin was escorted by a Marine from the Pentagon's east entrance through the building to an elevator that would take them to the bailiwick of SOLS. He was left at the door and he tapped on it, then stepped into the outer officer, where Kincaid and Zinkowski kept their desks. The young ladies—the former was twenty and the latter nineteen years of age—were collating the latest SPECOPS missions by date and location when Joplin made his appearance.

"Hello, young ladies," he said. "It's so nice to see you again."

"How are you, Dr. Joplin?" Zinkowski inquired as she slipped a training mission in Bosnia between a couple of Iraq agent insertions.

"I'm fine," Joplin replied. "You look busy this morning."

"We're busy every morning, Dr. Joplin," Kincaid remarked. She got up and went to the inner door, opening it to speak to someone on the other side. "Dr. Joplin is here, sir." A muffled voice sounded from within, and she turned. "Colonel Turnbull and Commander Jones are waiting to see you."

Joplin went into what was a small central meeting chamber, with Zinkowski following. The four doors inside opened up on the private offices of the staff members. Turnbull and Jones were seated at a table in the center of the room. A standalone computer sat on the table, and Zinkowski took the chair in front of it. One of the jobs she and Kincaid were tasked with was the downloading of classified disks onto the staff's CPU. This was done while the armed couriers who brought the data to the SOLS office waited. When the job was done, the couriers took the disks back to the vault, where they were stored under both electronic and human security measures.

Joplin reacted to an invitation to make himself at home by slipping into a chair. Both Turnbull and Jones were in their shirtsleeves with ties undone. They had the looks of men who had plenty to do that day and were impatient to get back to the tasks that awaited them.

"What can we do for you, Carl?" Turnbull asked.

"I've been approached by Zaid Aburrani," Joplin replied, knowing they had left some important work to take the time for this meeting. "I believe you're familiar with him."

"I don't know him personally, but his name has passed through here now and then," Turnbull conceded.

"Afghan, isn't he?" Jones asked.

"Yes," Joplin said. "He's got a sensitive situation in his home country involving one of the warlords. The man's name is Ayyub Durtami and he's holding a couple of their voter registration agents hostage. It would be to our advantage if the prisoners were rescued."

Turnbull wondered about the importance of rescuing such hostages, but he knew if it wasn't vital then Carl Joplin, PhD, would not be involved. "Would this warlord's name be the keyword in our search-and-find mode, Carl?"

"I'm not sure, John. But it would be a start." He looked over at Zinkowski, thinking that back in the old country she would be Zinkowska. "Try Afghanistan plus Durtami. The last one is spelled D-U-R-T-A-M-I."

Zinkowski's fingers flew over the keyboard, then she pressed ENTER. "It's come up," she announced.

"Print it out, please," Commander Jones said.

Seconds later the Lexmark Optra E312 printer buzzed on a table in the corner of the room, then began printing ten pages of data. When it finished, Zinkowski went over and got the document, carrying it to Colonel Turnbull. He read it, then passed it over to Commander Jones.

Jones took the pages. "Ah! A SEAL operation. A platoon is in the area to pick up a defector." He flipped over to the last page. "They're also expected to be ready for any additional missions assigned them. They're still in-country." He shoved the report over to Joplin.

The State Department undersecretary settled back and read the official cold, almost indifferent words that described a dangerous mission to pick up an indigenous defector. He knew the operative name Ishaq from other Middle Eastern missions. Joplin was intrigued by the contingency that the mission could be expanded because of the unstable situation in the OA. He took out his pen and wrote a few lines across the top of page one, then put his signature under it and on all the other pages. He nodded to Turnbull and Jones.

"You are now authorized to put in an order that the SEAL platoon in the area is to affect a rescue of the two hostages held by the Afghanistan warlord named Ayyub Durtami. Further instructions will follow."

Turnbull glanced at Zinkowski. "Do the paperwork."

"Yes, sir!"

WEST RIDGE BASE CAMP
16 AUGUST
0600 HOURS LOCAL

THE mortar round hit during the middle of the morning watch, detonating a hundred meters down the far side of the mountain. Since Delta Fire Team was on watch, Chief Matt Gunnarson was at the CP acting as duty petty officer. His LASH headset immediately buzzed with simultaneous transmissions from Adam Clifford and Bruno Puglisi.

"Ever'body shut up but Puglisi," he said back. "What the hell's going on?"

Another round exploded a hundred and fifty meters to the south. "There's some rat bastard moojee-hadeen shooting funny little mortars down in the valley from the base of East Ridge," Puglisi reported. "Looks like two crews. Are they coming in close up there?"

"Negative," Gunnarson replied. "They either can't hit shit or they're not sure of our exact location."

"It's prob'ly a little of both," Puglisi opined. "They're kinda spastic with them things."

"Can you reach them with your M-203?"

"Negative, Chief," Puglisi said. "They're out of range."

"You guys stand fast and keep your heads down," Gunnarson said. He glanced over at the Skipper, who was looking at him quizzically. He made a quick report. At that moment the senior chief came up, just as two shells struck on the opposite side of the mountain.

"Get your Bravos together, Senior Chief," Brannigan ordered. "That incoming is from a couple of mortars out there in the valley. You can get the exact locations from Puglisi. Evidently they're out of range of the M-203s, so you'll have to take 'em down with your CAR-15s. And that means paying them a personal visit."

"Aye, sir," Senior Chief Dawkins said. "Although I hate to just barge in without an invitation." He gave the Skipper a salute, then turned to trot over toward the Bravo positions while another explosion, too far away to do any harm, went off. "On your feet, Bravos. There's a couple of mortars that want knocked out."

In the passing of only a few short moments he was leading Connie Concord, Gutsy Olson and Chad Murchison on a circuitous route down the side of the mountain toward the valley.

0635 HOURS LOCAL

THE Bravos worked their way a short distance up the side of East Ridge, and found cover and concealment within a hundred meters of the mortars. They had an excellent view of the two weapons as the mujahideen made adjustments, then dropped the small shells down the tube.

"Jesus!" Connie Concord whispered through his LASH headset. "Them little mortars don't make hardly no sound at all."

"There isn't a flash either," Chad Murchison remarked. "And they don't just drop the shell down the tube. They pull a trigger there to fire it."

"That means a cartridge of some kind is involved," Connie said, thinking out loud.

Gutsy Olson, who had been sent a bit higher to recon the mountainside, now came back. "Them dumb bastards don't have no protection on the flanks. They're out there all by themselves just having a ball."

"Okay," Dawkins said. "Me and Murchison will take the far crew. Concord and Olson take the near one. Semi-auto. Let's make this fast. On my command." Everyone took aim, and an instant later the senior chief said, "Fire!"

Four of the six men on the site were hit by the single shots pumped into their midst. The other two, with one limping badly from a wound, abandoned the position to scramble higher up into the rocks. The SEALs rushed down toward the now abandoned mortar position, and the senior chief sent Gutsy and Chad to chase after the pair of escapees.

After examining the four sprawled corpses, Connie picked up one of the mortars. "I'll be damned!"

The senior chief gave it a close inspection. "I don't think I've ever seen anything like this."

"Me and Puglisi know this baby," Connie said. "We even fired it a few times when we went back to Fort Bragg for that weapons training at the Special Warfare Center." He tossed it to the senior chief. "See how light it is? Ten and a half pounds. It's nothing much more than a tube with little bitty base plate. See the carrying strap? You can sling that baby over your shoulder about as easy as a rifle."

"The damn thing is almost silent."

"Yeah," Connie said. "It's French. They call it the Fly-K. The ammo is fifty-one-millimeter and only weighs a couple of pounds."

Chad and Gutsy came back, and the latter made the report. "The wounded guy that was limping collapsed. I guess he bled to death. His buddy got up too high in them rocks for us to follow. He's prob'ly hauling ass over the top of the ridge by now."

"Okay," the senior chief said. "Our job is done here. Let's police up these two mortars and them ammunition pouches. How many of them is there?"

Connie counted. "Ten, Senior Chief. Each holds five rounds. That gives us fifty."

"There's a couple over here that are opened," Chad said. "One is empty and the other has three rounds in it."

"Bring it along," Dawkins ordered. "We can split up the weight between us. These sweet li'l babies could come in handy."

"Puglisi is gonna be surprised to see all this," Connie said.

"Yeah," Dawkins said. He smirked at Connie. "God! You said, 'Little bitty base plates.' You make it all sound so cutesy."

"Well, shit, Senior Chief," Connie said with a frown, "they *are* little bitty!"

BASE CAMP CP
1730 HOURS LOCAL

FRANK Gomez hurried from his commo site, across the ridge line to report to the skipper. He plopped down in front of the platoon commander and shoved a message pad page at him. "Big doings, sir!"

Brannigan took the paper and quickly perused the missive written in the radio operator's neat block printing style. "Damn!" He looked over at the small smokeless fire where Mike Assad and Dave Leibowitz were diligently boiling water for coffee. "Assad! Go fetch Lieutenant Cruiser and the chiefs!"

"Aye, sir!"

Mike leaped to his feet and rushed over to make a circuit of Bravo, Charlie and Delta Fire Teams. In less than a minute-and-a-half he was back with the lieutenant, Senior Chief Dawkins and Chief Gunnarson. He returned to his buddy Dave just in time to have a canteen cup of hot coffee handed to him.

Brannigan went straight to the subject at hand when he addressed his small staff. "Two things going down, gentlemen. When Commander Carey back in Isolation told us this mission had the potential to evolve into something a hell of a lot more complicated, he wasn't just whistling *Dixie*. We're getting a resupply drop at"—he checked his watch— "eighteen-thirty hours. That's less than an hour away."

"Great!" Cruiser commented. "I was starting to sweat the ammo and chow inventory."

"As was I," Brannigan said. "And I'm in no fucking mood to start living off the land." He scanned the message again. "Now this second bit is going to curl your toes. We are tasked with rescuing a couple of hostages being held down there in that warlord's compound."

"Our reconnaissance and the sketch map we updated will come in handy, sir," the senior chief said. "We noted they was two prisoners being held in one of them supply storage containers. They must be the hostages. We're gonna have to skirt the village and go through the vehicle park to get to it."

"Good to know," Brannigan said. "But first things first. We've got to concentrate on the resupply." He turned to Cruiser. "Figure out a good DZ up here on the ridge, and put out some panels. It'll still be light when the aircraft comes in."

"Aye, sir," Cruiser replied. "What kind of airplane is it going to be? And will they use parachutes or just dump the stuff out as they whip by?"

"Why should they give us all that information, Jim?" Brannigan said with a sardonic grin. "We're just the poor dumb bastards in the OA. If they dropped all that shit on our heads, we would be expected to be grateful just the same."

Cruiser got to his feet. "I'll get the panels."

"In the meantime, I'll use that sketch map to figure out some brilliant tactics to rescue those prisoners," Brannigan said. He nodded to the senior chief. "Stick around."

"Aye, sir."

1815 HOURS LOCAL

THE members of the crack AFSOC are little known by the American public. When the average citizen turns his mind to Special Forces, he thinks of SEALs, Green Berets, Rangers and Force Recon. He is unaware that there exist dedicated people in the United States Air Force who play a vital role in all SPECOPS. Those other, better known outfits would have a tough time without their courageous support. AFSOC provides infiltration and exfiltration services, resupply, fire support in combat situations and merciful MEDE-VAC and rescue services at the risk of their own lives.

One of the aircraft vital in these services is the MH-53J Pave Low helicopter. This extraordinary aircraft is equipped with FLIR that allows it to fly at low altitudes at night to arrive right on target. As well as having one of the most sophisticated navigation systems in the world, it can go six hundred miles without refueling. The choppers and their elite crews have proven themselves over and over, from the time of Desert Storm, where they led U.S. Army Apache helicopters in to destroy Iraqi radar positions, all the way through to the current campaigns in the Iraqi War and Afghanistan.

LIEUTENANT Bill Brannigan sat next to Frank Gonzales at the Shadowfire radio. He glanced out at the DZ that Cruiser and Chief Gunnarson had hastily organized with panels. They also had some smoke grenades handy, though no signal arrangements had been made for the use of the pyrotechnic devices. Brannigan had decided to follow the usual procedures, i.e., green smoke meant go, yellow smoke indicated go around again, and red was the signal to abort the mission.

The Shadowfire came to life with the voice of one of the Pave Low's six-man crew. "Delta Zulu, this is Chopper. We are fifteen minutes out. Supplies are on three pallets and will be pushed out the ass end at an altitude of zero-zero-low. We've been apprised of your coordinates, but we need an azimuth. Over."

Brannigan grabbed the mike. "Chopper, this is Delta Zulu. We have laid out panels indicating direction of flight. Use them as your first target. Azimuth is sweet and simple. Fly due north. Over."

"This is Chopper. Out."

1830 HOURS LOCAL

THE Pave Low could be seen flying south, then it made a slow turn and lined up on the crest of the ridge. Immediately it began spewing countermeasure flares that blossomed thickly and brightly around it. The pilot brought it in at such a low altitude that the aircraft appeared to be almost on the deck. Just as it passed over Cruiser's panels, the first bundled pallet slid out and hit the ground, skidding forward. Then a second and third quickly followed. With the load delivered, the power was increased and the aircraft made a rapid climb and turn as it sped back up to altitude.

The platoon members rushed out to the pallets, unbuckling the heavy nylon straps holding the bundles to the wooden platforms. The rations and ammunition issues were greatly appreciated. But the unexpected four cases of beer put there by the thoughtful Air Force crew elicited cheers of sincere gratitude.

2200 HOURS LOCAL

THE supplies—and beer—had been distributed among the four fire teams, and now the entire platoon was gathered in a semicircle around the CP for the briefing on the hostage rescue mission. All the extra weapons and ammo had been packed away, and the men, each with a six-pack of Michelob, were in a good mood as they waited for the skipper to begin the briefing for the upcoming operation.

Brannigan took a sip from a can of beer, then raised it high. "Here's to the magnificent guys of the United States Air Force Special Operations Command. God bless 'em!"

"God bless 'em!" came back the shouts with fifteen cans raised high in a toast to their comrades-in-arms of the flying branch.

"Now hear this!" Brannigan said. "Let's get down to business. The mission requires us to get into that warlord's compound and pull out two poor bastards he's holding there for ransom. I'll discuss the details of my OPORD following personnel assignments. Listen up!"

Both chief petty officers gave the platoon a careful look to make sure everyone was paying attention in spite of guzzling beer.

"A diversion will be created by the entire Second Squad," Brannigan continued. "Meanwhile the First Squad will move in and set up firing positions as close to the compound wall as possible. I will take Assad and Leibowitz with me over the wall and into the compound to the storage container where the prisoners are locked up. We'll get 'em out of there and over the wall. We'll join up with the rest of the squad and move to a rendezvous area where the Second Squad will join us. From there we come back here. Any questions so far?"

Chad Murchison raised his hand. "Are the hostages going to be exfiltrated from the base camp any time soon?"

"I don't know at this point," Brannigan said. "Once we have 'em here, we'll radio into SOCOM in Bahrain. Someone will have to make a decision." He checked his notes. "All right! Here's the execution phase of the mission."

Everyone instinctively leaned forward.

CHAPTER 8

THE entire Second Squad, under the command of Lieutenant Jim Cruiser, had spent three careful hours traveling across the barren area between East Ridge and the warlord's compound. The night vision goggles were helpful in finding their way under the cloudy night sky, and they traversed the terrain, showing green-white through the viewing devices, as rapidly as security precautions allowed. They knew the mujahideen would be nervous and angry in this volatile situation. That meant the ragheads on guard duty would be especially edgy and watchful at night. Thus, any careless sound such as an inadvertently kicked rock or one piece of equipment banging against another could bring salvos of incoming fire on the SEALs.

Now, sweat-soaked from the dangerous trek, the Second Squad was two hundred meters from the southeast portion of the walls around the warlord's compound. This put them in a position exactly opposite of where the First Squad would be located during the hostage rescue portion of the mission. Bruno Puglisi had one of the French mortars slung over his muscular left shoulder while his M-16/M-203 hung on the right. Joe Miskoski had been chosen to be his assistant gunner, and he had rigged haversacks from a couple of the ammo packs for use in carrying the shells. They both breathed the proverbial sighs of relief when the squad reached its objective and they could drop the extra weaponry to set up a mortar emplacement.

Cruiser, in his usual micromanagement style, personally selected firing positions for each man and the mortar. After the emplacements were scooped out of the ground with entrenching tools, the SEALs gathered brush to use as concealment around the fighting holes. Noise discipline was a must in those hours of darkness, when even the softest of sounds was amplified. It took extra effort to do the work in silence.

A half hour later, as soon as each man was ready, the lieutenant went to his own position and readied himself for the battle ahead. He checked his watch, observing the luminescent second hand work its way up to the 12. After one more glance around, he spoke in an excited whisper over the LASH headset to his mortar team.

"Fire!"

FIRST SQUAD
0045 HOURS LOCAL

THE firing of the first mortar rounds was a welcome sound to the First Squad. The Bravo Fire Team under Senior Chief Buford Dawkins was set up similarly to the Second Squad on the other side of the compound. However, the Bravos were charged with fire support only and were under strict orders not to shoot unless absolutely necessary. Brannigan wanted the mujahideen to think there was only one attack and it was coming from the southeast side. If this ploy failed, then the mission of the First Squad would deteriorate into a fighting withdrawal. In that disastrous event, Connie Concord was standing by with his M-16/M-203 ready to arc HE grenades at any potential attackers. Since he would have no time to employ one of the more effective French mini-mortars, the second of these recently acquired weapons had been left back on West Ridge.

"Let's go," Brannigan whispered, and he moved out toward the northwest portion of the compound wall. The rest of Alpha Fire Team—Mike Assad, Frank Gomez and Dave Leibowitz—followed after him. When they reached the mud fortress, Mike knelt down while Dave stood in front of him. Brannigan stepped on Mike's back and went up on Dave's shoulders then stepped up on the wall and slipped over, dropping to the ground. Frank did the same, but stayed on top of the wall to reach down and pull Mike and Dave up. In less than forty-five seconds they were all inside the compound.

The people of the village were already noisily reacting to the firing off to the southeast, and the men had sleepily stumbled outside, carrying their weapons. Their leaders shouted at them in the Pashto language, gesturing for them to hurry toward the sound of the fighting.

The Alphas skirted the outlying huts of the village and swung around to the vehicle park. They concealed themselves behind a Ford van and waited for a good opportunity to get over to the storage containers. The firing from the Second Squad had built up to a steady crescendo, and the loud detonations of mortar shells punctuated the rolling thunder of the fusillades. Jim Cruiser and his two fire teams were rocking and rolling with a vengeance.

Meanwhile, the women were out in front of their huts, obviously frightened out of their wits. They clung to their children, screeching at the boys who wanted to go join their dads and older brothers in the fighting. These were people who had endured attacks before, yet they could still panic into spasms of irrationality, to wander around where stray bullets could quickly end a life or cause grievous wounds.

But they did have the presence of mind to turn out all the lanterns in their quarters.

The Alphas waited a few minutes to be sure the villagers' collective attention was wrapped up in the developing battle. Then Brannigan whispered, "Let's have a jailbreak!"

He led his trio of men off to the shadows at the side of the vehicle park and over to an area where two large storage containers were situated in a row. The four SEALs came to a sudden stop when they heard excited male voices a few meters ahead. After determining that the speakers were stationary, they eased forward in the shadows to check the mujahideen's exact position.

The two fighters, obviously standing guard in the area where the hostages were held, stood looking toward the sound of the fighting. They seemed to be discussing whether to remain at their assigned sentry post or go join their brother mujahideen doing battle with the attackers. Brannigan pulled his K-Bar, pointed to himself and then to the man on the right. Next he pointed to Mike and the man on the left. Now Mike pulled his knife as Dave and Frank took the CAR-15s from him and the Skipper to hold while the owners tended to the bloody task ahead.

The two moved slowly toward their quarry, appreciative of the noise from all the shooting some hundred meters away. They stopped a scant two paces from the guards, then Brannigan nodded to order the attack. Both SEALs struck simultaneously with the viciousness of cobras, driving the blades of their weapons under the back of rib cages and up into the vital areas where organs and arteries were located. The knives were violently twisted to enlarge the wounds. Brannigan and Mike kept their hands over the victims' mouths, working the knives until the mujahideen went limp. At that point the dead men were lowered gently to the ground to avoid unnecessary noise.

"Shit!" Mike whispered. "The son of a bitch vomited."

"It's a messy job no matter which way you cut it," Brannigan said. "No pun intended."

They resheathed the K-Bars, retrieved their weapons from

Dave and Frank, then went to the first container. This was the one Senior Chief Buford Dawkins had reported as the one where two prisoners were being kept. Brannigan noted that there was no lock on the door; only a handle that slid through an eyelet to hold it shut. He pulled the lever on the handle and pushed the device to the side. The door cracked a bit, and he had to pull it the rest of the way open.

Two frightened young men looked up at him. The wide-eyed and openmouthed expressions on their faces made them appear weird in the night vision goggles. They cringed as if expecting to be shot.

Brannigan spoke quickly. "Do you speak English?"

"Yes," one said, puzzled. "We are speaking English. Who are you?"

"I'm the guy that's going to get you the hell out of here," Brannigan said, noting the overflowing bucket used for a night toilet. "Follow me out of this place."

"Oh, yes, sir," one said. "We are thanking you so very much."

"You are a nice man," the other added.

"Right," Brannigan said. "Now listen carefully. You can't see, but we're wearing night vision goggles. Do you understand? We can see perfectly in the dark."

"We are understanding what it is you are telling us," the first said.

"When we get outside, I'm going to have each of you grab the belt of one of my men to hold on to for guidance. We'll move rapidly as possible, but don't worry about bumping into anything. We'll be as careful as we can. We'll be going to a wall. We'll help you over, and then join the rest of my command. Now listen up! You must be quiet. Don't make any noise. Don't say a thing. Not a word."

"We are being quiet like little mouses," the second man promised.

Brannigan took them outside, handing one over to Frank and the other to Dave. Thus, prepared, they moved back through the vehicle park toward the wall.

SECOND SQUAD
0115 HOURS LOCAL

THE fighting on the southeast wall built up in intensity as more mujahideen joined their brothers-in-arms at the position. The tower at that corner of the fortification became unpopular with the warlord's men since the SEALs kept a steady fire on it whenever someone had the temerity to climb up in it to shoot down at them. The flares fired up by the defenders made them bolder than they should have been. Within short minutes, a total of eight dead men lay almost one on top of the other in the tower. By that time, none of the other mujahideen had any intention of occupying the place. They all stayed along the wall, firing from parapets built into the structure.

Bruno Puglisi and Joe Miskoski had to go through a vital learning process with the mortar, firing several rounds before they got the hang of the little support weapon. They were extremely inaccurate with the first three shots, but the resultant shell strikes scared the hell out of the mujahideen. But it wasn't long before the two impromptu mortarmen had the elevation and traverse down, and had found the range for the wall itself.

Joe slid a shell down the tube. As soon as it was positioned, Puglisi pulled the trigger. It responded with an "oomph" sound as it fired, and the intrepid mortar gunners made a count of "hut-thousand, two-thousand, three-thousand" until reaching "six-thousand." At that moment the shell fell on the wall, blowing chunks of mud and pieces of mujahideen straight up into the air. This strike was immediately followed by three more.

The defenders expected an all-out assault from a large number of attackers now that their wall was breached. They prepared themselves by quickly occupying positions where they could cover the ragged opening when the expected horde of infidels charged through it.

But Cruiser's Second Squad stayed put, throwing out short bursts of automatic fire. One of the senior mujahideen, feeling the power of Allah surging through his soul, organized a half dozen others into a small attacking force with wild screams of religious urgings to follow him. He led the small group through the wall and out into the open country. None of them made more than three steps before the combined fire of six CAR-15s cut them down.

Now Puglisi and Joe began to pace their barrages to make their supply of shells last as long as possible.

ALPHA FIRE TEAM

WHILE the Second Squad kept that part of the wall pinned down, Brannigan and his Alpha Team were on the opposite side of the compound, struggling to get the two hostages over the top of the earthen barrier.

Neither one was in particularly good physical condition, and the poor diet they had been receiving in the warlord's crude jail had not helped either. One was pudgy, with little athletic ability, and the other was skinny with a minimum of physical strength. When they reached the wall, Dave Leibowitz boosted his buddy Mike Assad up to the top. When Mike was positioned, he reached down, taking the hand of the pudgy hostage as he was pushed upward toward him. He pulled the guy hard, getting him astride the wall.

"Stay here," Mike ordered. He looked down at Dave. "Next!"

The skinny guy was quickly pulled up and positioned next to his buddy. Next the Skipper and Frank Gomez were hefted up. Both Frank and Brannigan reached down and grabbed Dave's wrists to haul him to the top. The SEALs leaped down to the opposite side of the wall, then turned and helped their charges to lower themselves to the ground.

With all the Alphas and the two hostages out of the fort, the group moved across the open ground to link up with the rest of the First Squad.

"How'd it go?" Senior Chief Buford Dawkins asked as they joined the others. "They was two of 'em, huh?"

"Right, Senior Chief," Mike answered. "They wouldn't be classified One-A by their local draft board so we'll have to make allowances for them while we haul ass the hell out of here."

The sound of the fighting to the southeast rose and fell, showing that the battle was still going at full speed. "Let's go, people!" Brannigan ordered. "Form a squad column with our guests in the middle. Move out!"

The small group headed southward to the scheduled rendezvous with Second Squad.

SECOND SQUAD
0145 HOURS LOCAL

LIEUTENANT Jim Cruiser checked his watch. It was now time to go into the fire-and-maneuver withdrawal phase to break contact with the mujahideen. "Puglisi! Miskoski!" he said over the LASH. "Make a final barrage. Six rounds."

"Aye, sir," Bruno Puglisi replied.

Joe Miskoski inserted the first shell into the tube, then Puglisi pulled the trigger. This was repeated five more times as the rest of the squad lay down heavy fire on the mujahideen behind the rubble of the wall. When the final mortar round was launched, Puglisi folded up the weapon and slung it over his shoulder, wincing at the feel of the hot tube through his BDU. Joe grabbed the haversack with the three remaining rounds.

"Charlie Fire Team!" Cruiser said. "Continue to fire! Delta Fire Team, withdraw!"

Joe joined his Charlie mates, adding his CAR-15 to the fusillades. Puglisi fell in with the Deltas now rushing rearward. They went some fifteen meters before turning and dropping to the ground. As soon as they began firing, the Charlies leaped to their feet and rushed back to join them.

This began a seesaw action of withdrawal and covering fire as the squad successfully broke off contact with the mujahideen. At that point, they turned west to meet up with the First Squad at the contact point.

THE PLATOON
0215 HOURS LOCAL

THE squads linked up at a point along East Ridge that was two kilometers south of the warlord's compound. The two hostages were exhausted from the quick run down the ridge line and were sitting on the ground breathing hard as the First Squad made its appearance. The fatter one gagged, then rolled over to his hands and knees to vomit.

James Bradley quickly checked him out. "He's just tired, sir," he reported to Brannigan. "I'll give them both stimulants."

"Do it quickly," Brannigan said. He looked the SEALs over, glad to note that they had taken no casualties. "Guys," he said, relieved, "this mission has been a piece of cake so far. Everything's going our way, but we've got to stay on our toes. I want everyone to concentrate on their assignments. This is the time that things can really get fucked up."

Jim Cruise glanced over at the hostages. "Do you think they can make it all the way back to the CP?"

"Bradley's getting them hopped up on some of his pills," Brannigan said. "At least they don't have to hump any heavy gear." He walked up to a point in front of the platoon. "Let's get the hell out of here! Platoon column! First Squad on the right, Second Squad on the left. Assad and Leibowitz take the point. Chiefs, each of you put a flanker out."

Dawkins nodded to Gutsy Olson. "Take the right flank."

Adam Clifford got the honors in the First Squad as he was ordered out to the left side of the column.

When they were all formed up, Brannigan signaled up to the front where Mike Assad and Dave Leibowitz waited. "Take us home!"

The platoon, with the officers and hostages in the middle of the column, moved westward into the darkness.

THE WARLORD'S COMPOUND
0730 HOURS LOCAL

THE devastation in the southeast corner of the wall was complete. The remnants of that corner of the earthen fortification were no more than piles of dirt with bits of mud brick mixed in. The mujahideen had pulled the corpses of their brethren from the wreckage and carried them back to the village area. Even now the loud keening of mourning women permeated the atmosphere with the intensity of bitch wolves howling in the mountains.

Warlord Ayyub Durtami stood on the roof of his residence with Ahmet Kharani, looking out over the valley between the compound and the ridge. "I have now lost almost a hundred men in these past days," Durtami said. "Who can those infidel devils be? And how many are they?"

"They could be getting reinforcements, *Amir*," Kharani suggested. "Perhaps they grow stronger as we grow weaker."

"They took the hostages!" Durtami exclaimed. "How in Satan's power could that have happened? Some of them actually came in here amongst us, killed two guards and took our prisoners away. What sort of demons are they? Do they have black magic to make them invisible?"

"They are not phantoms, *Amir*," Kharani assured him.

"Then we must do something or my men's fear will grow to panic! The unbelievers must be crushed as soon as possible. We can no longer tolerate this situation. It will cost many men, I fear, but an all-out effort would surely bring us a victory."

"Unfortunately, we do not know what part of the far ridge they are on," Kharani reminded him.

"I have a good idea what their position might be from the place the patrol of young fighters was wiped out," Durtami said. "And the mortar section that was massacred also gives us solid evidence of their campsite."

Kharani glanced over where the dead of the battle were now being prepared for burial. "You are right, *Amir.* The men are losing their courage. If we do not score a victory soon, your fiefdom will be lost to the infidel Americans and Europeans. The government in Kabul will send troops here. Your men will run away with their families. They will seek shelter and protection from your brother-in-law Hassan Khamami."

"I did not think the situation grave enough," Durtami admitted, "but now I recognize that I must proclaim a jihad—a holy war—to give the men the will and ferocity to sacrifice themselves for a final victory."

The words just spoken had an instant effect on Kharani. He was close to tears with religious fervor. "Praise Allah who is merciful and beneficent! He shall give us a magnificent victory and welcome our dead mujahideen to Paradise."

"Allah akbar!" Durtami exclaimed. "God is great!"

CP ON WEST RIDGE
1445 HOURS LOCAL

THE platoon, except for the men on watch, was at rest. Those off duty lounged on their foam mattresses, the more thrifty now consuming the final cans of beer they had hoarded from their six-packs.

The hostages were situated in good cover and concealment next to the CP. They were worn out, though revived slightly with MRE meals of spaghetti and meatballs. Now they sprawled in the shade of the camouflage, wrapped in poncho liners lent them by platoon members. The SEALs had been able to learn at least a little bit about their guests.

The chubbier one was named Ibrahim and his skinny buddy Hajji. Both were idealistic about the potentials of a democratic Afghanistan and had been enthusiastic workers for the new government. Unfortunately, at that moment the two were badly traumatized by their latest experience.

The incident of their capture had scared the hell out of them. Their bodyguards had been gunned down without mercy in a roaring metal hailstorm of automatic fire. Ibrahim and Hajji had expected the same, and the experience of awaiting an instant and sure death was something no human can endure calmly, even if he survives the experience. Their captivity had been unpleasant because of more than just bad food. Additionally, they were occasionally paraded through the compound, where the women and children shrieked insults and threw stones at them. With all that, they also had to endure for no apparent reason a good deal of physical punishment by surly guards.

The rescue had been unexpected and welcome, and going over the wall with burly, friendly Americans had given them a realistic hope for survival. But now they were on the top of a rocky mountain ridge, had no idea what was going to happen to them and had begun to seriously wonder if there was a possibility of being recaptured.

Before they fully succumbed to their exhaustion, they forced themselves to take care of one important matter. Using the poncho liners as prayer mats, they prayed to Allah, asking to be taken back to the safety of civilization.

CHAPTER 9

**WARLORD DURTAMI'S COMPOUND
18 AUGUST
1700 HOURS LOCAL**

THE Warlord Ayyub Durtami and his chief lieutenant Ahmet Kharani, along with a trio of bodyguards, stood on top of the warlord's residence. They gazed down at the sullen crowd of mujahideen gathered in the open space below. No women were present, as would be expected, but adolescent boys stood at the periphery of the crowd, the expressions on their faces exhibiting confusion and dismay. The youngsters sensed something was terribly wrong.

The dead were buried and the wounded were being taken care of as well as possible by people using basic medicines and bandaging techniques. With the blessings of Allah, perhaps 50 percent of the injured would survive the crude treatment, though some of them could be expected to end up permanently crippled human wrecks. Meanwhile, work on repairing the wall was under way. A trio of vans had driven over to the village of Herandbe, where a dozen unlucky farmers were rousted from their work in the fields to be brought over as a labor crew. Now they struggled to rebuild the corner of the fortification that had been pounded to pieces by mortar shells. Dark spots of blood showed on the smashed mud blocks and the ground where the dead and wounded had fallen.

Durtami nodded to the bodyguards beside him. They raised their AK-47s and fired off short bursts of automatic fire to get the attention of the muttering crowd. When all eyes were on the warlord, he raised his hands as if calling his fighters to prayer. "We have been invaded by infidels!" he proclaimed. "They serve Satan and have been sent by the Evil One to destroy us. For more than a week they have lurked unseen in these mountains and valleys, protected by the black magic of absolute evil. At first we fought them as we would fight mortal men. But we might as well have been naked under this onslaught of Satan's power as he sought to destroy us."

The mujahideen were visibly moved by this revelation. The warlord's words explained a lot about their recent failures in battle, and all now knew this had not come from their failings. Supernatural evil had brought this calamity down on them. Frightened expressions that had dominated their features had now turned to scowls of righteous anger.

"These defeats we suffered were like ancient plagues of locusts," Durtami continued. "Fighting the Evil One is beyond mortal men's capabilities. Therefore, in order to destroy the demons, I now, at this very moment, with the blessings of Allah the Merciful, the Beneficent"—he paused for effect—"I declare jihad—holy war!"

Now the mujahideen cheered, jumping and prancing around as they waved their weapons over their heads. In their minds this meant divine protection and guidance to achieve certain victory over this diabolical enemy. Several minutes went by and the bodyguards had to fire into the air to get them to simmer down. They turned their attention back to the warlord.

"What I have said to you is thus written in the Holy Koran!" Durtami shouted. "We shall know the greatest victory in the history of Islam!"

This was a hint for Kharani to step forward with the Holy Book. He opened it at a marked page and read loudly so all could hear. "When great wrong afflicts the True Believers, they should defend themselves! And when the True Believers defend themselves they do no wrong! The wrong is done by those who oppress the True Believers unjustly, and they shall suffer the most painful of punishments." He closed the Koran. "These words of Allah are proof that we shall win. Thus, have no fear, brothers, you will prevail over the Evil One's servants!"

Durtami took over again. "It is written that we are in the right by striking back viciously at the infidel followers of Satan! Allah looks down on us as we go forth on the holy mission! Fear not death, for if you die in this struggle you will immediately go to Paradise where seventy *houri* virgins will serve you and pleasure you throughout eternity. With this jihad now declared all of our brothers who have already died have received their rewards and now live with Allah and the Prophet. Prepare yourselves for this great battle that will destroy the demons prowling our land. You shall force them and their leader, Satan, back into the depths of hell!"

The mujahideen went back to wild cheering and more prancing around, their eyes wide with excitement. At first their shouting was intermingled and uncoordinated, but after a few moments chants began to emerge from the roaring voices.

"Jihad! Jihad!"

"Allah is great!"

"Death to the infidels!"

Over in the village, the women had gotten the gist of the warlord's speech, and now shrilled their warbling encouragement to the men.

WEST RIDGE
19 AUGUST
0545 HOURS LOCAL

THE mujahideen had gone en masse to the base of the ridge, looking toward their objective at the top. They moved quietly and slowly into what cover they could find in the rocks, to await the order to charge. There was no unit integrity among them, although they tended to congregate with special friends on this holy mission. The previous night had been spent fasting and praying as each prepared himself for the glorious struggle ahead.

Bashar Abzai was among the fighters. This man who had been made a sergeant was by himself in the crowd. His best friend, Sayed, had died on the wall, and now Abzai turned his thoughts to this departed comrade. Neither one of the young men had ever had a woman. Once, back when they were teenagers, an itinerate camel driver passing through with a caravan had photographs of naked females for sale. The sight of the rounded feminine bodies, with breasts, wide hips and hairy triangles between their thighs, caused them to tremble with a strange desire they could not fully understand. As they viewed the images, their penises grew hard and extended with a throbbing that was somehow as pleasurable as it was troublesome. This thing with women was confusing. By Islamic law the young men were forbidden casual fornication, yet Allah had made women so alluring.

But Sayed, now in his eternal life, knew all. At that moment he would be among seventy *houris,* and all would be naked as he enjoyed them to his heart's content under the blessings of Allah. Every day and night in the endless spinning passage of eternity, Sayed's secret passions would no longer be smothered. Instead he would have endless hours of the greatest pleasure known by man.

Abzai turned his thoughts to Paradise. It must be a wonderful place, where it was never too cold or too hot; where succulent meats, fruit, breads and cakes were available in unlimited quantities; and where sweet nectars and cold clear water slaked one's thirst. No hard winds drove gritty dust into one's face in Paradise. No hard work exhausted one's muscles until they cramped and burned. And those *houris*! Those wonderful, beautiful *houris*!

Abzai's reverie was suddenly broken by a loud shout from the rear. "*Allah akbar*! God is Great!" That was the signal to advance upward to kill Satan's demons. The young mujahideen leaped to his feet and began moving toward the summit of the ridge, joining the shouting of the other warriors of Islam.

"*Allah akbar!*"

THE BATTLE

JOE Miskoski was on the morning watch, looking out through the diminishing gloom of the night, when he heard the noises below. He looked downward, then grabbed his binoculars. Dozens of mujahideen moved up the side of the ridge toward him, looking like animated rag dolls.

Over to his right, Kevin Albee and Milly Mills reacted by firing down into the human targets bobbing among the rocks and boulders as they progressed upward. At almost that exact moment Chief Matt Gunnarson appeared among the trio of SEALs. After one quick look, he hurried over to the CP to alert the platoon.

BACK on the top of East Ridge, Warlord Ayyub Durtami and his entourage watched the attack across the valley. Ahmet Kharani held a pair of Soviet binoculars to his eyes. He spoke softly but in good spirits. "The fighters are doing well, *Amir*. They are filled with the holy spirit as they work their way upward toward the infidels."

Durtami was satisfied just looking at the distant figures of the mujahideen moving among the concealment of boulders and brush as they made a rapid advance to close with the enemy. "Today is our day, Brother Kharani," he said with uncharacteristic friendliness. "I hope we will find many weapons and ammunition bandoleers among the corpses of the infidels. Our stocks have shrunk over the past weeks."

LIEUTENANT Wild Bill Brannigan was at the firing line, moving from position to position as the SEALs fired single, aimed shots at the enemy advancing up the ridge in an uncoordinated, ragged assault. It was obvious the mujahideen planned on overwhelming them by sheer numbers. Automatic fire, even three-round bursts, would have been a waste of ammunition at that range. The platoon, with each man working within his individual field of fire, picked out targets of opportunity that bounded among the boulders. Now and then, after firing a well-aimed round, they were rewarded with the sight of an attacker suddenly staggering back and falling to the sloped ground as the strike of a bullet ended his life. Some rolled a few meters down, until their corpses collided with the rocks and brush scattered over the terrain.

Bruno Puglisi had no opportunity to set up the French mortars because Connie Concord, the other fire support man, was covering the opposite side of the ridge with Bravo Team. But Puglisi was able to use his M-203 to advantage when groups of mujahideen inadvertently congregated. Occasionally, the 40-millimeter grenades did a lot of damage, throwing shrapnel and shards of rock into the groups. But most times the targeted individuals had dispersed by the time Puglisi could get off a shot.

The attack pressed relentlessly upward, and the platoon began to have the disturbing sensation of shoveling sand against the tide. The ragged figures advancing toward them were rapidly closing the gap between the two battling groups of desperate men. Brannigan shouted encouragement to his men, urging quick, but carefully aimed firing.

Bravo Fire Team suddenly showed up from the other side of the base camp. Senior Chief Buford Dawkins threw himself down beside Brannigan.

"Sir," he reported, "they ain't nobody coming at us from the other side. They must be concentrating their whole effort on this part of the ridge."

"All right," Brannigan said. "Get your guys out on the perimeter here. The pressure is building."

"Bravos!" the senior chief shouted. "Follow me."

Within moments, four more weapons began firing into the attackers.

BASHAR Abzai hit the ground and rolled, ending up behind a large bullet-streaked boulder. He waited a moment, then stood up and fired two long fire bursts upward toward the infidel positions. His third salvo was cut short when the final bullet in the weapon was fired.

He pulled out the empty magazine and inserted a fresh one stocked with thirty rounds. The used one went into his bandoleer for reloading later. He glanced downward and could see mujahideen sprawled among the rocks. A couple were stirring slightly, while another sat up tending to a leg wound. Abzai turned back to the business at hand. He picked out some brush ten meters away to use as concealment. After a deep breath, he leaped to his feet and ran toward it.

Something hit him hard in the chest, and his legs gave out. He fell face first, rolling over on his back to gaze up at the morning sky. He knew at that moment that he was dying. He thought it strange that he should recognize the fact so quickly after being hit. It was also extraordinary that he was completely at peace about leaving the world of the living. Abzai thought about his friend Sayed. It would be good to see him again. Sayed would be interested in hearing about this day's battle, and would rejoice in the victory as much as if he had fought in it.

The dying mujahideen also thought about the *houris* even now anticipating his arrival in Paradise. As he lay on the mountainside with his life's blood leaking out into the hard-packed rocky terrain, he decided he would pick out one *houri* to be his favorite. She would be the most beautiful one, of course, and she would be delighted to be the number one. Abzai decided he would give her a name. Khesta Bibi. *Au*—yes! A perfect name: Beautiful Lady.

An exchange of gunfire sent bullets zipping over his body, but by then Bashar Abzai was unaware of what went on around his mortal remains.

CHAD Murchison and Milly Mills were sent back to the ammo dump next to the CP to pick up loads of ammunition to pass out on the perimeter. As they gathered the munitions, they could see the two hostages Ibrahim and Hajji huddled together back in the Skipper's camouflaged area.

Chad nodded to them. "How're you chaps doing?"

Ibrahim forced a grin. "Oh, we are doing fine. Thank you for asking."

"You are winning the battle, are you not?" Hajji inquired in a worried tone.

"Piece of cake," Milly said.

"No, thank you," Ibrahim said, misunderstanding what the American meant. "We are not being hungry at this moment."

Chad laughed and winked at the other SEAL. "C'mon, Milly, we must hurry."

They ran awkwardly under the weight of rucksacks stuffed with bandoleers of 5.56-millimeter ammunition and the extra HE grenades for Connie Concord and Bruno Puglisi. They skirted the perimeter, then split up going to their respective squads to drop off ammo for each man. When Chad reached Connie, he handed over the M-203 ammo. Connie happily took the explosives, asking, "What about the mortars? Has the Skipper said anything about 'em?"

Chad shook his head. "Nope. He only said to fetch some more grenades for the M-203s."

"Well," Connie said. "Me and Bruno wouldn't have time to zero 'em in anyhow."

Chad hurried over to the rock stand shared by the Odd Couple Mike Assad and David Leibowitz. Each took three bandoleers, placing them beside his firing position. "There's gonna be a long line at the gates to Muslim heaven today," Mike commented.

"Yeah," Dave said, "but them guys are gonna be disappointed. I got it on good authority that instead of seventy virgins, they'll get one virgin seventy years old."

Chad laughed, then hurried away when fresh volleys of fire came from down below. The Skipper was set up slightly behind the rifle positions, and he had called for Jim Cruiser and both chief petty officers to join him. He looked at Cruiser. "Give me a quick SITREP for Second Squad."

Cruiser, still panting a bit from running over from his position, replied, "The assault is slowing down noticeably. They're taking on a hell of a lot more casualties now that they've drawn closer. I think we've broken the back of the attack."

Senior Chief Buford Dawkins nodded. "Same with us, sir. Their firing is growing sporadic. It builds up real quicklike then peters out. There's also some periods when we get no incoming a'tall. But I don't think them dumb bastards has figured out they're starting to beat they heads against a brick wall."

"Okay," Brannigan said. "Get back to your guys and tell 'em to turn it up a notch. Maybe we can wrap this thing up within the next half hour."

THE mujahideen were out of steam. With high casualties and their ammunition running low, all the religious ardor they brought to the battle was fading with their energy and confidence. Most of them were no longer firing as they huddled behind bits of cover provided by the rocks and brush.

Fire from above began to build up until bullets slapped the air and kicked up dirt around them in what seemed a constant fusillade. The temporary encouragement brought on by the proclamation of a jihad continued to rapidly wane as the reality of the situation began to sink in.

One man suddenly leaped up and began running down the hillside. He kept going, gaining speed until he was out of range of the infidels. Another followed him. Then another, then a dozen, then more, until all the survivors ran for their lives, stumbling and staggering as they tried to make it down the hill. They leaped over their dead and wounded, only wanting to get out of the kill zone.

Warlord Ayyub Durtami watched impassively at the deterioration of his fighting force. He knew deep in his heart that he, his fighters and fiefdom were things of the past. None of this existed anymore. Ahmet Kharani, ever loyal, walked over and took his warlord by the sleeve. "*Amir*, we must go. The men will soon be climbing this ridge to get to the other side. We must get back to the fortress to make our plans."

Durtami took a deep breath. "That will not require much time, Brother Ahmet. I think we both know what we must do now."

"Yes," Kharani said. "It is best that you seek out your brother-in-law and put yourself and all of us under his authority. He leads a great force with many weapons."

Durtami pulled his arm free, turning to walk down the other side of the ridge.

ALL along the defensive line, the SEALs stood up to watch the disintegrating mujahideen force as it melted away from the battle. Brannigan walked forward to stand on a rocky outcrop that offered a good view. The rag dolls were now scattered thickly down the ridge, most lying still in death, while the wounded moved slightly in the shock and agony of their injuries.

Brannigan walked over to Alpha Fire Team's position and

yelled for Frank Gomez. The radioman hurried over to report to the commanding officer. "Yes, sir?"

"Give me your message pad, Frank."

"Aye, sir," Frank said, handing it over.

Brannigan took out a ballpoint pen and began writing in it. "We've got to get a quick SITREP back to Station Bravo in Bahrain," he said as he scribbled the message. "I'm curious as to what else they have for us to do around here."

Frank shrugged. "I hope they're gonna want to get those two hostages out of here, sir. They're a couple of useless mouths for us to feed."

Brannigan continued to write.

CHAPTER 10

THE convoy was colorful, noisy, diverse and filled with panic and the loud buzzing and chugging of engines. Vans, pickup trucks, motor-rickshaws and motorbikes made up the formation of travelers. Each was overloaded with people and possessions that made it dangerously top heavy as it rocked back and forth on the bucolic thoroughfare that led them all north to safety.

This was the entire band of Warlord Durtami abandoning their homes, compound and dead male relatives scattered on the eastern slopes of West Ridge. The widows and orphans of the slain mujahideen had been taken in by relatives for this exodus that was spurred on by unadulterated terror. In many cases old men who had years before surrendered their paternal authority to sons and grandsons were once again the masters of their families. The male descendents who died in the battle attacking West Ridge left behind widows and orphans to be taken care of by these dismayed grandfathers. A once settled and secure population had changed from permanent residents of a stable community to homeless refugees in only a matter of hours.

Rampant rumors of the imminent appearance of baby-eating demons who lusted for sex with human women ran through the throng of fleeing people. Those invincible servants of Satan were expected to appear at any moment and fall on the convoy in a frenzy of raping murder and child-devouring.

The fault for this calamity was laid on residents of the compound who were thought to be less devout toward Islam than the more righteous followers of the community. Surely these neighbors' irreverence was what brought Allah's wrath down on the people. This overwhelming fear, generated by a combination of religious myth and folklore, gave impetus to the people's terror. If it weren't for those sinners, their lives would have continued as before. But instead, they now ran like rabbits while mourning the deaths of most of their young men.

A special group of vehicles that included a Russian UAZ sedan led the way. This vehicle had been used by the murdered bodyguards of the lost hostages. It was now part of the entourage and families of Warlord Ayyub Durtami and his chief lieutenant Ahmet Kharani. Their vehicles were the best maintained of the whole group, and the distance between them and the common people increased rapidly as the exodus continued.

The road they followed was not much more than a wide track worn in the hard-packed earth. Parts of it had been washed away during flash floods that followed heavy rains, and the travelers made their way across the barely discernible areas by using a distant mountain peak as a reference for the proper direction of their destination. This was the fortress of the great Warlord Hassan Khamami and the sanctuary he could offer them.

THE ABANDONED COMPOUND
NOON LOCAL

MIKE Assad and Dave Leibowitz were on the point of the platoon as the SEALs slowly approached the compound. The remainder of the platoon was spread out in a skirmish formation, ready to react to any signs of resistance from the mujahideen community.

When they reached the wall, Mike and Dave were hoisted to the top by Bill Brannigan and Frank Gomez. The two scouts gazed into what was obviously a completely abandoned site. Mike laughed, looking down at the Skipper. "Sir, there's an open gate just around the corner. Do you want to use it or make the guys climb this wall?"

"The exercise would do them good," Brannigan said with a grin. "But I'll give 'em a break today. We'll go through the gate."

Frank Gomez, with the extra twenty pounds of the Shadowfire radio on his back, grinned. "*Ay, que bueno!* I was afraid I was gonna have to heft this fucking thing over the top."

While Mike and Dave dropped down to the ground inside, Brannigan signaled to the others to follow him as he headed for the gate. The fire teams, along with the two hostages Ibrahim and Hajji, moved toward the community. As soon as they arrived, the hostages immediately attached themselves to Brannigan as if they were under special protection while in his presence. They were uncomfortable in the fortress even though the mujahideen had departed the place.

The two scouts were waiting when the rest of the platoon entered the compound. Brannigan turned to his fire teams. "Bravos! Check out the village huts. Charlies! See what they've got over in that vehicle park. Deltas! Take a walk along the entire perimeter of the wall. Alphas! Come with me to check out the big building."

Brannigan led the way into what had been the warlord's residence. Some heavy ornate furniture that the former owners could not carry away sat abandoned throughout the building. Empty wardrobes had the look of having been hastily emptied, leaving discarded clothing lying scattered around the rooms. A look in the kitchen showed pots and pans of excellent quality. Brannigan turned to the hostages. "What do you make of this place?"

"Very nice furniture," Ibrahim remarked. "Maybe some of it is paid for, but most is probably stolen from somewhere."

"I am thinking so too," Hajji said. "This is looking like a country bumpkin was able to get some very nice things."

"Yes!" Ibrahim agreed. "Very nice things. Very nice. So expensive it appears to be."

After making a round of the place with the hostages at his heels, Brannigan took everyone back to the large foyer. "They sure as hell left in a big hurry," the Skipper remarked.

"Yes, sir," Dave agreed. "Did you notice there isn't a military look about the place? No desks, no file cabinets or computers."

"These guys were strictly gunmen," Mike said. "A lot like the Mafia, I guess."

"We'll have to ask Puglisi about that," Dave said with a grin.

"Right," Brannigan agreed. He turned to Frank. "There's a ladder there leading to the roof. Take the radio up there and contact SOCOM. Tell 'em we've run off the bad guys and have moved into their garrison area. You might add that I estimate that the surviving mujahideen are not very numerous. However, I have no idea how many women and children got away."

"Aye, sir," Frank said, heading for the ladder with the Shadowfire weighing heavy on his back.

Meanwhile, the Bravos carefully went through each hut in the village, finding the same things the Alphas had in the residence, except these discarded belongings were fewer and cheaper. Gutsy Olson found a burqa that needed mending and slipped it over his head. Chad Murchison laughed at the ludicrous sight. "I'll wager you're much more attractive than the woman who belonged to that covering."

"I always been suspicious that Arab men insist that their women wear these things 'cause they're uglier'n the south end of a northbound mule," Gutsy said.

Over in the vehicle park, the Charlies had discovered some useful transportation left behind. The government van belonging to the hostages Ibrahim and Hajji was there along with a motor-rickshaw and four motorbikes in various states of disrepair. Joe Miskoski and Kevin Albee gave the bikes a quick inspection.

"Are you thinking what I'm thinking?" Joe asked.

Kevin nodded. "Does the word 'cannibalizing' ring a bell?"

They studied the little vehicles for a few moments more. "Oh, yeah!" Joe said. "I figure two damn good bikes could be made out of the four."

"Sounds like a fun project," Kevin said.

"Hey!" Lieutenant Jim Cruise snapped at them. "You guys can fart around with those later. The skipper wants this place scoped out."

"Aye, aye, sir!" the two would-be mechanics responded quickly and simultaneously. As they turned back to the work at hand, they looked at the motorbikes in happy anticipation of tinkering with them.

Several 100-liter fuel drums were found. One of them had a pump in the top and appeared to be about half full of fuel. Three others were full and unopened. Milly Mills summed it up nicely. "Three hundred fifty liters of gasoline ain't nothing to sneeze at."

The Deltas walked along the top of the wall, around to the area bombarded during the attack by the Second Squad. Bruno Puglisi was particularly interested in seeing the effect of the mortar rounds that he and Joe Miskoski had fired at the fortification that memorable night of the attack. He emitted a low whistle of self-admiration, saying, "By God, me and Joe did some knocking down!"

"I'll say you did," Chief Gunnarson agreed. "Looky there! Somebody has been working on rebuilding that section of the wall."

"Sloppy bastards," Adam Clifford criticized. "They wasn't doing as good a job as the guys that built it in the first place."

The hospital corpsman James Bradley noted the dried pools of blood. "These guys took a lot of casualties during the few hours we were out there."

"There's a sexual lesson in that," Puglisi said.

"What do you mean," James asked, "sexual?"

Puglisi laughed. "They learned not to fuck with the U.S. Navy SEALs."

"Okay, funny guys," Gunnarson growled. "Let's go over and report in to the Skipper."

By the time all the fire teams had assembled in the warlord's residence, Frank Gomez was climbing down from the roof. "Sir," he said to Brannigan, "SOCOM wants us to occupy the village south of here. It's supposed to be a small farming community about five miles away. That want us to report in as soon as we take over the place."

"Sir," Cruiser interjected. "We won't have to walk. We discovered a van and a motor-rickshaw in working order in the vehicle park. There's plenty of fuel available too."

"Don't forget them motorbikes, sir," Joe said. "Me and Kevin can build a couple of good ones out of the four in about two hours."

Brannigan grinned. "Get on the project. Why walk when we can ride?"

VILLAGE OF HERANDBE
1700 HOURS LOCAL

THE van was the first vehicle into the village square, followed quickly by the motor-rickshaw and the two motorbikes carrying Mike Assad and Dave Leibowitz. They brought up the rear of the group, acting as rear guard for a change rather than the point. The fact they were on the bikes created a bone of contention between the Odd Couple and the amateur mechanics Joe Miskoski and Kevin Albee. Since they had done the work of creating the two operative bikes, they felt the ownership was theirs by right. However, Lieutenant Bill Brannigan wanted his recon team mounted on them, and that pretty much settled that hassle.

The old farmers who always sat at the well were in their usual spot when the small convoy made its unexpected appearance. They already knew what had happened to the warlord and his people. Two families of surviving mujahideen had arrived the night before seeking hiding places with relatives in the village. When the elderly men noted the armed SEALs spilling out of the back of the van and the motor-rickshaw, they struggled to their feet with intentions of fleeing the scene as fast as their ancient legs could carry them. Any attempts to get away were blocked when Mike and Dave zoomed in and braked to sudden stops as they flanked the oldsters. All the SEALs fanned out to form a tight security perimeter around the immediate area. They faced outward, weapons at the ready, keeping their eyes on the surrounding huts.

Ibrahim and Hajji were the last to get out of the van. They walked up to the oldsters speaking in Pashto. Brannigan was not pleased with that. "Hey! You two don't say anything—not a single fucking word—unless I tell you to. Understand?"

Both the ex-hostages immediately shut up. Hajji turned to the SEAL commander. "We are sorry, sir. But our bodyguards were murdered here while these old men are looking at it without a warning to us."

"I understand your anger," Brannigan said. "I want you to tell the old guys that we have no intention of harming them if everyone in the village does as we say."

"Yes, sir," Ibrahim said. He turned and spoke sternly to the elderly men, translating Brannigan's words.

"I want everyone to come out of their huts and gather around the well," Brannigan ordered. "Now!"

One of the oldsters spoke hesitantly, and Ibrahim translated. "The old man he is saying that there are men working in the fields. Only old people and the women and the children are being here."

Brannigan raised his voice in anger. "Then get 'em out here! And tell him we're going to search the houses, and if we find anybody hiding, there's going to be big trouble."

Again Ibrahim, enjoying the villagers' discomfiture, translated. The old men hurried away, and began going from domicile to domicile banging on doors and yelling loudly. People looked from their doorways at the SEALs, hesitating to leave the safety of their homes. But the old men kept yelling at them, and within ten minutes all the villagers were crowded together in front of the Skipper. The women instinctively drew their veils tighter around their faces since they were being observed by infidel males. Senior Chief Buford Dawkins noticed a couple of young men among the group. He pushed his way through the crowd and grabbed the youths, dragging them out.

An exchange of words between Ibrahim and the elders began until Brannigan grew tired of the chattering. "What the hell's going on?"

Ibrahim explained, "The villagers are frightened about these men who do not live here. They are saying they came from the warlord's fort yesterday and stayed with kin."

"Take 'em as prisoners, Senior Chief," Brannigan said. "Second Squad! Start going through the huts! And be careful. If anything looks suspicious, shoot first and we'll sort it out later."

Lieutenant Jim Cruiser led his men into the village and they began kicking doors open. They discovered no people, but immediately found weapons, tossing them out of the huts. It took half an hour to complete the process that revealed more than a hundred firearms. Most were modern AK-47s, but a few pistols and even a half dozen ancient muzzle-loading rifle muskets were among the arms the SEALs discovered.

While the little community was brought under control, Frank Gomez set up his radio and informed SOCOM that the area was occupied. After an exchange with the commo center, he closed the transmission and reported to Brannigan. "Sir, we're gonna get some visitors from Kabul tomorrow morning. Official types to take a look at things."

"I expected that," Brannigan said. "Did they say anything about us being relieved?"

"No, sir."

Brannigan sighed. "I expected that too."

21 AUGUST
1000 HOURS LOCAL

THE night before had been uneasy for everyone. The villagers had returned to their huts right after the initial introduction to the platoon, and the men who had been working in the field were met by Charlie Fire Team who ordered them into their huts with warnings not to come out. However, these were farmers not mujahideen and they hadn't the slightest intention of making trouble.

Wild Bill Brannigan put his men on 50 percent alert, keeping both stationary and mobile sentry posts in operation throughout the hours of darkness. By dawn he had changed the guard to a squad at a time standing around the outskirts of the village at vantage points in case someone tried to leave.

THE approaching helicopter could be heard long before it came into sight over the distant mountain ridges. When it arrived, the MH-6K Blackhawk came in with a dust-scattering roar, setting down lightly just outside the entrance to the village. When the engine was cut, two figures came out of the troop compartment and hurried over to where Brannigan and Jim Cruiser waited. Ibrahim and Hajji stood respectfully to the rear of the officers, happy at this event that would get them closer to returning to their homes in Kabul.

One of the arrivees was a civilian in casual clothing that included field boots and a wide-brimmed boonie hat. The other was a U.S. Army lieutenant colonel wearing desert tan BDUs. He returned the salutes rendered him by the two SEAL officers.

"How are you, gentlemen?" he said with a wide smile. "I'm Colonel Latrelle from the military mission in Kabul. Allow me to present the honorable Zaid Aburrani. He is a special envoy of the Afghanistan government."

"This is my Two-I-C Lieutenant Cruiser," Brannigan replied after identifying himself. He gestured to the ex-hostages. "These are the government agents we freed."

Ibrahim and Hajji salaamed respectfully. Aburrani took the behavior as his due, but he gave them a friendly smile. "I am pleased you are safe."

"Shukhriya," they replied, expressing their gratitude in the Urdu language.

Brannigan continued. "I've set up a CP in the first hut over there. We can discuss things better inside."

Ibrahim and Hajji went to the well to wait while the other four men walked over to the impromptu command post. Inside, the little mud building was void of furniture except for a thick carpet. Neither Latrelle nor Aburrani seemed fazed by this lack of modern conveniences, and they settled down on the rug, crossing their legs.

"I don't have any refreshments," Brannigan said. "I could get some MREs, but somehow that doesn't seem appropriate."

Latrelle chuckled. "Don't bother, Lieutenant. I'm strictly a staff officer from Civil Affairs, and I came here with a full stomach after a good breakfast that followed a full night's sleep."

Brannigan had noted the lack of either a parachutist badge

or combat infantryman's badge sewn above the man's left breast pocket. He knew that in the Army, that meant Latrelle would never wear general's stars on his collar or epaulets. However, later on he could well be one of those retired colonels who appeared as military pundits on TV news shows.

The SEAL looked at the Army officer. "What can we do for you, sir?"

"The first thing is a 'well done' to you and your men," Latrelle said. "When you wiped out Warlord Durtami and his band of thugs, you did a lot of people a hell of a big favor."

"We didn't exactly wipe him out," Brannigan said. "He managed to escape with his surviving people to the north."

"He will be joining his brother-in-law," Aburrani interjected. "That particular gentleman will be ten times the trouble getting rid of." He shrugged. "But, alas, we will have to deal with him. And that will be soon, I fear."

"At any rate," Latrelle said, "the rescue of these two hostages has raised morale considerably in the voter registration program."

Aburrani nodded enthusiastically. "That is most important, Lieutenant. Our people now know we will make strong efforts to liberate them. These are not the first of these dedicated people to be taken prisoner. And a few have been murdered. They are most courageous to continue their dangerous work in the democratization of Afghanistan."

"I'm glad we could help," Brannigan said. "In the meantime we are waiting for orders. I don't know if we're going to be relieved or continue to carry the load here."

"You'll be continuing to carry that load, Lieutenant," Latrelle said. "Right now SOCOM has no one to send in to take your place. And all the conventional forces in this theater are hard at working trying to find terrorist camps and cells hiding out in the wilderness. And, of course, the hunt for Osama Bin Laden continues." He turned to Aburrani. "By the way, I noticed some poppy fields when we flew in here. What is being done about them?"

"They are scheduled to be destroyed," Aburrani said, covering up the truth about the opium industry. "We wait only for funds from the American government to pay the farmers. I fear they will not readily submit to losing their best cash crop without having money in hand to make up for the loss."

"I can't say that I blame them," Latrelle said. "These poor people have endured hardships for decades. We certainly don't wish to add to their suffering by making them wait for badly needed cash."

"That is most understanding of the American government," Aburrani said. He nodded to Brannigan. "Colonel Latrelle and I would like to visit the site of Durtami's old fortress. We wish to take photographs for an official report."

"Certainly," Brannigan said. "I assume it will be all right if we use the Afghan government van outside. Or would you prefer your helicopter?"

"The van would serve our purpose better," Latrelle said. "A close-up inspection of an OA is always advantageous."

"Certainly, sir," Brannigan said, thinking that only a staff weenie would think a quick cross-country drive would familiarize him with an active OA.

The four men got to their feet and went outside.

CHAPTER 11

THE KHAMAMI FIEFDOM

WARLORD Hassan Khamami was a muscular, handsome man with a heavy beard and lively green eyes that reflected his high intelligence. He was also a lusty warrior chief with three wives, and further enhanced his sex life with two concubines from the lowly Dharya Clan of the Pashtun people. He maintained these playmates in a hut away from his family.

The warlord ruled his holdings from a sturdy wooden castle called Al-Saraya. Unlike his brother-in-law Ayyub Durtami, who allowed his people to live within the walls of his fortress, Khamami mandated that his followers keep their village outside his rustic palace grounds.

Many outsiders thought that the warlord had come to be the commander of his private army through heredity since his father was also a great leader of mujahideen. In truth, he gained control of the fighting force not through the peaceful legalities of his father's will, but by violently turning on two of his half-brothers who also had ambitions to control the armed band. Their sire had a total of four wives who had presented him with three sons and ten daughters. All the women in the old *amir's* household were proper Muslim women who had no ambitions toward acquiring leadership. The third wife, however, saw the advantages of having her two sons take over the fiefdom, and she urged them to contest Hassan's claim to the throne.

This set off a mini civil war that went on for three years before Hassan's superior skills in field command smashed the opposition. Both half-brothers were hanged in public executions held outside the castle walls. Their domineering mother was beheaded in front of the gallows even as her sons' corpses hung there. This was the traditional punishment of adulteresses, and Khamami jokingly remarked that this was her proper due since she loved power more than his father.

The macabre event was stark evidence to the rest of the people that their new leader was not to be trifled with. Khamami assembled the opposition's frightened followers and gave them a blanket pardon if they swore their faith to him in the name of Allah. These grateful fighters became some of his most loyal soldiers. When the dust settled, the warlord had a large mountain stronghold and close to two hundred armed men at his beck and call.

Within a year Khamami added to his holdings by conquering some minor warlords in the area. These men resented the intrusion into their domains, and did not submit meekly to Khamami's authority. Consequently, they were dispatched in secret assassinations that included shootings, ambushes and even a couple of poisonings. These deaths left their people confused and lost. It was only natural that they turned to the most powerful leader around for protection. None realized this was the very man who was responsible for the murder of their chiefs.

This doubled both Khamami's land holdings and his army. The one person to whom he showed mercy was Ayyub

Durtami. Durtami, a low-grade chief, was saved because one of his sisters was Khamami's favorite wife. He let Durtami slip off to the south after securing an informal nonaggression pact with him. Durtami was smart enough not to try any treachery toward his brother-in-law, who had emerged all-powerful in that area of Afghanistan.

Under normal conditions, Khamami would have gone as far as any man could before he would eventually run into other more powerful warlords who would defeat him. Then it would be his turn to dangle from a gallows. Surprisingly, it was a political event involving a superpower that catapulted Hassan Khamami into becoming one of the most powerful leaders in Afghanistan. In fact, he almost became a king.

Soviet ambitions led to the destruction of the Afghan monarchy in 1973. Mohammed Daoud became prime minister with the help of local Communists, but instead of moving into the Soviet sphere, he adopted a neutral attitude toward both the East and West. He didn't last long under those conditions, and was assassinated in order to be replaced by a leader who was more cooperative with Moscow's desires. All this was instigated by Soviet KGB agents who were experts in meddling in the affairs of weak foreign nations. Nur Mohammed Taraki was the reds' fair-haired boy, and he was chosen by the Kremlin to take over Afghanistan in their name. He ran the nation along Communist atheistic lines.

This was a bad mistake, since the population would barely tolerate a secular government, much less a godless one. They revolted against the new ruler, and this led to war with the central government. Units of the Soviet Army were quickly dispatched to put things right. After months of futile campaigning, the situation turned out to be the Russians' Vietnam. They abandoned the disaster after being bogged down in an unwinnable counterinsurgency war. Luckily for Warlord Hassan Khamami, he had fought on the side of the victorious rebels.

Khamami had been one of those local leaders chosen by America's CIA to supply and support. He received funding and weaponry from the American intelligence organization as he fought viciously against the Russians. By the time the conflict came to an end, his personal army was twice as strong as it had been before the conflict. The warlord used this power to overcome a few additional weaker neighbors. For several months, however, it appeared that he might have bitten off more than he could chew. Vast territories and a large fighting force are terribly expensive to maintain. Since his people were overwhelmingly poverty-stricken farmers, Khamami didn't have much of a tax base to finance his ambitions.

Then he got into opium poppy cultivation.

This stroke of luck was almost accidental, when a smuggler who had been operating before the war came back to renew his association with the people he'd dealt with in the past. Unfortunately for him they were all gone. Fortunately for Hassan Khamami, he was in the right place at the right time to fill the vacuum. Deals were made with the smuggler, and a group of farm villages were recruited and organized to begin a big-time cultivation and production business. Now great amounts of money rolled in to fill the warlord's coffers. His personal army was stronger and better structured than ever due to these unexpected, substantial opium revenues.

Additionally, the intelligent and perceptive Khamami had learned much about strategy and tactics during the long fight against the Russians. He also accumulated large stocks of Soviet weapons, uniforms and equipment. But the most important commodity Khamami acquired was knowledge.

During the struggle against the Soviets, the warlord quickly realized that mass, disorganized attacks almost always ended in disaster, and he recognized the advantages of breaking his army down into subordinate units coordinated along a chain of command. He created squads, divided them among platoons; organized the platoons into companies; and the companies became part of battalions—all under his leadership. Khamami also developed tactical skills in such things as patrolling, fire support, ambushes, attack and defense. But most importantly, he learned to pick the right times to fight and how to safely break contact and withdraw when things went wrong.

Arms was another phase of warfare he took note of. Khamami gathered all the weapons given him by the CIA and combined them with the arms he'd looted from the Soviet Army. He even had no less than three Soviet Hind Mi-24 troop-carrying helicopter gunships at his disposal, and the pilots to fly them.

Additionally, he acquired a spiritual leader to back up his activities. One day a hermit appeared at Al-Saraya after fifteen years of living and wandering in the mountains. This was Khatib the Oracle, who claimed he was the new prophet of Allah who had been sent to lead the faithful in a struggle to destroy all the infidels in the world. Khamami was aware that the old man was as crazy as a flea on a goat, but he recognized the oldster's potential usefulness. Khatib the Oracle had a way of mesmerizing the crowds who listened to him speak. The warlord told the pseudo-prophet that he would be welcome to remain in the fiefdom if he slanted his sermons to teach the audiences that Khamami was a warrior guided by Allah. That was fine with the elderly fellow, who recognized a good meal ticket. Thus he acquiesced wholeheartedly to the warlord's program. Consequently, the people obeyed Khamami's every command with a reverent adoration.

The last bit of resistance Khamami had to deal with was the Dharya Clan. These Pashtuns were a small group of dissidents who tried to set up their own poppy cultivation on lands controlled by the warlord. They paid a terrible price for the affront. After a vicious attack that decimated their numbers, the survivors were place into slavery, and held there with many of their young females put into enforced concubinage—the worst fate for Muslim women. According to Islam, they were as much if not more to blame for this shameful situation as the men who violated their bodies.

Because of this, they would never know freedom from the warlord or forgiveness from their male relatives.

THE REFUGEE CAMP
KHAMAMI FIEFDOM
22 AUGUST

AYYUB Durtami and Ahmet Kharani were off to the side of the convoy that by now had deteriorated into a miserable, milling mob. Although there was no shouting or struggling, the people who had fled the compound in the south were bunched together in an instinctively protective manner. The motors of the vehicles were now turned off while everyone waited nervously to find out what would happen next. They were tightly surrounded by an armed detachment of Warlord Hassan Khamami's mujahideen, who glared at them as if daring the refugees to try to disturb the peace and tranquility of the fiefdom.

Durtami and Kharani sat in the back of the Soviet sedan. Their bodyguards, who normally stayed close by, had wandered off, as if wishing to put a great deal of distance between themselves and their former chiefs. The former warlord and his lieutenant were plainly worried, and both had AK-47s within easy reach. If Khamami was going to kill them, the men he sent would pay dearly for the assassinations.

Kharani rolled the window down a bit to let some air into the old Soviet automobile. "Perhaps we are worrying over nothing," he murmured, to himself as much as to his companion.

Durtami shook his head. "I do not know what to think. We are defeated, Brother Ahmet. We show up here with naught but what we have in our vehicles. Even our fighting force is down to almost nothing."

"Surely we and our men have some value," Kharani said. "And is your sister not still the favorite of Warlord Khamami's wives?"

"I do not know," Durtami said miserably. "Perhaps he has gotten younger, prettier ones."

"But she gave him four sons," Kharani said. "Surely a man would honor such a wife for as long she lived."

"Maybe she no longer lives," Durtami said. "I have had no news from here in two or three years. She could have sickened and died."

"Allah help us!"

AL-SARAYA CASTLE
1400 HOURS LOCAL

NO less than a squad of riflemen had gone to the refugee camp to fetch Ayyub Durtami and Ahmet Kharani for an audience with Warlord Hassan Khamami. The leader of the unit was brusque to the point of being rude and threatening. This behavior made the two even more apprehensive than they had originally been.

After being hurried from their vehicles and through the village to the gate of the castle, they were almost trembling with fear. By then they figured the best they could hope for was a quick and painless death. When the gate was opened, the castle guards took them in hand, escorting them into the interior of the two-story building. They stopped by a door in one of the inner hallways. The senior guard stepped inside and closed it. A moment later he appeared. "The *Amir* Warlord Khamami deigns to speak with you. Enter!"

Durtami and Kharani hurried inside the room, where the warlord sat on a throne-like teak chair flanked by a pair of guards. The two reluctant guests threw themselves down, touching their foreheads to the floor. It was now time for them to practice *nanawatey,* the act of total submission in the Pashtun culture.

Durtami, as the senior, spoke for them both, his voice quavering. "*Amir!* We appear before you humbled and defeated.

We beg your mercy and submit to your authority and power without hesitation or limits."

Kharani added, "*Amir!* It is written in the Koran that Allah loves those who show mercy to the believers."

"Don't tell me what is written in the Koran!" Khamami bellowed in fury. "I have Khatib the Oracle to advise me on religious matters."

"Of course, *Amir!*" Kharani acknowledged in cold fear. "Forgive my rude audacity, I beg you!"

"And here you are, driven from your lands by Infidels!" Khamami said. "Both of you have disgraced Islam with your ineptness and cowardice. Why do you come to me instead of remaining to martyr yourselves against the enemy?"

Durtami had anticipated that line of questioning, and he quickly replied, "We have come to join your army, *Amir!* We wish to continue the fight under your command."

Khamami was secretly amused by their fear. It fed his ego to observe two people literally begging for him to spare their lives. "And why should I accept you into my army and my fiefdom?"

"I have come here with more than a hundred armed men, *Amir,*" Durtami said. "I also have money from my treasury."

"A pittance," Khamami scoffed.

"We have behaved badly and admit it with great shame, *Amir,*" Kharani said. "We beg you for mercy."

"Mmm," Khamami said, acting as if he were deep in thought. More than two minutes passed before he said, "Very well! I have decided to take you under my rule if you swear allegiance to me."

"By the grace of Allah I swear a full allegiance to your authority, *Amir,*" Durtami said. "I speak for my people and you may hold me responsible for their actions."

"I most certainly will do that," the warlord said. "However, until you have proven yourselves, you and your people will live beyond the village in the wilderness. I will give you no food, no water and no shelter. All these problems are for you to solve."

"Shukhria!" they said simultaneously in their gratitude. "You are dismissed!"

Durtami and Kharani scurried backward on their hands and knees until reaching the door. Only then did they get to their feet and flee the throne room.

REFUGEE CAMP
KHAMAMI FIEFDOM
1500 HOURS LOCAL

THE mood in the camp was one of utter despair. When the people were informed they would have to remain where they were, they instinctively glanced northward to where the frigid winds of winter would descend from within weeks. It had rained the night before and everyone had gotten wet. The lucky climbed into the backs of the motor-rickshaws for protection from the elements, but most had to cover themselves with blankets that had quickly grown sodden from the rain. Coughing children were already in evidence.

The men now ignored Durtami and Kharani. They formed up in family groups to make plans for hunting in the nearby hills. With no rations being issued to them, this was their only way of obtaining food. They pooled their available cash to send the women to the nearby farming villages to buy food. With the growing season already over, the best they could hope for was dried vegetables and flour.

All this activity came to a halt when a platoon of Warlord Khamami's mujahideen appeared, shouting for everyone to gather at the far edge of the camp. A strange individual was with the fighters. He was rail thin with a wispy beard and of undeterminable age. His attire was simple, with a tattered *pukhoor* wrapped around his spindly body. In spite of his self-effacing appearance, he had a fierce fire in his eyes. His presence made the refugees uneasy, while many of the women shrank back in fear from the walking scarecrow who glared at them, baring his rotting teeth in a fierce grimace.

When everyone was gathered, he stepped up on the hood of the Soviet sedan. After an angry glare at the assemblage, he spoke in a reedy but loud voice. "I am Khatib the Oracle! I serve the faithful here as their spiritual guide. I have lived alone in the wilderness of the mountains for fifteen years. I fasted and prayed for weeks at a time without stopping. I was celibate, without thoughts of lust disturbing my devotion. Other men would have starved or gone mad under such circumstances and abused their genitals. But Allah had chosen me to prove my devoutness to Him and Islam."

Now the old fellow had become downright frightening. Mothers pulled their young children closer to them, and the men gave one another worried glances.

Khatib the Oracle continued. "You are all miserable sinners, cast from your homes and your lands and your herds for your faithless disregard of Islam. Now you are here among true believers seeking comfort and alms. You will receive all the aid that can possibly be rendered unto you, for that is the way of Islam. Though you are fallen, Allah has been merciful and sent you to us to be put back on the right path."

The crowd remained silent, fully recognizing that they were completely and utterly at the mercy of this zealot, and the most frightening aspect of the condition was that this had undoubtedly been done with the approval of Warlord Khamami.

"But before your well-deserved misery is relieved," Khatib the Oracle pronounced, "you will have to atone for your sins. Husbands and wives will live apart and not know each other. You must fast and pray, eating nothing during daylight hours and only one meal after the sun sinks over the western lands. Make yourselves pure in thought and deed. Do not dwell on your thirst or your hunger! Do not let your unrelieved passions give you unclean thoughts! If there are those who die from these conditions, then give thanks to Allah for their deaths. He will have relieved them of their mortal burdens and taken them up to Paradise, as they have truly atoned for wrongdoings! The sinners among you will continue to live in this misery. So be it!"

He abruptly ceased his speech and nimbly stepped down to the ground. He hurried away, walking so rapidly that his mujahideen escort had trouble keeping up with him.

The people turned away and went miserably back to their campsites.

KHATIB the Oracle lived in a far corner of the castle. His apartment was isolated by narrow hallways that led to the roof. When he returned to his quarters after delivering his revelations to the refugees, he was met by his old servant. The ancient retainer salaamed respectfully. "Welcome home, Holy Khatib."

"Is the Dharya girl still here?" he inquired, speaking of one of the captive concubines.

"Yes, Holy One," the servant said. "I have not yet had her taken back to the bordello."

"Send her to me."

"Yes, Holy One."

Khatib the Oracle went to his sleeping room and slipped out of his *pukhoor*. A moment later there was a rapping on the door. The servant opened it and motioned a young girl to step inside. After the old man left, she began disrobing, numbly accepting the inevitable rape that she would endure in a matter of moments.

CHAPTER 12

DUST swirled violently off the ridge top as the two Blackhawk helicopters came in for landing. The roar of the engines frightened the buzzards feeding on the dead mujahideen farther down the slope, and the large, obnoxious birds rose in dark clouds of feathered flight at the thunderous disturbance. They scattered through the sky, their indignant squawking loud and obscene at this interruption in their gruesome feasting.

As soon as the wheels touched down, each squad of Brannigan's Brigands disembarked from its aircraft, quickly forming relay lines. The crewmen inside began handing boxes and bundles of gear and ammo to waiting hands, and the supplies were passed from man to man toward the side area where Senior Chief Petty Officer Buford Dawkins and Chief Petty Officer Matt Gunnarson neatly stacked the goods prior to proper stowage. Among the usual issue of ammunition and rations were camouflage netting, shovels, picks, empty burlap sandbags and an assortment of uniform items to replace what the SEALs had been wearing for almost three weeks. The fresh, unused skivvies were the most appreciated, but not quite as much as eight cases of Budweiser officially donated by the Army Post Exchange Board in Kabul. The Brigands didn't receive enough alcohol to get roaring drunk, but they were appreciative of this second gift of beer just the same.

Connie Concord and Bruno Puglisi were also happy with the addition of an M-224 light mortar system to their small arsenal of support weaponry. The platoon commo was enhanced greatly with each officer and chief petty officer being furnished with a PRC-112 radio to enhance his command and control capabilities. These sets also broadcast beacons that all military aircraft monitor on their guard channels to provide an automated method of calling support to particular points of the globe. It was a handy and quick way to get help when needed.

As soon as the Blackhawks were given the all-clear signal, their rotors whipped back up to flying speed, and they lifted off the ridge, turning toward their home base. The ensuing quiet was broken by the hoarse shouts of the chief petty officers, who set the men to work constructing storage sites for all the new gear. This would include the erection of camouflage netting to enhance the cut brush the platoon had been using for concealment since their arrival.

The Odd Couple, Mike Assad and Dave Leibowitz, were the lucky ones in the activities. The assignment of recon patrol duties saved them from the pick-and-shovel work. They happily donned their combat vests, grabbed their CAR-15s and headed down the ridge to check out the area.

When the new equipment was covered and concealed, the next order of business was the improvement of the present fighting positions. Now, with better digging implements than entrenching tools, the SEALs set about deepening and strengthening the field fortifications that surrounded the immediate area. This included filling the sandbags to build up higher parapets.

With the work under way, Lieutenant Wild Bill Brannigan called a staff meeting with his 2IC and chief petty officers. Rather than go into the CP, they stood outside for the session, gazing at the men working hard at their various tasks.

Brannigan liked what he saw. "That's real discipline."

Chief Gunnarson frowned in puzzlement. "What are you talking about, sir?"

"Some people—especially civilians—think military discipline is a combination of harsh training and punishment," Brannigan replied. "Chickenshit stuff, y'know? Like making guys spit-shine boots and Brasso their brass. But real discipline is the voluntary spirit to be willing to do whatever it takes to make yourself the best man in the best unit in the best service of the Armed Forces. And that's especially true when what you're doing is pissing you off or busting your balls. Like the platoon out there."

"Yes, sir," Senior Chief Buford agreed. "Guys in outfits like ours put out a hundred and ten percent without a boot up their ass."

"Your statement may be grammatically flawed," Lieutenant Cruiser said, "but it is filled with volumes of truth."

The senior chief grinned. "As long as I'm understood, sir."

"Well, understand this," Brannigan interjected. "We're up here for the long haul, and I've reached the conclusion that nobody anywhere in any SOCOM has the slightest idea of what is going to happen around here. They've stuck us on top of this fucking mountain and are waiting to see what kind of shit is going to be thrown at us."

"They must expect a lot of trouble," Gunnarson said. "Why else would they give us all these extra goodies, not to mention have us improve the fortifications on this ridge top?"

"If they expect a lot of trouble," Cruiser said, "why don't they reinforce us or send in a larger unit?"

"Because nobody else is available," Brannigan replied. "Whatever happens here is going to drop right in our laps."

"Ouch!" the senior chief said with a wink. "That's where I keep my balls."

"I was just thinking the same thing," Brannigan said. "Now! Let's organize the Watch Bill, shall we?"

"Aye, sir," the other three answered together as the administrative side of the session began.

1115 HOURS LOCAL

THE Odd Couple, dirty and sweating, returned to the ridge after struggling up from the valley below. They climbed over Bravo Fire Team's improved defensive positions and looked around.

"Wow!" Dave Leibowitz said. "What the hell have you guys been doing?"

"Working our asses off," a disgruntled Gutsy Olson replied. He and Connie Concord were filling sandbags. "How was your stroll?"

"Oh, God!" Mike moaned. "We're gonna need to see psychiatrists after this."

Chad Murchison stopped his shoveling. "So what's driving you two into the depths of derangement?"

"Them buzzards, man," Dave said. "They're eating those dead mujahideen down there."

"And they're just about finished," Mike added. "They're picking the last bit of meat off the bones."

"Shit!" Gutsy said. "That's worse than a horror movie. Don't tell me no more."

Mike felt wicked. "They're even eating the eyeballs right out of the sockets."

Gutsy scowled. "You make me fucking sick!"

"We must've really kicked their asses," Dave said. "Not only did they leave their dead behind, but all their weapons and gear are laying around too. All that shit's gonna be covered all winter by the snow when the blizzards come."

"That'll be quite a sight next spring when the sun melts the ice," Mike commented. "It'll look like something out of hell with skulls and rusty weapons all over the place."

"Godamn it!" Gutsy said. "Ain't you guys got a report to make or something? Don't you think you should take care of it?"

"Yeah," Mike said. "We better get over to the CP." He grinned at Gutsy. "Have a nice day."

"Sure," Gutsy said, shoveling angrily. "Thinking about dead humans being eaten by big birds will make the time pass faster."

The Odd Couple left the position, cutting across the top of the ridge to check in with the Skipper.

AL-SARAYA CASTLE
THRONE ROOM
NOON LOCAL

THIS visit was much more pleasant than the previous one for Ayyub Durtami and Ahmet Kharani. They sat cross-legged at a small table, each with a dish of deep-fried yogurt and flour called *jalebi,* to be washed down with *sabz chai,* green tea. Warlord Hassan Khamami sat across from them, sharing the dishes in a magnanimous gesture of hospitality. Two bodyguards, however, stood behind the warlord, glaring at the guests to let them know they were still second-class residents of the fiefdom.

Durtami took a sip of tea. "We thank you for your kind-ness and consideration in sharing this bounty of delicious food and drink with us, *Amir.*" Like his people in the refugee camp, Durtami and Kharani had been almost starving on the one meal a day allowed them by Khatib the Oracle.

"Yes!" Kharani said. "May Allah shower you with ten thousand blessings, *Amir.*"

"You are welcome at my table," Khamami said insin-cerely. Rather than exchange any preliminary pleasantries with his guests, he impolitely moved the conversation to the reason behind the invitation. "I wish to find out exactly what happened in your fiefdom these past weeks."

"It was a treachery brought upon us by Satan," Durtami said. "By the time I had declared jihad, their black magic had grown too strong."

Khamami, who was not in the least bit religious, picked up a *jalebi* and bit into it. "Perhaps it is as Khatib the Oracle says. You and your people had sinned so much that you angered Allah, who is all merciful and beneficent. Thus he would not come to your aid." He enjoyed the oxymoronic aspect of the statement he had just uttered. It was an expression of disrespect for the tenets of Islam.

Before Durtami could say anything rash, Kharani interjected, "We would not argue with one so spiritually inspired by the Oracle, *Amir*."

Khamami had already recognized that of the two visitors, Ahmet Kharani was the most intelligent. The warlord was silent for a moment, appearing to be thinking deeply as he considered the past conduct of Durtami. "Tell me, brother-in-law. How many of these infidels were arrayed against you?"

Durtami, almost speechless with pleasure at finally being recognized as a kinsman of the warlord, leaned forward. "At least a thousand, *Amir*. Perhaps more."

"That does not seem possible," Khamami remarked. "Such a number of foreign devils could not enter these lands without my being informed of them."

Kharani, no longer fearful of Durtami, spoke boldly to his new warlord. "I have heard that the infidels have special fighting forces that are most skillful in the more clandestine aspects of making war."

"Did they make massive attacks against you?" Khamami asked.

"Yes!" Durtami exclaimed.

"No," Kharani answered calmly, making an obvious contradiction.

Durtami turned and glared at his companion. "Was it not a mighty force that attacked those walls when the hostages were taken from us?"

Khamami stifled a laugh. "Were those the hostages whose ransom you were going to use to pay me for the French mortars I sold you?"

"Oh, no, *Amir*," Durtami said desperately. "My finances were never so strained." He changed the subject quickly. "A very heavy attack against our walls breached them. They even fired mortar shells into my fortress."

"Those were the same mortars you purchased from the *Amir*," Kharani said. He turned to the warlord. "They were stolen from us by the infidels."

Now Khamami knew he wouldn't get any reliable information out of Durtami. "You are both dismissed!" he snapped.

"Your will is our command, *Amir*," Durtami said.

The two quickly got to their feet, bowing deeply before backing toward the door. Just as they reached the exit, the warlord spoke directly to Kharani. "You may move your family into the village beside the castle walls."

Kharani was almost giddy with happiness. "My gratitude toward you will last ten thousand eternities, *Amir*!"

The two exited the room. As soon as the door closed, Khamami looked up at the bodyguards. "See that Captain Sheriwal is brought to me."

"Yes, *Amir*!" they said, immediately rushing toward the door. When the great warlord issued an order, he expected immediate and enthusiastic obedience.

Khamami took a deep sip of tea. The situation in Durtami's former fiefdom was precarious and worrisome. It was time to go to war.

WEST RIDGE OP
24 AUGUST
0930 HOURS LOCAL

A rocky outcrop of bare ground extended from the ridge, which offered an excellent view down into the valley. The area below could be seen from the north all the way around

to the southeast of the base camp. This position had been ignored before, since it would have been too difficult to maintain a firing position there. But with the receipt of camouflage
covers and sandbags, the SEALs were able to establish an
excellent OP where the eastern valley and East Ridge could
be kept under surveillance.

It was the forenoon watch and Charlie Fire Team was on
duty as the other platoon members continued to expand and
improve the positions put in the day before. Joe Miskoski
was doing the honors at the new OP, staying undercover as
he used binoculars to scan the eastern side of West Ridge.
The number of buzzards feeding and scolding one another
among the dead mujahideen had diminished noticeably, and
many had despaired of the dwindling food supply, soaring
away in search of more abundant carrion.

Joe had been teamed with Connie Concord and Bruno
Puglisi on the new 60-millimeter mortar, and the three had
spent most of the previous evening running through crew
drill as they rotated the jobs of gunner, assistant gunner and
ammo bearer. They had plenty of shells, but the Skipper had
not allowed any live firing. He was concerned about alerting
any unfriendlies who might be lurking within the OA looking for them. The Skipper wanted to conceal this heavy
weaponry as a big nasty surprise for any mujahideen who
might come looking for trouble.

Joe put the binoculars to his eyes for another look at the
top of East Ridge across the valley. It was a comfortably
warm morning, with the sun already making the air under
the camouflage stuffy. He shook his head to chase the
drowsiness away, then stopped. A distant "chop-chop" sound
came from the north, and he swung his gaze in that direction. Within moments he could see a helicopter flying
straight at the mountain. He picked up the PRC-112 radio.
"Charlie Papa, this is Oscar Papa. Over."

Frank Gomez's voice came back immediately. "This is
Charlie Papa. Over."

"We got a chopper of some sort coming right at us," Joe

reported. "It's flying at an altitude of maybe a hundred or so feet higher than the ridge. I can't determine the type, but the engine sound isn't familiar to me. Over."

"Roger," Frank replied. "Wait." A few moments passed, then he spoke again. "We're going under cover. Stay down. Out."

Within ten minutes an old model Soviet Mi-24 helicopter flew slowly, almost nonchalantly across the ridge top. Lieutenant Wild Bill Brannigan studied it through a small gap in the camouflage across the top of the CP. Senior Chief Buford Dawkins, beside the Skipper, could also see the intruder. The senior chief was confused. "That's an old'un, sir."

"It sure is," Brannigan agreed. "It's a Soviet Mi-24 Hind model, and it's not fully equipped. There's nothing on its weapons wings."

"A machine gun barrel is sticking out the front," Dawkins observed. "That seems to be just about all he's packing."

"As I recall, those Hind choppers have a crew of three," Brannigan said. "The pilot and gunner sit side by side in the upper cockpit while the navigator is in the lower position."

The chopper went out to the south, then turned and came back for a run in the opposite direction. As it swept by, both men could easily discern only two men in the aircraft. One was in the pilot's seat and the other in the front cockpit manning the machine gun.

"They've jury-rigged that baby to work with what's in their arsenal," Brannigan remarked.

"It's prob'ly Afghan Army," the senior chief opined. "I'll bet my next payday that them guys is stuck with surplus equipment left over after the Soviets pulled out."

"That means the stuff they've got is more than twenty years old."

After buzzing the base camp for a few more minutes, the helicopter suddenly turned and headed off onto a northern course, slowly flying off in the distance.

"Okay, Senior Chief," Brannigan said when the sound of

the engine had faded completely away. "Secure the men from cover and get them back to work."

"Aye, sir!"

AL-SARAYA CASTLE
1015 HOURS LOCAL

THE pilot eased the chopper into a turn, lining up with the helicopter pad near the rear portal of the fortification. A well-trained technician used hand signals to direct him in, monitoring the landing to completion. When the engine was cut, the young guy smiled and proffered a sharp salute. The gunner, a trained mujahideen, opened the Plexiglas cockpit cover and stepped out to drop to the ground. The pilot unbuckled himself and went down to the troop compartment door opened for him by the technician.

"Did you find the infidels, Captain?" he asked eagerly.

The pilot, Captain Mohammed Sheriwal, answered affirmatively. "They were most skilled with their camouflage, but I was able to spot a few positions."

"You must have flown very slow, Captain."

"Yes. In cases like that it is necessary to appear to be looking and looking without finding," Sheriwal said. "In that manner, the enemy thinks you cannot see him, as you seem to aimlessly go hither and thither."

"Very clever, Captain!" the technician exclaimed in unabashed admiration.

A young mujahideen officer walked up and saluted. "Captain, the *Amir* awaits you."

"Then let us go to him immediately," Captain Sheriwal said. "I have important news."

MUHAMMAD Sheriwal had been born Gregori Ivanovich Parkalov in the suburbs of Moscow. His father was a machinist in Manufacturing Plant 21, which specialized in home appliances, while his mother worked as an X-ray technician in a neighborhood clinic. Gregori was an average kid growing up in the Soviet Union. He belonged to the Young Communist League and joined the paramilitary Volunteer Society for Assistance to the Army, Air Force and Navy of the USSR when he was fifteen. This cumbersome title was reduced to the acronym дОСААф (DOSAAF). It was in this organization that the Soviet youth were introduced to the various aspects of military service. DOSAFF even tested the young members' aptitude to see where they might best fit into the armed forces when it came time for them to do their bit for Mother Russia. These examinations and interviews determined that Gregori Parkalov was a natural to become a helicopter pilot.

When Gregori was eighteen, he reported to the local draft board for the obligatory two years' service in the Soviet Army. However, because of his DOSAAF file, rather than being assigned to a motorized rifle division, as were most conscripts, he was posted to the Army's tactical helicopter training center. This was a lot better than having to deal with the brutal bullying and hazing of older soldiers as a recruit in the infantry.

The helicopter training still included plenty of discipline and political indoctrination, but it concentrated on turning the students into excellent military chopper pilots. The downside of the situation was that instead of serving two years, he would be required to put in five. But he and his comrades consoled themselves with the knowledge that when they completed their terms of service, they would be eligible for good-paying jobs as professional helicopter aviators. This meant prestigious positions in Aeroflot, the civil air organization in the People's and Worker's Paradise of the Soviet Union.

But Gregori Parkalov did not complete his five years. After being sent to Afghanistan in 1980, he flew dangerous missions delivering detachments of Spetsnaz Special Forces far into the hinterlands of the mujahideen rebels, to attack them where they lived and hid. After many close calls from numerous Stinger barrages fired at his aircraft, the young Russian was eventually shot down by one of the American-furnished weapons. It was all he could do to control his aircraft as it spun crazily downward to crash. He managed to bring it to the ground in one piece, but he and his crew were captured.

This was when he met the Warlord Hassan Khamami, who had been fighting the Soviets and their Afghanistan puppets for several years. Khamami had scored significant victories, and mujahideen flocked to his unit to share in the glory and spoils of successful ambushes and raids. The warlord had amassed a great amount of war booty while being paid plenty of American dollars by CIA personnel who supported him and his growing personal army.

Most prisoners were executed outright when they fell into the mujahideen's hands. But helicopter pilots were something else. Khamami had given standing orders that they were to be brought directly to him. This was how Gregori Parkalov and the Afghanistan warlord met.

When the Soviets finally withdrew from their futile war, they left behind a plethora of weaponry and other material. Among these were helicopters. Khamami needed all this if he was to fulfill his personal plan of ruling at least half of Afghanistan within a decade. His army commanders were handpicked, combat-proven leaders who had been well trained by the CIA. As infantry officers they were excellent, and as guerrilla leaders they were superlative. What Khamami needed now was an air force. He had three pilots from the Afghanistan Army, but it was obvious they had received little technical training in the maintenance and repair of the Hind model helicopters. However, the Soviet prisoner of war had already demonstrated a great deal of expertise in the mechanical side of that phase of aerial warfare.

Khamami gave Gregori Ivanovich Parkalov a choice. Stay behind and serve him as his airforce commander or be executed by beheading. Gregori chose to keep his head on his shoulders, and was made an auxiliary member of the warlord's army. He was never fully trusted, however, and during those times he actually piloted a helicopter, an armed mujahideen accompanied him with orders to kill the Russian if he tried any tricks such as flying toward the border of any of the Soviet socialist republics.

After six months of the arrangement, it dawned on Gregori Parkalov that he had an excellent chance to become wealthy. Aside from the war patrols, there was also plenty of flying in opium smuggling. In spite of the suspicion he worked under, the Russian was given a full share of the spoils. With his sights set on making even more money, Gregori went to Hassan Khamami and swore allegiance if the warlord would make him a full member of his army rather than a hostage. To prove himself, the Russian agreed to convert to Islam. Such a gesture was definite proof of his sincerity; not so much because of the religious aspects, but because it required circumcision without the benefit of anesthesia. Khamami happily accepted the offer, even throwing in a direct commission in the rank of captain for the ex-Soviet pilot.

Thus, Gregori Ivanovich Parkalov became Mohammed Sheriwal, who now had personal quarters in the castle, where he kept his three wives and one Dharya concubine. Also, through the aid of Zaid Aburrani, Sheriwal had been able to send 750,000 euros to a secret Swiss bank account. Now all he had to do was figure a way to get out of Khamami's fiefdom to get the money. Then he could return to Russia for a life of luxury.

WARLORD Hassan Khamami eagerly awaited Mohammad Sheriwal's arrival in the throne room. He had heard the helicopter land and needed the pilot's report before he could seriously begin a campaign against the infidels who had driven Durtami from his fiefdom.

Sheriwal was admitted into the warlord's presence, and reported to Khamami with a proper Soviet salute. This was a habit he had never been able to break. *"Amir,"* he said in fluent but accented Pashto. "I have returned from the reconnaissance patrol over the suspected enemy area."

"And what did you find, Captain Sheriwal?" Khamami asked with undisguised impatience.

"The ridge is occupied by an armed force," the experienced combat pilot reported. "I am not sure of the exact size. They are definitely under battalion strength. I think at the most they might be a reinforced detachment or company."

"At the most?" Khamami asked. "Are you saying there is a chance they might be less than company size?"

"Yes, *Amir*. In truth, I would say they number somewhere between a dozen to perhaps two dozen that are cleverly camouflaged and dug in on that mountaintop."

Khamami broke out in loud laughter. "So! Those are the *thousands* of infidels who routed Durtami and his miserable band of hill bandits, eh?" He began laughing again, barely able to control his amusement. After a couple of minutes he calmed down enough to speak. "I can tell you one thing, Captain. The easy life the invaders have enjoyed up to now is about to come to an abrupt end."

"My men and helicopters are at your service," Sheriwal said.

"And so are my eight hundred mujahideen infantrymen," Khamami pointed out.

CHAPTER 13

CHARLIE Team had the responsibilities of the morning watch, but they didn't have to sound the alarm to wake the platoon when the loud "chop-chop" of helicopter engines broke the early morning silence.

Everyone stayed under cover as per SOP, looking to the east in the direction of the disturbance. The noise grew steadily louder, but the sun's low position on the horizon made it difficult to see the exact positions of the aircraft or what nationality they might be. Then suddenly three dark shapes could be discerned approaching the ridge in trail.

The lead Mi-24 turned to the north and the others followed, maintaining exact distances between themselves in the formation. This was skillful, precise piloting, and in less than a minute they made a leisurely turn toward the south, perfectly aligned with the ridge line. Then the noses dropped and the speed increased as they sped toward the base camp.

The rapid staccato of heavy machine gun fire from the first chopper broke out as slugs kicked up the dust on the ridge top. The gunner, sitting in the front cockpit, swung the barrel back and forth as he hosed the ground below. Immediately the second chopper followed suit, sending steady fusillades to splatter heavily along the top of the mountain's apex. The third did the same, then the small group swung out to turn for another run.

"Keep you heads down!" Brannigan bellowed so loud that even Kevin Albee on the OP could hear him.

The Hinds came back three more times, skillfully covering areas that had been missed. Cartridge cases rained down, some bouncing off the camouflage netting and colliding with one another as they made little pinging sounds. A couple bounced into Bruno Puglisi's fighting hole and he grabbed them, being careful not to burn his fingers.

"Soviet," he said to himself. "Twelve point seven millimeter. Big bad shit!"

The helicopters flew away as quickly as they'd arrived, leaving an eerie silence over the Afghanistan countryside. The next sound was Chief Matt Gunnarson's voice. "Corpsman! Clifford's hit!"

James Bradley grabbed his medical kit and leaped from his fighting hole. He ran past Bruno to where the chief stood by Adam Clifford's position. James pulled the netting off the emplacement, and could see Adam slumped over with his back against the earthen wall. A quick check for a pulse found nothing, and when James pulled the bloody BDU jacket open, he could see there was no chance for survival. The entry wounds were large and the exit wounds even more ghastly. Bits of flesh and lung were plastered against the side of the position behind the corpse.

James looked up at the chief, who waited for the word. "He's dead."

"Shit," Gunnarson said. He went into the hole and checked for himself. Violent death puts a certain expression on a man's face at times. It's neither shock nor anger, just a sort of dazed, slack-jawed appearance. The chief got Adam's poncho and poncho liner and tossed them out. James laid them out properly as the other SEALs gathered around. He helped the Chief bring the corpse out, and they laid it on the covers.

Lieutenant Jim Cruiser walked over and knelt down. "Our first one." He'd seen it before, but in a new outfit it was almost as shocking as the first time he had gazed down at a dead SEAL who had been under his command.

Lieutenant Bill Brannigan joined the crowd. "He'll have to be buried ASAP," he said, hoping he wasn't sounding too sanguine about this first casualty. "No telling how long we'll be up here."

"I'll have him interred and we can note the exact location of the grave with a GPS," Cruiser said.

"Have your squad take care of it," Brannigan ordered. "I need a word with you and the chiefs."

Frank Gomez came up with an apologetic expression on his face. "Sir. The Shadowfire radio was hit. It's nothing but a piece of crap now. Sorry."

"It wasn't your fault," Brannigan said. "You couldn't have done any more to protect the commo gear other than keep it under cover." He turned and walked toward the CP. "Let's go, team leaders."

They stayed on their feet outside the CP's confines as they gazed back at the Second Squad beginning the burial process for their buddy. Brannigan sighed, then got back to the business at hand. "Did anybody note an insignia of any kind on those choppers?"

"No, sir," Cruiser replied. "Too bad we didn't know the enemy had aerial attack capabilities."

"Yeah," Brannigan said. "At any rate, we're cut off. We got no anti-aircraft weapons, but I guess nobody thought it would be necessary. We've also lost our long-range commo. There's an unknown enemy facing us and you can bet your asses that the sons of bitches are going to want to take this mountain."

Senior Chief Petty Officer Buford Dawkins jerked his thumb toward the supply dump. "At least we got lots of ammo, sir, even if none of it is AA. It's more'n enough to knock down a whole bunch of jihad jerks."

"It may or may not be that easy, Senior Chief," Brannigan said. "Right now it appears we're caught dead in the middle of one of those battle-of-attrition scenarios. And if they have more men than we have bullets, we'll have a real load to carry around here." He turned and looked out over the terrain. "Get back to your units and do like they say in the Bible. Gird your loins for battle." He nodded to Cruiser. "We'll want to say a few words over Petty Officer Clifford. Let me know when you're ready for the services."

"Aye, sir," Cruiser said.

The 2IC and the chiefs headed over to their squads and teams.

WARLORD DURTAMI'S FORMER COMPOUND NOON LOCAL

THE trio of Mi-24s came in and landed in an echelon right formation. As soon as they touched down, the troop compartment doors opened and twelve fully armed mujahideen fighters quickly exited each aircraft. As soon as all were off to one side, the choppers took off, once more turning toward the fiefdom of Warlord Hassan Khamami.

Although the thirty-six men wore the traditional Afghanistan *puhtee* caps, the rest of their uniforms were modern military. This was brand-new Russian Federation *kamuflirovani kurtki* pattern camouflage garb as was issued to the Federation's Border Guard outfits. The men also had their features streaked with black and green face paint, and they sported AK-47 assault rifles with plenty of bandoleers of ammunition.

The leader of this group was Warlord Khamami's senior field commander, Major Karim Malari. He was a graduate of the Soviet Army's Infantry Academy and had taken other military training courses in the USSR. The officer had not been home for very long before he defected from the Democratic Afghanistan Army to join the mujahideen to fight the foreign invaders from the Soviet Union.

Now he took the handset of the R-108 tactical radio from his commo man and raised the station back in Al-Saraya Castle. "This is Field Command," he said into the mike. "First three helicopters are on the ground and all troops deplaned. The aircraft are on their way back to pick up the next lift. Out."

One of the sub-unit leaders joined him just as the major handed the handset back. The lieutenant saluted. "My men are ready to move out, Major Malari."

"Excellent," Malari said, glancing over at what was left of Durtami's compound. "Those infidels seem to enjoy a good fight. Look what they did to Durtami's old home."

The lieutenant smiled confidently. "I think the unbelievers have a big surprise in store for them. We're not a bunch of country bumpkins they can push around."

"I agree," Malari said. "They're confidence is going to be badly shaken when they discover they're facing the disciplined, well-trained troops of *Amir* Khamami." He checked his watch. "Alright, Lieutenant. Move your men out. Stay out of sight and take a good look at the terrain features leading up to the infidels' position. We'll run a night reconnaissance patrol after dark. I want everything ready by the time the rest of the command is here."

"Yes, sir!"

The young officer hurried over to lead his men up on East Ridge, where they could put the target area under observation.

WEST RIDGE OP
1500 HOURS LOCAL

LIEUTENANT Wild Bill Brannigan sat in the OP with Mike Assad and Dave Leibowitz watching the helicopters coming in from the north, then disappearing behind East

Ridge to land. So far they had counted ten flights of three choppers each for the past three hours.

Brannigan took the binoculars from his eyes. "They must be setting down at the warlord's compound over there."

"That's something SOCOM didn't figure on," Mike remarked.

"Yeah," Dave said. "It really torques my jaw that nobody knew these ragheads had choppers."

"That helicopter model is more than just a gunship, y'know," Mike said. "They're troop carriers too."

"Yeah," Brannigan agreed. "If I remember correctly, those are Mi-24s and can carry about eight troops each. That means a total of two hundred and forty men have been brought in."

"There's probably more than that, sir," Dave pointed out. "Have you ever seen how many of those people can crowd into one of those motor-rickshaws? I'll bet they have at least twelve guys crammed into each of those troop compartments."

"Mmm," Brannigan mused. "That would mean three hundred and sixty or so of them."

"And I don't think they've finished yet," Mike commented.

"We're gonna be outnumbered big time," Dave said. He shrugged. "At least we have plenty of ammo. We can mow those shrieking mujahideen down in rows if we have to."

"More food for the buzzards down on the slope," Mike said. "Those birds have been on triple rations since we got here."

"All this reminds me of an uncle of mine," Brannigan said. "He was an infantryman in the Army during the Korean War. He used to talk about human wave attacks made by the Red Chinese. He was a gunner on a Browning light machine gun. He said he'd burn out barrel after barrel hosing fire bursts into those crazy bastards. Now I know how he felt."

"What are our tactical choices, sir?" Dave asked.

"Well," Brannigan said thoughtfully, "we can stay up here and hold out as long as we can. Maybe when somebody back at SOCOM notices our radio silence, they'll send out an aircraft to investigate."

"That's what those PRC-112s are good for," Mike said. "They can home in on the beacons."

"What if they're a little slow in reacting to our predicament?" Dave wondered aloud.

"Then we'll have to make what is known as a strategic withdrawal," Brannigan said. "That means sneaking out of here under the cover of darkness, hoping we can make it through a strong enemy force that has us surrounded."

"What about Adam Clifford?" Mike asked.

"We always bring our dead and wounded out," Brannigan said. "But we're not keeping one foot in the water like we used to. We'll have to note the burial site and come back for him."

"Or have someone else do the job," Dave commented.

"Damn shame," Mike said glumly.

The three fell into silence as the noise of helicopters ascending into the sky suddenly came from the other side of East Ridge. Within moments all three choppers rose into view over the mountain, turning north.

"Well, there they go again," Mike said, "to pick up another twenty or thirty assholes for us to shoot at."

"And to fire back at us," Dave pointed out.

26 AUGUST
0230 HOURS LOCAL

THE platoon was on 50 percent alert, and Chad Murchison and Bruno Puglisi had been assigned to the OP for the mid-watch. Bruno was asleep while Chad took his turn keeping an eye on things. The night vision device gave him the usual eerie green-white environment to gaze into, and he studied the terrain in front of him with an intensity brought on by the heavy helicopter activity the day before. It was a sure sign that the local situation was going to liven up quite a bit.

Chad had been able to get up a bit higher since it was dark, and he had an excellent view of the boulders and vegetation that swept out and down from the position. Suddenly a stone clicked as if it had been dislodged or accidentally kicked against another one. The SEAL instinctively brought his CAR-15 up as his eyes scanned the terrain in front of him. The disturbance could have come from a jackal who had come back to see if there was anything left to eat on the bones of the dead mujahideen scattered down the slope of the ridge.

A movement to the right caught the SEAL's attention. A moment later he saw the crouching figure of a mujahideen who had evidently just stopped. The guy wore no night vision equipment, so he was working in the deep darkness under a severe handicap. Yet his ability to be silent impressed Chad as he once again began moving upward. The man carefully put his foot down to test the ground in front of him before placing his full weight on it. Then he repeated the movement with the opposite foot while sweeping his eyes in short jerks to see as well as possible in the night's blackness.

Chad thought first of trying to take him prisoner, but that wasn't feasible. He would have to go out to get him and that could bring him in contact with the guy's buddies. So he did the next best thing. He raised the CAR-15 to his shoulder, aimed and fired.

The mujahideen doubled over like he had been mule-kicked in the stomach, then fell to the rocks. There was no return fire, and the sounds of the enemy patrol withdrawing could be heard. They were moving as cautiously and as rapidly as they dared.

Now Puglisi was wide awake. He joined Chad to add his firepower in case of an attack, but now there was nothing but the night's natural silence. Moments later Lieutenants Bill Brannigan and Jim Cruiser appeared at the OP. "What the hell happened?" the Skipper asked.

"Enemy recon patrol, sir," Chad said. "I got one guy that was getting too close. After I fired, I could hear the rest of them making a rapid descent down the slope toward the valley."

Brannigan looked down at the corpse sprawled only a few scant meters away. "The guy is wearing a camouflage uniform and his face is painted. No extra noisemaking gear on him."

"Obviously a reconnaissance," Cruiser commented. "And they broke contact and withdrew just like a recon patrol is supposed to when contact with the enemy is inadvertently made."

"Shit," Brannigan said. "You know what, guys? We're facing some disciplined troops here."

"Obviously," Cruiser agreed. "It would seem the rules of the game have changed."

"But not to our advantage," Brannigan said dryly.

WARLORD DURTAMI'S FORMER COMPOUND
DAWN LOCAL

THE patrol leader squatted in front of Major Karim Malari, who was seated on his Soviet Army–issue groundsheet. Both sipped from cups filled with *dudh chai* tea as the subordinate made his report to the field commander.

"We were able to go completely around the infidels' defensive perimeter, Major," the patrol leader said. "Allah was not with my point man. He stumbled on a rock and was shot dead on the spot. We withdrew without further casualties."

"What was the result of your reconnaissance?"

"I estimate they are no more than a platoon force of forty men at the very most," the patrol leader said. "They are in a circle defensive formation that runs around the entire top of the ridge. They make no unnecessary noise and their positions seem no more than field fortifications. We detected no bunkers."

"Then they are susceptible to mortar fire," Malari commented thoughtfully. "It is good that our battery is set up and ready to go into action."

"How soon do we attack, Major?"

The major chuckled. "I suggest you finish your tea as quickly as possible."

CHAPTER 14

LIEUTENANT Bill Brannigan recognized that any attacks on the base camp would most likely come from the east. To make sure it was the strongest point of his defense, he placed the entire First Squad along that side of the perimeter. Connie Concord and Bruno Puglisi set up the 60-millimeter mortar in a circle of sandbags fifteen meters down from the OP. A camouflage covering across the top of the position could be quickly pulled off in the event of fire missions.

Charlie Fire Team has been assigned to cover the western side of the ridge top. Chief Matt Gunnarson and James Bradley, now the only available members of Delta Fire Team since Puglisi was assigned to the mortar and Adam Clifford was KIA, had situated themselves in a fighting hole near the mortar position. These two SEALs were ready to move to any side of the fighting line where their extra firepower would be needed.

Everyone in the platoon knew that combat was imminent and unavoidable. They waited with dry mouths and sweaty palms as a combination of anticipation and apprehension dominated the SEALs' collective mood. However, the tension was relieved from time to time when one of the Brigands told a joke that had suddenly come to mind, or made a humorous remark to cut the tension. There was also some very creative bitching about life in the Navy, headquarters pukes, staff weenies and ragheads.

On the practical side of the situation, the platoon had ammo bandoleers with fully loaded thirty-round 5.56-millimeter magazines laid out in handy spots near their positions. Each man also had a half dozen deadly M-67 fragmentation hand grenades within reach. These nasties blew steel pellets out some fifteen meters from the point of detonation. This made the explosive devices excellent defensive weapons.

As everyone did his best to settle down, the butterflies in the stomachs were worse than those prior to a parachute jump. Senior Chief Buford Dawkins summed it up with one simple remark:

"This is what they're paying us for, but at times like this we should go on time-and-a-half."

0645 HOURS LOCAL

THE mortar shell ripped through the sky, going completely over West Ridge before slamming into the valley on the western side. The explosion was sharp, the sound echoing in waves across the open country below. It was immediately followed by a second that hit on the western slope of the ridge. Everyone in the platoon hunkered down, their jaw muscles tense and teeth tightly clenched.

A mujahideen mortar was zeroing in on the ridge top.

A couple of moments passed, and the SEALs knew the raghead gunners were using the time to adjust elevation and traverse knobs. The third explosion was dead in the center of the SEALs' position. Over on East Ridge the mujahideen forward observer was satisfied. He got on the old Soviet field radio to let the chief of the mortar battery know they had the range.

A half dozen detonations announced the arrival of the first real barrage of the exploding inferno to come. From that point on, the rounds began coming in separately, but spaced close together, giving evidence that the mortar battery was now doing independent fire. The ground shook like dozens of California earthquakes as the bombardment went into high gear. Sharp pains and a ringing in the ears dulled everyone's hearing as the incoming hell continued. Sometimes the nearness of a hit would create a vacuum that seemed to suck the air out of the lungs of anyone in close vicinity of the detonation. The spraying shards of shrapnel struck sandbags with hundreds of loud thuds and ripping sounds.

Lieutenant Wild Bill Brannigan checked in with Mike Assad, Frank Gomez, and Dave Leibowitz over his LASH headset, then spoke into the PRC-112 to his team leaders. "Report!"

They in turn contacted each man over the LASH headsets, then responded to the skipper in the proper order.

"Bravo Team okay," Senior Chief Buford Dawkins said.

"Charlie Team okay," Lieutenant Jim Cruiser stated.

"Delta Team okay," Chief Matt Gunnarson said, then added, "All two of us."

"Mortar Crew okay," Connie Concord reported. "How about some counterbattery fire, sir?"

"Negative," Brannigan said, knowing their 60-millimeter mortar was outgunned and outnumbered. "This is the place, but it sure as hell isn't the time. Everybody stay down!"

0715 HOURS LOCAL

THE sudden silence caused the buzzing in the men's ears to intensify. The incoming from the enemy mortars had suddenly ceased, leaving the SEALs with concussion headaches to go along with the discomfort of their punished eardrums. Then new sounds erupted from skyward. Three helicopters came in at an altitude that would take them a couple of hundred feet above the ridge top. This aerial attack was obviously coordinated with the mortar barrage.

The aircraft were in a tight echelon right formation, and as soon as the first passed over the SEAL positions, the gunner in the front cockpit cut loose with the 12.7-millimeter heavy machine gun, pounding the SEAL positions with slugs. Within a beat his two buddies joined him.

Dozens of large steel bullets smacked into the shell-pocked ground, ricocheting off boulders with angry whines. Like the shrapnel from the mortars, these smaller projectiles ripped into sandbags, making the dirt within spurt out in dusty gushes. The SEALs had no choice but to maintain their crouching positions with heads down. The choppers pulled away and turned for a second run. Senior Chief Buford Dawkins took a chance for a quick look to the east. He ducked back down and got on the PRC-112.

"Skipper, this is Bravo," he said. "They's a shitpot full of them ragheads coming over the top of East Ridge! The sumbitches is headed right for us and they's spaced out proper as skirmishes. These ain't crazy-ass suicide shitheels. Them bastards is coming on like proper soldiers!"

"Roger," Brannigan said. He and his men were caught in a classic situation of being pinned down flat while the enemy maneuvered to close with them. The next time he took the platoon on a mission, he was going to make sure there were at least a couple of Stingers in their arsenal to handle aerial assaults.

If there was a next time.

Once more the trio of Mi-24s began their attack in nose-down positions to give the gunners the best view of the target area. They swept in, firing sweeping salvos that once more splattered the ridge top. Kevin Albee of Charlie Fire Team looked up through his camouflage netting just as the second passed over his position. He impetuously stood up and cut loose at the departing Hind with his CAR-15 on full-auto. The range was less than fifty yards, and the 5.56 slugs bit into the old aircraft, punching into the engine and transmission behind the pilot. The helicopter veered off to the right and dove downward on the west side of the ridge, hitting the steep terrain and exploding.

Kevin had no time to see the result of his quick shooting. The third chopper's gunner gave a long burst that hit the SEAL in the back, slamming him with the intensity of a dozen sledgehammers. Kevin was kicked forward, falling half in and half out of his fighting hole.

"Corpsman!" Lieutenant Jim Cruiser said over his LASH system. "Albee's down!"

James Bradley leaped up and rushed toward the Charlies' positions, taking no notice that the two surviving helicopters had pulled away. He stopped at the hole, kneeling down to examine the casualty. The 12.7-millimeter slugs had done their worst. Kevin was raw, bleeding hamburger between his neck and waist. The hospital corpsman looked up as Cruiser joined him. "He's dead, sir."

"Fuck!" Cruiser said. "A good kid. Man! A good fucking kid. He got himself killed to destroy an enemy aircraft." He got on the LASH. "Skipper, one of the choppers is down, but we've lost Kevin Albee. He shot the son of a bitch out of the sky."

"Are you under ground attack on that side?" Brannigan asked.

"Negative, sir."

"All right," Brannigan said. "Get back to your position, but first tell Bradley and Chief Gunnarson to get their asses over here. We're about to engage what looks like a two-company force!"

"Aye, sir."

"I'm real sorry about Albee, Jim."

"We all are, sir."

0730 HOURS LOCAL

CHIEF Matt Gunnarson and James Bradley were both loaded down with bandoleers and grenades, and they rushed to the First Squad's perimeter, sounding like a couple of pack horses. The two members of Delta Fire Team took a couple of auxiliary fighting positions that flanked those of Mike Assad and Dave Leibowitz.

"Glad to see you," Mike said to James. He pointed below. "Take a look."

James glanced in the indicated direction and could see mujahideen skirmishers moving steadily up the slope toward them. These men were not shrieking zealots engaged in a running suicide charge. They moved carefully under the command of squad leaders as they took advantage of all the cover and concealment offered by the rugged terrain.

James studied them, and commented, "They're still out of range, aren't they?"

"Yeah," Mike said, "And I kind of wish they'd stay that way."

Lieutenant Bill Brannigan was over on the left side of the line, between Frank Gomez and Mike Assad. He had taken time to figure out what routes the different attack elements of the mujahideen were taking in their approach toward the top of the ridge. Now he spoke into the LASH. "Mortar Crew, we need some rounds dropped on the eastern slope. It's minimum range, so your tube is going to be almost vertical. Fire one round for effect."

In less than thirty seconds the sound of a sharp "crump" came from the mortar position. A couple of beats passed, then an explosion came from below. Brannigan liked what he saw. "Give 'em two dozen more."

Now Connie Concord and Bruno Puglisi went to work.

WARLORD KHAMAMI'S CP
EAST RIDGE
0745 HOURS LOCAL

WARLORD Hassan Khamami held the Soviet Army *polevoi* binoculars to his eyes as he watched his troops make their way up the side of the mountain opposite his CP. Several moments before, he had received an oral report via radio of the skeletal remains of Ayyub Durtami's dead mujahideen that lay scattered across the rocky slope. Such a situation was abhorrent to any Muslim. The dead of the faithful must be properly buried according to the dictates of the Holy Koran. Even the secular Khamami considered this important and respectful to those who died.

Now his radio operator, wearing an R-100 pack radio, spoke up. "*Amir,* the chief helicopter pilot has entered the net desiring to speak with you."

Khamami let the binoculars dangle around his neck by the strap as he took the handset. "Yes, Captain Sheriwal?"

"*Amir!*" Mohammed Sheriwal said in his Russian-accented Pashto. "We have lost the number two Mi-24. It was shot down by the infidels."

"May they rot in hell for two eternities!" Khamami hissed angrily, using a traditional Pashto curse. "Do they have Stingers?"

"I don't think so, *Amir,*" Sheriwal replied. "It was either a lucky hit from infantry arms or they have an automatic anti-aircraft weapon."

"Ground the other helicopters and do not fly them over the objective," Khamami said. "I shall let the ground fighters take care of those interlopers."

"How goes the battle, *Amir*?" Sheriwal asked.

"Our men progress upward in a proper, prudent manner," Khamami said. "They continue toward a sure victory. I must turn my attention back to the attack." He gave the handset back to the radio operator, and once more gazed across the valley through the binoculars.

MUJAHIDEEN ATTACK FORCE
WEST RIDGE
0750 HOURS LOCAL

THE platoon and section leaders kept in close contact with the men as they moved upward, firing well-aimed volleys toward the area where the infidels were dug in. Mortar shells had been coming slowly but regularly, and caused a few casualties, but the barrage did not amount to much. It was quite evident that the unbelievers had no more than one such support weapon, and it was of a minimum caliber. However, they had managed to slow the assault with accurate drops of shells in key locations.

But now the warlord's fighters were getting closer to the crest of the ridge, and the effect of the small arms fire from above was beginning to tell. The incidents of mujahideen crumpling under the impact of rifle bullets grew more numerous with each passing moment.

The commander, Major Karim Malari, ordered a halt when they reached a place where numerous stands of boulders offered good cover. At that point, the men settled in and began trading shot-for-shot with the defenders.

Malari gestured to his radio operator to join him. He took the handset and raised the warlord. "*Amir,* we have reached a place where it is most perilous to continue the advance without suffering very heavy casualties."

"I understand, Major," Khamami replied. He had total faith in whatever tactical decisions or opinions his field commander might express. "Are you completely stopped?"

"Not at all, *Amir,*" Malari assured him. "We could score a victory here within an hour or an hour and a half, but I fear our casualties would be close to fifty or even sixty percent."

"What is it you wish to do?"

"I respectfully request that you send the two companies in reserve around to the opposite side of this mountain, *Amir,*" Malari said. "When they are in position, we can launch simultaneous attacks from both directions. The infidels' volume of

fire would be reduced by having to defend two sides. I estimate a victory could be accomplished before dark even if we
are most sensible and cautious. By carefully advancing upward, our losses would be more acceptable."

"I will issue the necessary orders to Captain Tanizai immediately," Khamami said. "Hold your position and keep
the enemy busy. I suggest a few rushes up toward them to
keep the dogs distracted."

"I hear and obey, *Amir*," Malari said. He switched
over to his own command net. "All units began rapid fire at
the enemy for a period of ten seconds, then cease. Platoon
Two and Platoon Four! As soon as the firing stops, make a
bold attack to test the mettle of the enemy. Begin immediately!"

The sound of firing picked up in intensity as all mujahideen began shooting at the enemy above them. As soon
as the fusillades lessened, the two platoons ordered to attack
leaped from their positions and rushed upward toward the
infidels' defenses. They immediately came under fire, and
several of them were hit by the accurate shooting from
above. Then three hand grenades were tossed by the defenders. The explosive devices hit the rocks, bounced once, then
detonated. A half dozen attackers wilted under the solid
steel hail of the M-67 grenades' deadly pellets.

"Platoons Two and Four!" Malari radioed. "Break off the
attack and return to your original positions." The field commander now realized that the infidels were much more desperate and skilled than he had at first thought.

The surviving mujahideen gladly broke contact and
stumbled back to where they had launched the attack.

0910 HOURS LOCAL

THE convoy of ten Soviet ZIL-157 transport trucks
came to a stop a kilometer southwest of West Ridge. Each
vehicle had twenty mujahideen packed into the back, and

when the tailgates were dropped, the fighters quickly leaped to the ground, forming up by platoons.

The commanding officer, Captain Lakhdar Tanizai, wasted no time in facing the men toward the mountain occupied by the unbelievers. "Double time!" he bellowed. *"March!"*

The double column moved out quickly, anxious to do their part in changing the assault to a two-pronged operation.

WEST RIDGE BASE CAMP
0925 HOURS LOCAL

LIEUTENANT Jim Cruiser spoke rapidly but calmly into the PRC-112. "Charlie Papa, this is Second Squad. Approximately two companies of enemy troops have moved into the area just below our positions. Expect an immediate attack. Over."

"Roger, Second Squad," Lieutenant Bill Brannigan radioed back. "I'm sending over the reserves." Then he added, "Both of 'em. Out." He pressed the throat mike of the LASH. "Chief Gunnarson! Bradley! Get over to Second Squad and report to Lieutenant Cruiser. Out."

The two grabbed grenades and bandoleers, then rushed from the First Squad's perimeter to dash across the open space to where their squad mates were preparing for the impending mujahideen blitz.

1015 HOURS LOCAL

THE attack from the west side of the ridge was carried on like the one on the east side. The mujahideen took advantage of the cover to fire-and-maneuver their way upward. And like their comrades on the opposite side, they became bogged down under the intense and accurate fire of the SEALs. Hand grenades and the sporadic mortar shells that came from Connie Concord and Bruno Puglisi also slowed their advance.

Khamami, back on East Ridge, knew he could overwhelm the defenders anytime he wished. The problem was that it would cost him dearly in casualties. As the general of a private army, he did not have the luxury of a draft board or the populations of large cities from which to draw replacements. If he behaved rashly, he could well end up almost as bad off as his idiot brother-in-law who stupidly sacrificed almost two hundred men and gained nothing for it. He turned to his radio operator and took the handset.

"Major Malari! Captain Tanizai! Pull your men back to more secure positions and hold them there until further orders." Khamami paused long enough to take a deep breath before continuing. "Mortar Battery! Renew your fire mission! Fire at will! Twenty-five rounds each gun! Commence firing!"

1600 HOURS LOCAL

THE day's fighting had been unmitigated hell for the SEALs. A total of three mortar barrages had pounded them into near insensibility while the time between the shellings was occupied with fighting off probing attacks by the warlord's infantry. These assaults, though not pressed to completion, ate up valuable ammunition and grenades.

Empty cloth bandoleers littered the fighting positions and those that held full magazines were rapidly becoming fewer. The SEALs, for all their amazing physical conditioning, were close to exhaustion. If the mujahideen kept up the pressure through the night, Brannigan's Brigands would be reduced to a token force barely able to defend themselves. Senior Chief Buford Dawkins, as usual, summed it up with one of his sardonic Alabama country-boy comments that were not meant to be humorous:

"By tomorry morning we're gonna be reduced to throwing rocks at them raghead sumbitches."

But the fighting suddenly came to a halt. Mike Assad in the OP could see the mujahideen withdrawing farther down the slope, then stopping and digging in.

2215 HOURS LOCAL

THE pressing need for watchfulness made the preparations of MREs an inconvenience. Most of the SEALs turned to the energy bars for nourishment as they went into another 50 percent alert.

Brannigan called Cruiser and the two chief petty officers to join him in the CP. The four spoke quietly, sipping water from their canteens to get some fullness in their stomachs as they munched their snacks.

"Things are going downhill," Brannigan said candidly. "And we've just about struck rock bottom. We've got two KIAs, but at least nobody's been wounded. We won't have to go through the shit of making a choice to leave the WIAs behind or try to carry them with us."

Chief Matt Gunnarson finished off his oatmeal bar. "You're talking like we're getting the fuck out of here, sir."

"That's the next item on our agenda," Bannerman said. "We've got a real hairy operation to pull off tonight. We're tired, relatively low on ammo, and are completely cut off. But we've got to make a withdrawal under the cover of darkness. It's going to be tough sledding, gentlemen, but if we can get off this mountain and into the terrain to the west, we'll have a chance of breaking contact."

"I agree, sir," Cruiser said. "There's a lot of deep ravines and forested areas for cover and concealment on the other side of the valley."

"Right," Brannigan said. "It also offers us a better chance to put up a fight. We can even set up some ambushes. Or if they give us a hard knock, we can use the terrain features for cover to haul ass. That'll give us enough time and space for a quick counterattack to keep 'em off balance."

Cruiser was thoughtful for a moment before expressing an important concern. "Didn't you say Al-Qaeda could be in that area?"

"Yeah. But we have no other choice," Brannigan said. "It's like we're damned if we do and damned if we don't."

"When do we move out, sir?" Senior Chief Dawkins asked.

"Oh-one-hundred hours," Brannigan answered.

Cruiser checked his watch. "That'll give our guys damn near three hours to rest up for the ordeal."

"Rest up?" Brannigan remarked. "We've got two graves to hide, not to mention digging caches for the mortar and third line equipment. We're hauling ass with little more than weapons and skivvies. You guys turn to and get those items taken care of. If it's done fast enough, the men will maybe have a twenty- or thirty-minute breather to rest up for the withdrawal."

"Luxury!" Cruiser said with a grin. "You're spoiling the platoon, sir."

"Yeah!" Brannigan said with a humorless chuckle. "Who said it was tough in the SEALs?"

CHAPTER 15

THE task of caching extra gear such as the 60-millimeter mortar system and everyone's third line equipment had taken longer than Wild Bill Brannigan estimated. It was difficult to do the work properly because of having to rely on the night vision system goggles to make sure the excavations were undetectable after being filled in. It was even necessary to eliminate boot prints as much as possible so the mujahideen could not make a ballpark estimate of how many people had occupied the mountaintop. The two chief petty officers made damn sure nothing was left to chance. Everyone's life literally depended on keeping the mujahideen guessing.

The most difficult part of the activity involved the graves of Kevin Albee and Adam Clifford. The idea of abandoning these resting places of their buddies seemed near sacrilege to the SEALs. As if this wasn't bad enough, the knowledge that some miserable raghead would tread over the graves gave Brannigan's Brigands a sense of shame tinged with a deep grief. The fact that it was a tactical necessity did not lessen the emotional pain.

Although the Skipper had ordered the noise of the shoveling be kept to a minimum, he wasn't that concerned about it. If the mujahideen detected the sound of digging, they would only assume the infidels on the ridge top were reinforcing their fighting positions. This would serve well in giving the impression they were staying put. It was of the utmost importance that they conceal the fact that an escape off the mountain was in the offing. But the work took extraordinary effort, and nobody in the platoon was able to get any rest before it was time to abandon West Ridge for the questionable safety of the ravine country to the west.

0100 HOURS LOCAL

THE entire platoon was stripped down to their combat vests, taking only first and second line equipment, along with extra ammunition bandoleers, the PRC-112 radios, and hand and M-203 grenades. As soon as everyone was checked out, the chiefs formed them up to begin the withdrawal. The order of march was Alpha, Bravo, Delta and Charlie Teams. The point was manned as usual by the intrepid Odd Couple, while Joe Miskoski and Gutsy Olson acted as rear guards. Since the route would be through the deep ravines of the foothills, Brannigan didn't bother to station flankers out on the sides of the column. Security would have been seriously compromised if anyone walking in the open above the deep gullies was spotted by enemy reconnaissance patrols.

Mike Assad and Dave Leibowitz led the way down the ridge slope, moving slowly and carefully as they peered into the darkness through the night vision devices. Behind them, the rest of platoon followed noiselessly, being extra careful to avoid the rattling of equipment and bandoleers of ammunition. They knew the mujahideen would have OPs scattered throughout the area, and the need for total alertness was super critical. A safe withdrawal could only be made if they stayed vigilant and cautious. Fate would not be kind to the careless.

The platoon reached the valley floor, and Mike signaled a halt while Dave went forward a few meters for a quick recon. He came back and whispered over the LASH. "There's an OP manned by two ragheads approximately twenty-five meters ahead at ten o'clock. There's a way around them, so follow us real careful."

"Carry on," Brannigan whispered back.

The two point men led the way farther to the north for a hundred meters before turning back west toward the foothills. A half hour later the Odd Couple eased back to the original direction, but they hadn't gone far before Joe Miskoski at the rear spoke urgently. "Enemy patrol! Left flank!"

"Everybody down!" Brannigan ordered, thinking about what a relief it would be when they finally reached the concealment of the ravines. There would be constant danger of contact with the enemy until they left this open, flat country.

Within moments a six-man patrol of mujahideen could be discerned moving carefully in the opposite direction. They had no night vision capabilities, but were doing an excellent job of maintaining their course and speed without any unnecessary noise. The only sound came when one grunted slightly after making a misstep on the uneven terrain. A few more nervous moments passed before Joe spoke again. "All clear!"

"All right," the Skipper said. "Move out!"

Mike and Dave stood up and renewed the westward trek.

TOP OF WEST RIDGE
0720 HOURS LOCAL

THE door of the Mi-24 helicopter's troop compartment was open, and Warlord Hassan Khamami stood in it, looking down at the place the enemy had defended with such ferocious determination and skill. They had chosen the spot well, he concluded, and he noted that they had an excellent view of the valley on all sides of the mountain. When the chopper touched down, Khamami leaped to the ground and hurried over to where his field commander, Major Karim Malari, waited.

The major saluted. *"Asalaam aleikum, Amir."*

"Greetings," Khamami said. He looked around at the bare area, seeing no indication of anyone having recently been there. "What is the situation here?"

"The infidels seem to have walked off the face of the earth, *Amir,*" Malari replied in an apologetic tone. "We know they were here because they constructed field fortifications, yet there is no evidence of anything else. Not even boot prints or latrines." He gestured in frustration. "It is pristine, as if no one had been here for decades."

"What about equipment?" Khamami asked. "Surely they could not carry everything they had away with them."

"There was not as much as a single cigarette butt," Malari said. "Not even a thread or button. It seems the entire ridge top has been carefully swept over by some diabolical giant with a huge broom. As Mohammad is the prophet, they must have buried things, but my men cannot find any evidence of it, no matter how hard they search."

"At any rate we don't have the time or need to start digging around here," Khamami said, angered by the situation. The foreigners were indeed a clever enemy. "The only direction they could have gone is west."

"I agree, *Amir.* The foothills and ravines leading to the western mountain ranges offer excellent concealment."

"Prepare some men for aerial transport out to the foothills ahead of where the enemy must be," Khamami ordered. "Meanwhile I shall dispatch the helicopters to make an aerial search for them. The foreigners are not invisible! We will find where they are eventually."

"Au, Amir!" Malari said, again saluting. "I shall order

two platoons to ready themselves for air transportation. They will be waiting when the aircraft return from their scouting mission."

Khamami turned and trotted back to the helicopter to order the aerial reconnaissance to begin. Now there were more than material reasons to destroy this elusive enemy. He had grown to hate them in a cold, calculating way. The warlord was ready to apply his own tactical talent, and the tenacity of his mujahideen, to destroy these maddening foreigners.

THE FOOTHILLS
1045 HOURS LOCAL

THE platoon could hear the helicopters long before they made an appearance. Brannigan ordered a halt, then scurried up to the top of the ravine and looked toward the eastern sky. Two dark shapes, flying in a zigzag search pattern, drew closer. It was obvious they were scouting the foothills and surrounding terrain. And the Skipper knew exactly who they were looking for with such painstaking diligence.

"Now hear this!" Brannigan said over the LASH. "Get into the shadows at the side of the ravine. Keep your heads down and don't move!"

He slid down to the ravine floor, heading back to his position between Frank Gomez and Senior Chief Buford Dawkins. The senior chief patted his CAR-15. "D'you think we ought to shoot 'em down if they come in low enough, sir?"

"Negative," Brannigan said. "If they receive fire, they'll radio their positions immediately. I don't want the bastards to have any idea of where we might be. Our best hope is remaining phantoms."

Frank Gomez grinned. "Maybe they'll end up thinking we're figments of their imaginations."

"Not likely," Brannigan said. "I'm sure they've counted their dead and treated their wounded. Imaginary enemies don't inflict casualties." The sound of the chopper engines was much louder by then. "Everybody down!"

The Mi-24s came in cautiously, knowing better than to get too close to where these particular infidels might be concealed. One of their comrades had already paid for that carelessness with his life, the life of his gunner, and a helicopter. The aircraft went past, made a sweeping turn, then came back. After a half dozen runs, they took one final look and headed eastward.

The sound of the engines gradually faded away. Brannigan let fifteen minutes pass, then stood up. "All right, guys. Let's haul ass out of here. Assad and Leibowitz, step out sharply!"

"Aye, sir," the Odd Couple replied simultaneously. The fourteen-man column was once again on the move.

TOP OF WEST RIDGE
1105 HOURS LOCAL

WARLORD Khamami and Major Malari watched as the two helicopters came in for a landing. They turned away from the clouds of gritty dust the rotors kicked up, waiting for the engines to be cut.

Captain Mohammed Sheriwal, as the senior pilot, left his aircraft to make a personal report to the warlord. "*Amir,* we could not find the infidels. The terrain is cut up by numerous ravines and some stands of trees. They had no trouble in remaining concealed from us. But they are out there. There is no doubt of that."

Malari pulled the Soviet Army map from beneath his jacket and knelt down to spread it out. "Show us where you went."

Sheriwal joined him, putting his finger on the topographical chart. "We flew in a search square. I kept us together, since the more sets of eyes we had, the greater the chance of spotting the infidels. We went a hundred and fifty kilometers on both sides of this area."

Khamami stood with his arms crossed on his chest, looking down at the map. "Excellent. I agree with your search pattern, Captain Sheriwal. The enemy would not be so stupid as to wander too far north or south."

"The problem is the loss of our number two aircraft," Sheriwal said. "It cuts our capabilities by a third."

"Yes," Khamami said. "I must get a replacement helicopter as quickly as possible."

"I could go to Kabul," Sheriwal said. "It would not be too difficult to steal an Afghanistan Army aircraft there. A small bribe to a guard would allow easy access. I could fly it straight back here."

"It would do us no good without a third pilot," Khamami pointed out.

"But if we were able to obtain a helicopter, you could hire another, *Amir*," Sheriwal argued.

Khamami smiled sarcastically. "You have amassed a great deal of money since joining my army, have you not, Captain Sheriwal?"

"Of course, *Amir*," Sheriwal replied. "I shall be eternally grateful to you for the opportunities you have given me to enrich myself."

"The opium smuggling was the best paying of all your activities, *na*?"

"Yes, *Amir*," Sheriwal answered.

"You are a good servant and soldier, Mohammad Sheriwal," Khamami said. "But if you ever withdrew from my presence, I would not trust you to come back."

"I would come back!" Sheriwal said. "I swear, *Amir*!"

"I am aware of the money you have sent to Switzerland," Khamami said.

Sheriwal swallowed nervously. "But . . . but . . . that is for my old age, *Amir*."

"Some men are old at thirty-five," Khamami said. Now he knelt down and studied the map for a few moments before

looking at Major Malari. "Take careful note of that canyon
that is shown far to the west."

Malari looked. "Yes, *Amir*. I know the place. It is the
Wadi Khesta Valley."

"The enemy must pass through it if they are to successfully evade us," Khamami said. "I want two platoons flown
to the far end to take up positions. Understood?"

"Au, Amir!"

"Additionally, I want one more platoon between here and
that canyon," Khamami said. "That way the enemy will be
caught between that one platoon and the two-platoon force.
Those devils will have no escape, and the rest of our fighters
can join up with the single platoon to crush them."

Malari smiled. "You plan to attack the enemy from two
sides, do you not, *Amir*?"

"You have read my mind like a bazaar magician,"
Khamami said. "Prepare the platoons for this mission."

Malari got to his feet. "I shall assemble the men immediately, *Amir*." He picked up the map and refolded it. "Captain
Tanizai! Assemble the Third Company. Have them ready to
leave here within fifteen minutes!" The order set off a flurry
of activity among the mujahideen.

The warlord looked straight into Sheriwal's eyes in a
threatening manner. "Did you understand the orders?"

"Au, Amir!" the pilot answered quickly. "I am ready to
perform my duties!"

"I always keep my eyes on you, Sheriwal."

"I am pleased, *Amir*. That way you will truly know of my
trustworthiness."

THE FOOTHILLS
1600 HOURS LOCAL

BRANNIGAN brought the forced march to a halt. The
helicopters were back flying in the vicinity, but were not
conducting any searching activities. It became obvious that

they were flying to a point ahead of the column and to another location in the rear; landing, then taking off again and flying eastward. After a half hour or so, they would reappear to repeat the process.

Senior Chief Petty Officer Buford Dawkins had been watching carefully, making mental notations of the goings-on. He hurried down the line to report to the platoon commander.

"Sir," the senior chief said. "I've counted a total of seven lifts by them choppers. They's been five to the front and two to the rear. Seems kinda strange, don't it?"

"Yeah," Brannigan commented dryly. He spoke into the LASH. "Jim. Chief Gunnarson. Front and center." He waited for the two to join him and the senior chief. "Has anybody figured out what's going on with those fucking helicopters?"

Jim Cruiser nodded. "I figure they're landing troops to both our front and rear."

"Give the man a cigar!" Brannigan said. "And there're more to the front than to the rear. That would mean they want to draw us into an escape attempt back in an eastward direction. It would be easier that way since resistance would be lighter, but eventually we'd run into their main force. If we try to avoid both ends and move out of the cover of the ravines for a cross-country run, we'd be caught flat-footed and helpless as a herd of deer facing a wolf pack."

"That'd be some bad shit, sir," the senior chief commented. "Then they'd know they's only fourteen of us. It wouldn't be long afore they was all over us like stink on shit."

"We'd last about as long as that proverbial snowball in hell," Cruiser agreed.

"No fucking doubt about that," Brannigan said bitterly. "So we'll do the unexpected. The platoon will move toward the stronger enemy group until contact is made after dark. That will be the Odd Couple's job. When they've scoped out the enemy position, we'll make a three-pronged attack in the darkness."

"What's the order of battle, sir?" Chief Gunnarson asked.

"The Alphas and Deltas will form up to hit the enemy straight on," Brannigan replied. "Charlie Team will go out of the ravine, then get into position on the right flank. Bravo Team will do the same on the left. When everyone is ready, I'll give the word and we'll make a simultaneous attack. From the number of helicopter flights, I estimate we'll be going against maybe eighty or ninety men. But we'll have three big things in our favor. The first is the element of surprise. The second, and most advantageous, is our night vision capability."

"What's the third advantage we enjoy?" Cruiser asked.

"That we are SEALs," Brannigan replied. He pressed the LASH throat mike. "Assad! Leibowitz! Report to me!"

2230 HOURS LOCAL

MIKE Assad and Dave Leibowitz were not close enough to see or hear the mujahideen. They became aware of the enemy's proximity through the tingling nerves that come from a strong awareness of imminent danger. These instincts had developed over countless combat patrols and hours spent on point in hostile territory. They glanced at each other, then came to a halt. Mike tapped Dave's shoulder, and pointed to the left. Dave nodded his understanding then waited while his buddy led the way out of the ravine to higher ground.

Their senses sharpened even more when they reached the exposed area. They stepped slowly and deliberately, scanning the immediate vicinity in all directions. It was Dave who sighted the OP first. He grabbed Mike's sleeve and pointed. Mike then led them farther to the left, then turned in slightly past the mujahideen position. When they stopped, they could see the bivouac. Both quickly and silently estimated that there were seventy-five or eighty men down in the ravine. All were either seated or lying down, obviously waiting for some expected event—such as a group of infidels stumbling into them.

Mike and Dave retraced their steps, went back down into the ravine and headed in the direction of the platoon.

THE MUJAHIDEEN POSITION
2330 HOURS LOCAL

THE fighters were tired and hungry. Their field rations had been no more than balls of rice, and they'd not even had tea to wash down the meager meals. Only the tepid water in their old Soviet canteens was available to satiate their thirst. Most had been badly unnerved not only by the dangerous, skilled enemy they faced, but also by the bones of Durtami's mujahideen that were scattered across the ridge they had to climb in the dangerous attempts to reach the enemy positions. Some of the men claimed the sound of the wind across the mountains was not from the usual gusts; instead it was the weeping moans of the lost souls of dead Muslims whose flesh had been consumed by jackals and buzzards.

Most of the men slept fitfully, enduring the discomfort of having to lie down on rocks and bumpy ground to slumber. A few were awake, nervous about the unusual chain of events that had brought them to this strange place in the foothills.

These were the ones that heard the slight but sudden sounds of pings and dull thumps.

They didn't realize these were from the seven hand grenades that had just been tossed into their midst. As soon as the detonations began, heavy firing came from the front. This was quickly joined by salvos from the right and left that sent dozens of rounds to sweep through the two mujahideen platoons.

Now Alpha and Delta Teams moved in from the front, raking the prone enemy with automatic fire bursts of three rounds. Bravo and Charlie Teams slid down into the ravine from their attack positions to join their platoon mates.

The entire platoon charged through the position, leaving dead and wounded mujahideen as they rushed out the other side to continue rapidly down the ravine.

CHAPTER 16

LIEUTENANT Wild Bill Brannigan had decided there wasn't much to be gained by simply running like a herd of zebra being pursued by lions. As the Brigands continued through the foothills, his mind raced with ideas on how to keep any pursuers not only off balance, but nervous as hell in the bargain. A hesitant enemy was a less dangerous enemy. Unlike the zebras, the SEALs had some pretty sharp fangs of their own.

The skipper considered sending out patrols since that was the normal manner of harassing bad guys. The activity also served to keep tabs on what kind of trouble the sons of bitches were trying to stir up. But he had to keep in mind that the platoon was involved in a vital retrograde movement and they really had to get the hell out of the area as fast as possible. This precluded any possibility of standing still while sending out fire teams to observe or hassle the mujahideen.

Then the solution to the problem of keeping the enemy

on edge came to him in a flash. An ambush would serve that purpose just as well if not better.

The art of sneaky deadly ambuscades was the most tried and true means of shocking an enemy ever applied throughout military history. Although harassment was the secondary purpose of ambushes—destruction of the enemy was the primary motive—it would serve the platoon well. A small unit like the Brigands would have a distinct advantage over even a much larger one in a well-planned attack from concealed positions. Most of the time, the unit suffering the assault overestimated the number of attackers and reacted accordingly in subsequent combats. After suffering a bloody ambush, they would conduct their operations in a much more prudent and wary manner.

The only regret Brannigan had was that with only fourteen men, he would be unable to organize a baited trap ambush. If they were a stronger force, the SEALs could use the original ambush as bait to draw in enemy relief forces. These would be hit by one or more harassing ambushes as they rushed to aid their pinned down buddies. The harassing elements did not have to destroy the targets, only delay and disorganize them while inflicting casualties. The tactical situation that developed would dictate the method for breaking contact and melting back into the countryside. But with a little more than a dozen men, this was not going to be feasible.

Brannigan came to the conclusion that in the future if the SEALs were going to be participating in longer in-country missions, the platoons were going to have to be reorganized and beefed up. This would be something to put in his after action report.

0845 HOURS LOCAL

WILD Bill Brannigan kept his thoughts to himself until they reached a perfect site to lay an effective ambush. When he perceived the possibilities of the location, he viewed the area with a ferocious happiness. The ravine narrowed and deepened slightly, with excellent areas of cover and concealment along the top. During a potential ambush, if the victims decided the best course was to charge through the incoming fire, they would be slowed when they tried to crowd themselves through the confined space at the end.

Brannigan spoke into the LASH. "Let's hold it up. Point men report to me."

The SEALs went into a defensive posture, covering all sides as Mike Assad and Dave Leibowitz came back from the point and trotted down to where the skipper waited for them.

"Hey, guys," Brannigan said. "I've got a short recon for you. I need to have the top of this ravine around the immediate area checked out. See what's up there. Cover and concealment is what I'm interested in."

"Aye, sir," Dave replied.

Brannigan and Frank Gomez boosted them up so they could climb out of the deep gulley. While the Odd Couple was gone, the Skipper decided to take the opportunity to have a stroll down the platoon column for an informal visual inspection. He visited the Bravos first, finding Senior Chief Buford Dawkins restless as usual. He was standing up while his only companion, Chad Murchison, sat comfortably on the ground with his back resting against the ravine wall. Gutsy Olson, normally a member of Bravo Fire Team, had been sent over to the Charlies, then further dispatched to accompany Joe Miskoski on rear guard.

The senior chief eyed the Skipper somewhat suspiciously. "What've you got on your mind, sir?"

Brannigan grinned. "What makes you think I've got something on my mind, Senior Chief?"

"You got a devious look in your eye, sir," Dawkins said with country-boy candor. "You look like an ol' bear that's just sighted a beehive of honey."

Brannigan lowered his voice. "I'm thinking of springing an ambush."

Dawkins glanced around the immediate area. "This looks like a pretty good place. What's up on top?"

"I've sent the Odd Couple to find out," Brannigan said. "Hang in there. I'll be getting back to you."

"Aye, sir."

Brannigan went on down to where Chief Matt Gunnarson, Bruno Puglisi and James Bradley, the hospital corpsman, were strung out along the ravine. The chief also gave him a shifty look, so Brannigan beat him to the punch by saying, "I'm seriously considering setting up an ambush right here."

"All right, sir!" Gunnarson exclaimed. "Is that why you sent Assad and Leibowitz topside for a look-see?"

"You bet," Brannigan said. He nodded at James. "The guys may be getting pretty tired before this is all wrapped up."

"I've got some pep pills that will give them some oomph," James said. "I think we might end up with a water problem though."

"Nothing is ever easy in this line of work," Brannigan remarked, moving down the line.

Lieutenant Jim Cruiser nodded a greeting to the platoon commander as he approached. "Welcome to the aft end of the column, sir."

"Thank you," Brannigan said. "How's it going?"

"Fine, thanks," Cruiser said. "Milly Mills and I are hanging in here while Joe Miskoski and Gutsy Olson are playing tail-gunners. I thought it would be a good idea if Milly and I relieved them for a while. They need a break."

"Don't bother about it right away," Brannigan counseled. "I'm working on setting up a special reception for the ragheads at this spot. I'll be getting back to you later."

He walked back toward the front, reaching Frank just as Mike and Dave slid back into the ravine. Mike did the talking. "There's a flat area about a kilometer to the front where we could go after we break contact from the ambush."

"I didn't say anything to you two about an ambush," Brannigan said.

Dave shrugged. "Hell, sir, it was obvious as hell."

"Right, sir," Mike agreed. "Me and Dave found a place where it'd be easy to get back into the cover of the ravine."

"Right," Dave agreed. "We'd be long gone by the time the bad guys recovered from the attack."

"What about cover and concealment along the top of this area?" Brannigan asked.

"It couldn't be better, sir," Mike said. "You can look right down into this fucking ditch without having to worry about anybody spotting you from below."

"Okay," Brannigan said. He pressed the throat mike of the LASH. "All right! Listen up. We're going to set up an ambush here. I don't want to waste grenades since the mujahideen are going to be pretty much confined in this space. They'll make very easy targets."

Senior Chief Buford's voice came over the system. "What kind of ambush do you have in mind, sir?"

"A line ambush," Brannigan said. "To refresh your lessons from Ambush 101, let me remind you that means we will be deployed parallel to the bad guys' direction of travel. In other words, we'll be positioned for flanking fire. And that means it has to be heavy."

"But no grenades?" Bruno Puglisi asked.

"You'll have to control your base emotions, Bruno," Brannigan said. "You'll do more damage with your M-16. Anyhow, there'll be too much of a chance that those steel pellets would fly back in your face in this confined space. Okay. Listen, guys. Here's the order of battle. The rear security force will be the Deltas, with the responsibility to see that none of the enemy escape back in the direction they came from. Understood, Delta Leader?"

"Yes, sir," Chief Gunnarson responded.

"The front security force will be the Charlies," Brannigan said. "It's your job to make sure no bad guys charge forward to safety. Okay, Charlie Leader?"

"Got it, sir," Jim Cruiser said. "Right now we're under strength since Kevin Albee is KIA and Gutsy Olson and Joe Miskoski are assigned to rear guard."

"Thanks for reminding me," Brannigan said. "Olson and Miskoski, you will rejoin the Charlies. After this thing goes down, you can be the rear guard again." He waited a moment. "The entire First Squad—I say again—the *entire* First Squad will be the attack force. That means delivering heavy fire into the target. Remember, men, we don't want any of those sons of bitches getting through the ambush at the front or running away at the back. Got it? Good! The firing will commence when Charlie Fire Team sees that all the bad guys have passed into the kill zone."

"When does the firing halt?" Milly Mills asked.

"When every one of those raghead bastards is dead," Brannigan said. "Now let's climb up there on the edge of this gulley and get set up."

The platoon began scrambling to get out of the ravine.

0930 HOURS LOCAL

CHIEF Matt Gunnarson had spent a bit more than half an hour keeping an eye on the location where the enemy would enter the ambush kill zone. Now he tensed as he watched a three-man point team of mujahideen walk slowly into the killing area, pausing to take a careful look down the ravine. A couple of beats later they resumed their walk, moving toward the end where the Charlies formed the final firing line.

When the main column of ragheads came into view, they were relaxed and confident with the certainty that their point crew had cleared the way ahead. Gunnarson waited patiently, noting when the last of the group came into view. One of the mujahideen was a tall, lanky guy who reminded the chief of photographs he had seen of Osama Bin Laden. When Gunnarson determined this was the last guy, he aimed carefully at his upper body. At the exact moment the mujahideen came to a point to his direct front, the SEAL gently squeezed the trigger. The jolt of the bullet slammed the raghead against the far wall of the ravine, and he crumpled to the ground.

Immediately the First Squad—seven men strong—opened up with three-round automatic bursts of 5.56-millimeter. The salvos whacked into the mujahideen, shaking them violently as they toppled to the ravine's floor. The enemy point team panicked and made a run forward, but the weapons of Charlie Fire Team blasted an instantaneous volley of a dozen shots that cut the trio down before they went five meters. Then the Charlies raised the barrels to blast into the front of the enemy column. The air was filled with the ear-shattering reports of a dozen CAR-15s and two M-16s.

It was all over in ten seconds.

Thirty mujahideen were down, slumped and sprawled in piles of two and three. The sounds of moaning could be discerned coming from the fallen men, while a few twitched in the agony of their death throes.

Brannigan spoke firmly into the LASH. "Cease fire!" He got to his feet and surveyed the scene for a moment. "All right! Assad and Leibowitz on the point. Charlie Team take the rear guard. Let's go, people! Move out!"

The platoon hurried forward a kilometer along the flat terrain before slipping back into the cover of the ravine.

1000 HOURS LOCAL

CAPTAIN Lakhdar Tanizai watched the wounded being carried out of the ravine, back to a wider area in the gulley for treatment. There were no proper stretchers to transport the stricken mujahideen, so they were rolled onto blankets for an uncomfortable, jarring trek of fifty meters back to where the medics had set up a treatment center. With only the barest of medical supplies available, the injured men were quickly divided into two groups. The first was made up of wounded who might survive to fight another day. They were given top priority. The poor bastards who didn't have a chance for recovery were laid out to survive or die as dictated by Allah the Beneficent, the Merciful.

Tanizai had sent the rest of his company forward of the ambush site to occupy the ravine and the high ground on each side. They went into a purely defensive mode, nervously wondering if the infidel devils would reappear from nowhere to deal more death and maiming to them.

Tanizai heard his name called, and turned to see Major Karim Malari hurrying toward him with his radio operator closely following. The major's distress was evident in his eyes. He looked past the captain at the carnage, then turned to him. "What has happened here?"

"My men were ambushed, Major," Tanizai said. "I am shamed to report that there are fifteen dead, ten wounded and"—he pointed over to the side—"six dying."

Malari's face reddened with anger. "Why are you not pursuing the unbelievers, Captain? You are letting an opportunity slip by."

"I made an effort, Major," Tanizai explained in a sorrowful voice. "But they went down into another ravine, then into a valley, and finally beyond. I have lost so many men I did not wish to risk another disaster."

Malari sighed. "I suppose you took the best course, Captain." He got his map out and studied it for a moment before snapping his fingers to signal his radio operator to hand him the handset. He pressed down the TRANSMIT button and made instant contact with Warlord Khamami back on the mountain.

"*Amir*, this is Malari. I regret to inform you that Captain Tanizai has suffered a great tragedy. Heavy losses, I fear. The infidels ambushed him. He feels the situation is too precarious to risk a pursuit. I must say that I agree with him."

Khamami's voice came back. "I must turn these circumstances over in my mind for a moment. Wait."

Malari looked over at Tanizai. "The *Amir* is pondering this disaster."

"I appreciate your kindness in expressing approval of my tactical decision," the captain said sincerely.

Malari had started to reply when Khamami's voice came back over the handset. "Here are my orders to both you and Captain Tanizai. You will follow after the enemy, but keep your distance. Do not make contact with them at all costs. If they turn aggressive, you must withdraw as quickly as possible. Do not engage the dogs in battle!"

"I understand, *Amir*," Malari said.

"That is most important," Khamami emphasized. "Above all, avoid sustaining more heavy casualties. I have a solution to this dilemma that will save us further losses and guarantee a resounding defeat of the enemy."

"Yes, *Amir*," the major said. "I understand and will pass on your orders to Captain Tanizai."

OUTCAST CAMP
THE KHAMAMI FIEFDOM
1730 HOURS LOCAL

KHATIB the Oracle strode alone into the camp of former warlord Ayyub Durtami, as he had done many times since their arrival in Khamami's fiefdom. The hungry, miserable people regarded him with fear and hatred. His visits were not to comfort them or deliver them from merciless punishment; rather he came to make sure they were not getting extra food and that the men and women—including husbands and wives—lived separately. This self-styled mullah had even ordered a special observation tower, with a platform five meters above the ground, constructed for him in the middle of the wretched bivouac. Each time he came to the place, he climbed up onto the structure to glare down in righteous fury at the sinners.

This time, standing on the obscene perch, he surveyed the people for a few moments, then called out in a loud voice. "I want all males over the age of eleven and under the age of forty-one to come forward and gather around me. I have a special message for you from the Warlord Khamami that was passed to him from Allah the Beneficent, the Merciful. Thus, the significance of what I shall tell you today is the holiest of all that is holy."

All boys and men from twelve to forty years of age dutifully moved forward, crowding around the platform. Their eyes were downcast and they expected yet one more announcement or proclamation that would add even more suffering to their already miserable lives. The Oracle's raspy voice scolded them. "You are under a curse for leaving behind unburied Muslim dead as you made a cowardly flight from infidel devils. You thought more of your mortal lives than the existence you would someday endure throughout eternity after your souls had passed on to either divine reward or retribution. And surely your terrible sins would have caused you to enter Satan's domain and live in fiery agony forever. But Allah the Beneficent, the Merciful, has now provided you with a grand opportunity to save your wretched souls."

The males of the camp felt a sense of hope, but only a faint one. None trusted the Oracle to show them kindness or mercy.

Khatib knew they were pondering his words, and he enjoyed viewing the pitiful pleas in their eyes as they regarded him. He renewed his address in a louder voice. "At this moment the Warlord Hassan Khamami is locked in a mighty struggle with those same unbelievers who disgraced and humiliated you. Allah has decreed that if you join the *Amir*'s army and fight bravely without regard for your lives, He will forgive your great transgression against His laws. If you come back victorious, the married men will once again be allowed to know their wives. If they or any of the bachelors die, they will be granted entrance to Paradise, where the *houris* will await to pleasure them through time that knows no end."

The men and boys were shocked into stupefaction by the revelation. After a few moments they recovered, breaking into cheers and waving their arms while praising Allah's glory in loud shouts. The horny husbands considered the opportunity for sex with wives or *houris* particularly attractive.

"You go from here to the other side of the castle," Khatib said. "There you will be strengthened by a great feast, then armed for war. Tomorrow, helicopters will come to carry you to be tested in battle against Satan's warriors. It is there that you will know either the glory of victory or the grandeur of Paradise."

He pointed toward the castle, screaming, "Go! Go now! Now!"

The crowd immediately rushed out of the bivouac, running as fast as they could across the bare, scrubby terrain toward the good food that awaited them. The older men, remaining behind in the company of the women and children, enviously watched them depart.

BRANNIGAN'S BRIGANDS
THE FOOTHILLS
2145 HOURS LOCAL

THE SEALs were exhausted.

It was more than the physical fatigue of strenuous and continuous activity; they also felt the deep mental bite of nervous weariness that is brought on by a deteriorating tactical situation. They had been forced into a retreat toward safety after the loss of two good buddies whose bodies had to be cached like pieces of equipment. All this while on a mission that had been originally laid on as a simple link-up and extraction operation. But that had deteriorated into a complicated mess in which they battled two warlords without the addition of a single reinforcement. Those are circumstances that do not exactly raise morale.

They had stumbled on relentlessly into the hours of darkness, unspeaking and numb until Mike Assad called back via LASH to inform Lieutenant Wild Bill Brannigan that he and Dave Leibowitz had discovered a small spring. The Skipper told them to wait at the site, and he brought the rest of the platoon up to join them. He didn't bother to put out security right away. Instead, he and Lieutenant Jim Cruiser, with the two chiefs following, went from man to man checking the status of the platoon's ammunition supply. They seemed to be in reasonably good shape, with each Brigand packing an average of ten magazines holding thirty rounds each. This was backed up by the forty-two M-67 fragmentation grenades they had among them. A few had extras, and the devices were evenly divided among all fourteen SEALs, so that each would have three. With the ammunition check done, the senior ranking men of the platoon withdrew for a confab with the Skipper.

Brannigan summed up the obvious. "These guys are dog tired to the point of almost being fed up with this mission."

"I think in the Army this is a situation they call soldiering," Cruiser remarked.

"Whatever it's called, it sucks," Brannigan said. "The next time we're attacked, the situation could easily deteriorate into something worse than a risky battle. It would be a last stand."

"That's another word for massacre," Cruiser pointed out.

"We'll have to be careful, sir," Dawkins said. "The guys are going to need a lot of looking after."

"Right," Gunnarson agreed. "This is one of those times when a word of encouragement or a joke does more than putting a boot in somebody's ass."

"I can't argue with your logic, Chief," Brannigan said. "So here's the skinny. We're going to drink water from this spring until our bellies slosh. God only knows if there're any more sources available to us. We'll bunk down here on fifty percent alert until oh-five-hundred hours. At that time we want all canteens filled for the ordeal ahead. Then we'll saddle up and move out. Any questions? All right then. Get back to your guys."

The team leaders walked down the ravine to their men to pass on the word.

THE KHAMAMI FIEFDOM
29 AUGUST
0830 HOURS LOCAL

THE disabled senior mujahideen, taken from active campaigning because of a leg crippled by a Soviet sniper, yelled angrily as he formed up two dozen men for transport in the pair of Mi-24 helicopters coming back for another lift. Forty-eight of Durtami's former mujahideen had already been flown out to the battle area and dropped off. It would take another five lifts to get the rest of the group out.

Every man was armed with an ancient British bolt-action Lee-Metford Mark II rifle. Although the magazines were designed to hold ten cartridges, this group had been issued only three for each weapon. They had no additional ammunition, and after discovering that they would be sent against an enemy with modern automatic weaponry, the men knew that within a short time they would be bedded down with *houris* in Paradise.

One of the riflemen's buttocks flared in pain. He was a newlywed who had been impetuous enough to ask Khatib the Oracle if he could visit his new wife one more time before going off to battle. The enraged mullah had him given a caning of fifty strokes for his weakness of the flesh.

Now, as the choppers came in, the two groups were sent out to cram themselves into the troop compartments for the flight out to join Major Karim Malari's field force.

CHAPTER 17

THE platoon had been on the move steadily since leaving the area of the spring twenty-four hours previously. Lieutenant Bill Brannigan reluctantly came to the conclusion that they had reached a point where the forced march had to be brought to a temporary halt. The men had done about as much as could be expected of them. The Skipper called for a seven-hour rest break. In reality there was only three and a half hours of actual relaxation per man since they were on a 50 percent alert. The exception was the Odd Couple—Mike Assad and Dave Leibowitz—who had been excused from standing watch. The two point men had been constantly on the go during unit movements, going forward then returning to make periodic reports to Brannigan. Consequently, they walked almost twice as much as anyone else during each day's movement.

Under Senior Chief Buford Dawkins's less than gentle leadership, the men on watch turned to waking up the sleepers.

One indication of a man's excellent physical conditioning is the ability to make a rapid recovery from prolonged and demanding activity. The SEALs were much better rested than the average human male would have been after long hours of pushing himself through ravines with all possible speed. But there is a limit to even superbly conditioned individuals, whether they are professional fighting men or athletes. And the one person with this on his mind was Hospital Corpsman Third Class James Bradley.

James began going from man to man as they prepared for the coming day's activities, making inquiries about how each was doing. Naturally all put on shows of manly vigor, saying they felt absolutely froggy and ready to jump, but James wasn't buying that line of bullshit. He knew the extent of their fatigue, and advised each to eat an energy bar as quickly as possible. These high-calorie bars of sustenance would get some nutrients flowing through their badly used bodies. The corpsman augmented his field therapy by passing out pep pills from his medical kit to each SEAL. These amphetamine derivatives not only gave bursts of energy and a feeling of well-being, but also suppressed the appetite. That might prove a blessing later on if the rations ran low. Unfortunately, the drug also caused dryness in the mouth. The water acquired at the spring would last only so long, and they would soon be running low on the precious H_2O.

Brannigan slipped into his combat vest and glanced up and down the column. He turned to the radio operator, Frank Gomez. "Turn on the PRC-112's beacon."

"It's always on, sir," Frank replied. "I've hoarded some extra batteries for it."

"All right!" Brannigan said approvingly. He turned his attention back to the men, satisfied that they were ready to renew the trek. He glanced up and sighted the Odd Couple looking back at him from the point. He spoke into the LASH. "Let's go."

Mike Assad and Dave Leibowitz turned and led the platoon out for that day's travel.

WARLORD KHAMAMI'S CP
WEST RIDGE
0515 HOURS LOCAL

A complex of a half dozen tents had evolved in the area the SEALs had used as a temporary home when they first arrived in the OA. The field headquarters of Warlord Hassan Khamami hadn't been this well organized since the war against the Soviets. The reason for the enhanced efficiency and attention to detail came from the fact that Khamami had developed a special respect for the men he now fought. The ambush sprung on Tanizai's troops the day before had been skillfully planned and executed, and the warlord had no doubt that he faced a determined and expert enemy.

Now, in the early hour of dawn, Khamami climbed from his blankets and walked to the front flap of his tent. His instincts, developed during years of fighting in this sort of rugged, isolated terrain, gave him a solid feeling of optimism. Somehow he did not think he faced an enemy that was particularly numerous. He could tell by their actions that there was no chance they could overwhelm him. That was the reason for the ambush and sudden withdrawal. Had they been a stronger force with support weapons, they would have stood fast and slugged it out with the mujahideen.

On the other hand, they were well practiced in the type of warfare the Westerners called unconventional. But with both Major Karim Malari and Captain Lakhdar Tanizai in the field, Khamami was confident that victory was only a matter of time. Malari and Tanizai were veteran combat commanders and were now using every tactical trick they knew to track down the foreign devils who had intruded into this land. The situation his foes faced reminded him of what he had learned about a certain infamous American general who fought Indian warriors in that country's West many years before. The commander's name was Custer. Good luck in past battles had made him reckless, and the day finally came when he paid for that overconfidence with his life and those of his men.

A servant scurried forward with a hot bowl of *cha* tea for the warlord. Khamami took it, treating himself to a sip of the stimulating brew. He glanced over to where his air force of two helicopters stood waiting for the day's activities to begin. Just beyond them were the one hundred men of the disgraced Ayyub Durtami. Their former warlord had joined the ragtag group in time to come out on the last airlift. He and his mujahideen lay sleeping with their ancient rifles, eager to atone for their past actions, both in Khamami's eyes and those of Allah.

This was one of those times that Khamami was most appreciative of religion. Not because of any personal devoutness on his part; but because such beliefs made it easier for him to send men to their death on his behalf. There was nothing like a good jihad to pep the lads up. He took another drink of tea as he looked at the sleeping men who faced a battle they could not possibly survive.

Their bodies would soon be soaking up bullets as sponges do water.

WADI KHESTA VALLEY
0800 HOURS LOCAL

WHEN the Odd Couple rounded a sharp turn in the ravine, they came to a sudden stop. Stretched out to their direct front was a large valley that appeared to be at least an eighth of a kilometer wide. Although it did not have a lot of cover along the tops, scrub brush grew abundantly on the gentle slopes of the sides.

Mike Assad stayed as security while Dave Leibowitz went back to the column to report to Lieutenant Bill Brannigan. When he met the platoon coming toward him, he went straight to the Skipper.

"Sir, we've just run out of ravine," Dave said. "There's a pretty big valley about fifty meters ahead. It ain't the Grand Canyon, but it's maybe a hundred meters wide. We don't know the length of the place, but there's lots of vegetation on the sides. That could be a sign of water."

"I sure as hell hope so," Brannigan said. "We're about to start having a great big fucking problem with thirst if things keep going the way they have been." Most of the men had popped at least one pep pill, and the resultant dryness in their mouths was becoming uncomfortable. They were forced to resort to the old Apache Indian trick of sucking on a couple of pebbles to keep the saliva flowing. Brannigan felt a little better now. "Let's take a look at this magnificent terrain feature you and Assad discovered."

The column began moving again, going on down the ravine. They turned the same corner of the big gully as Mike and Dave had, stepping into an extremely wide valley that had a varying depth of between ten and fifteen meters. The feeling of security the platoon had formerly enjoyed in the ravines quickly evaporated. They felt positively exposed, and instinctively went on the alert, hoisting their weapons to high port.

Senior Chief Buford Dawkins trotted up to the Skipper. "Sir, what do you make of this?"

Brannigan shrugged under his combat vest. "I was hoping we'd find some water, but the farther we go the less I think that's going to happen."

"This ain't a place for water, sir," the senior chief commented. "Them thorny shrubs around here is the type of bushes that don't need a lot of water. That's why it's growing so good up on them dry slopes."

"I was afraid of that," Brannigan said. "You better pass the word to the men to take it easy with the canteens until further orders."

"I already did, sir," Dawkins said. "But most of 'em had figgered that out already."

"All we can do is keep moving and hope for the best. And suck those pebbles."

"Right, sir. See you later."

Dawkins turned and headed back down toward Bravo Fire Team.

THE WADI KHESTA VALLEY

ABDULLAH and Ashraf were veteran mujahideen who had spent their entire lives in the wilds of Afghanistan. Both were small men, wiry and illiterate but possessed of a natural intelligence and cunning that made them the best scouts in Warlord Hassan Khamami's army.

As Pashtun boys they had been raised in the warrior traditions of their people, living hard lives of deprivation and poverty in an unforgiving country where the weak and unwary succumbed early in life. Their nameless home village was precariously perched on the side of a mountain, the crude homes built of the natural rocks that abounded in the area. A single well served the population of ten families, and three out of five babies, born to women worn by cruel toil, died before attaining three months of age. These were people who took nothing for granted. Bad weather was more than an inconvenience; it could herald natural disasters such as drought, howling windstorms, and thunderclouds that sent immense sheets of water to splash down across the mountains, causing avalanches and flash floods. Additionally, an injury that would only be bothersome in gentler living conditions could kill the unlucky with infections and gangrene. However, anybody reaching the age of ten could reasonably expect to live to the ripe old age of thirty-five or forty, since their bodies had proven to be resistant to all the illnesses and diseases of that environment.

Abdullah and Ashraf, like all the boys, were introduced to firearms early in life. They took their turns standing guard at night, watching for marauding bandits who might raid their village. Their weaponry consisted of old flintlock smoothbore muskets, a few percussion muzzle-loading rifles, and bladed instruments of war that included Indian shamshirs, Arabian scimitars and even some heavy British cavalry sabers taken during a nameless battle over a hundred years before.

Hunting was not a sport for the Pashtuns. It was a way of obtaining protein. The favorite game in those barren mountains was gazelles, but the meager herds had been hunted to near extinction. Now the most numerous animals were hares that had stringy, hard-to-chew meat on the haunches and back legs. Another, better source of meat was the domestic animals of other villages obtained through outright thievery. It was this latter activity in which Abdullah and Ashraf developed their skills in reconnaissance and raiding.

By the time the big troubles with the Soviets came along, the two friends were in their teens. They joined Warlord Khamami's band to fight against the invaders, and found themselves in a world of constant warfare. One of their main jobs was to dog Russian patrols to keep track of the activities and whereabouts of the infidels. Even though they were daring to the point of recklessness at times and had many close calls, Abdullah and Ashraf were never discovered by their prey, and guided many detachments of mujahideen to successful ambush and attack sites.

0830 HOURS LOCAL

ASHRAF moved slowly down the valley, at times bending over almost double as he studied the spoor he had picked up more than two kilometers back. He noted dislodged rocks, a bent twig on a bush or a scrape along the ground where a misstep had left a boot mark. It was Abdullah's turn to carry the R-100 pack radio, and he watched his friend doing his best to pick up clues of the men they tracked so relentlessly.

Ashraf suddenly stopped, then pointed to the side of the valley. A fresh smudge in the dirt showed where somebody must have stumbled and bumped against the earthen wall. Abdullah saw it too, and nodded to indicate he thought it a very significant sign. This was more than just the evidence of a recent passerby to the skilled eyes of the Pashtun friends. It was a clear indication that the enemy they followed, though skilled and crafty, was growing tired and careless. Both could remember when even the elite Soviet Spetsnaz troopers, highly trained and motivated, compromised themselves at times during long, arduous missions. Their carelessness was mostly dropping cigarette butts when their senses were dulled with exhaustion. They also urinated anywhere they pleased, leaving wet spots in the ground easy to identify if one stuck one's finger in the dampness and sniffed it. Human piss is much different from that of animals.

Abdullah stood beside Ashraf, also noting things that would be invisible to the uninitiated. He put his mouth close to his friend's ear and whispered, "This is fresh, *ror!* They cannot be far away."

"Au!" Ashraf agreed. "Stay here with the radio. I shall go ahead and take a look."

He slowly and silently ascended the wall of the valley. When he reached the top, he went down flat on his stomach and snaked his way through the brush. After carefully raising his head for a look at the surrounding countryside, he quickly ducked back down. He had seen the head of a man wearing a brimmed cap made of camouflage material. It was not like the *kamufliron kurtki* pattern of the Russians; instead it had brown spots of various shades on a tan background. Ashraf took one more quick peek. Now he saw another fellow beside the first. He crawled carefully backward, reached the edge of the valley and noiselessly lowered himself to where Abdullah waited. He signaled to his friend to follow him, and they moved a few meters back in the direction they had come from. Ashraf lifted the radio handset out of its cradle.

"Amir!" he said in the informal manner of mujahideen communications. "We have located the infidels!"

WARLORD KHATAMI'S CP
WEST RIDGE
0850 HOURS LOCAL

WARLORD Hassan Khamami sat cross-legged on the carpet in his tent. He leaned forward as he studied the Soviet map of the area in which he once again was waging war. His radio operator spoke into the microphone of the R-108 radio, then held out the handset for his commander's use.

"I have contacted Major Malari, *Amir*," the commo man said. Then he sat while he patiently listened to what seemed to him a one-sided conversation as the warlord spoke to his field commander.

"Yes, Major, I have good news. We have located the enemy. They are well into the Wadi Khesta Valley. Yes. It is reliable information. They were found by Abdullah and Ashraf. Ha! Ha! Yes, they are. The foreigners are now trapped. There is only one way for them to reach safety. They must continue to travel westward by following the valley. Their only alternative is to go up into the high, flat country where there is neither cover nor concealment. Now listen to me, Major. We are going to advance some companies to their front. They can move on foot, and we will fly the helicopters back and forth between their column and the target area. The movement will go very fast. That is Phase One. Phase Two will be simultaneous with Phase One, and other companies will move to the rear of the invaders. Both groups will occupy the valley as well as the flat land above. That is right, Major. There will be no escape for the enemy. No matter which direction they turn, we will have them covered and outnumbered. Now! Listen to this carefully. Do not attack. I say one more time, do *not* attack! I have a special assault group to throw at them first. Who? Durtami's bunch of miserable beggars, that is who! They will soak up a great deal of the foreigners' ammunition. The attack they make will also confirm the enemy's exact location. Do you understand all I have told you? *Der khey*—very good! I will give you orders by radio to let you know what to do and when to do it. Any questions, Major? Excellent."

He handed the handset back to the radio operator.

"Will you want to contact anybody else, *Amir*?" the man asked.

Khamami shook his head. "*Na*. But fetch me Sheriwal and the other helicopter pilot. *Os!* Now!"

WADI KHESTA VALLEY
0930 HOURS LOCAL

LIEUTENANT Bill Brannigan called a halt. The men were dragging their feet now, thirsty and sweat-soaked from the heat. He knew they hadn't much more than a few ounces of water in their canteens. This was a worst-case scenario when it came to heatstroke. Even an adult male in the pink of condition would crumble fast when he became dehydrated, with his body temperature soaring while he was unable to perspire. Brannigan hoped a half hour in the shade of the valley sides would cool them down enough to continue the tortuous hike.

Mike Assad and Dave Leibowitz joined the platoon commander. They sank down wearily beside him. Mike licked his dry lips before he spoke. "Any special orders, sir?"

"Yeah," Brannigan said. "Find some fucking water!"

Neither of the Odd Couple bothered to make a reply. That's all they'd been thinking of as they moved forward on the point. But the valley was as dry as the proverbial bone.

Senior Chief Buford Dawkins walked up slowly and stood silently beside the trio for a few moments. Finally he asked the same thing the Odd Couple had inquired about. "Any special orders, sir?"

"Put out the word," Brannigan said. "We've got no choice now but to avoid any further contact with the enemy."

Dawkins shrugged. "I don't know how the hell we're gonna do that, sir. We're gonna run into 'em sooner or later."

"Well, then, godamn it, Senior Chief, if we do make contact we're going to have to take some pretty fucking drastic steps, aren't we?"

Dawkins nodded, ignoring the Skipper's angry sarcasm. "I'll pass the word, sir."

Brannigan watched him walk away to inform the fire teams. He pulled out his canteen, then stuck it back in its carrier without taking so much as sip. "When you find yourself down deep in a shit hole, you got to stop digging."

The Odd Couple looked at their commanding officer, then each other. Mike yawned. "I think I'll take a nap."

"Good idea, Assad," Brannigan said. "I'll call you in about two minutes."

"Thank you, sir," Mike said. "Being surrounded and out-numbered by a vicious enemy, thirsty as hell and as hungry as a starving bear is a great inducement to sleep."

"Y'know," Dave mused, "compared to this, Hell Week wasn't really all that bad, was it?"

Mike was already snoring quietly in his slumber.

CHAPTER 18

THE FOOTHILLS WEST OF WADI KHESTA VALLEY
30 AUGUST
1400 HOURS LOCAL

CAPTAIN Lakhdar Tanizai's two-company force was slightly under strength at 150 men, but he had been more than adequately augmented with the addition of three Soviet 82-millimeter mortars and plenty of shells. At that moment his mujahideen struggled through the afternoon heat on a forced march of twenty-five kilometers. They were close to exhaustion from fatigue and exposure to the sun as they hiked across the open country above and alongside the Wadi Khesta Valley. It could have been worse, but the movement was being made with minimum equipment of nothing more than personal weapons, a basic field ammunition load and canteens of water. The rest of their gear had been flown ahead by helicopter to the location where they were to set up a defensive position that would block the far end of the valley. This was their portion of the operation Warlord Khamami had devised to hem in the infidel invaders.

Tanizai walked at the head of the column, doing his best to set a good example for his fighters in the demanding situation. The officer was a firm believer in maintaining excellent physical conditioning, and he personally supervised an exercise regimen that he had designed for his men.

Now he kept up a steady, confident pace, forcing himself to endure the fatigue with no sign of discomfort. The captain finally allowed himself to relax a bit when he sighted two figures up ahead through the haze of heat that shimmered off the terrain. He increased the pace, impatient to reach the scouts Abdullah and Ashraf, who had been waiting for them.

Ashraf, always the spokesman for the duo, performed a Russian-style salute when Tanizai walked up to him. "Greetings, Captain. It is only another kilometer to where the equipment awaits you."

"Thanks to Allah!" Tanizai said in relief. He turned toward the column, shouting as loudly as he could. "Your packs and rations are just ahead. Step lively!"

The word was passed down the line, and the mujahideen happily put forth some extra effort to hurry forward to the place where they could regain possession of their gear. The company formation began to spread out as they stepped up the rate of march in their excitement. The sub-leaders immediately regained control of their men, keeping them in good order as they neared the final destination of the speed march.

When they reached the temporary supply dump, each platoon was brought to a halt, then ordered to dress right and cover down as if on parade. Under the philosophy of discipline established by Warlord Hassan Khamami, there would be no disorderly stampede to retrieve the gear. As soon as they were under tight control, one group at a time was marched in an orderly fashion to retrieve the equipment, then return to their platoon to await the next order of business.

When everyone was once again fully equipped, Captain Tanizai took personal command of the company and marched them down to the western egress of the valley. The mujahideen were ordered to ground their packs, then begin digging defensive positions that covered both the valley and the ground above. The mortars were arranged a few dozen yards to the rear to organize for short-range barrages. The crews' aiming stakes were quickly deployed to align all the tubes on the proper azimuth.

Weariness dogged Tanizai as he walked slowly along the platoon perimeters that faced the direction the infidel enemy would come from. The valley was sealed shut, and anyone approaching them would come under the combined fire-power of both light and heavy infantry weapons.

THE WADI KHESTA VALLEY
1500 HOURS LOCAL

THE going was easy for the SEALs. The valley was wide at that point—approximately half a kilometer—and the ground was flat and firm. They had noticed the flights of helicopters that traveled from east to west, but noted there had only been two lifts flown before the aerial activity ceased. That would mean that if a mujahideen unit had been taken ahead to lay an ambush, there could not be more than fifty of the enemy positioned for an encounter.

Lieutenant Wild Bill Brannigan hoped the bastards were waiting to engage the platoon. It shouldn't be too difficult to deal with them from the valley, and the canteens the mujahideen undoubtedly had with them would be a godsend. The lack of water was a situation that grew more serious with each passing hour. The highly disciplined SEALs took only small sips from their canteens when they should have been gulping down large swallows to replace the body fluids being sweated away in the pressing heat.

Brannigan noted the men were beginning to look like candidates toward the end of Hell Week during BUD/S. The situation they now endured was the exact reason why SEAL aspirants were driven to the utmost in spiritual and physical limits during training. If the fainthearted were able

to successfully complete SEAL training and win the coveted
Trident badge, any weaklings among the platoon would have
succumbed to the hardships days before. Even the ancient
Roman legions recognized the importance of a tough, unre-
lenting training program, and the centurions who led the le-
gionnaires did their best to make the training more difficult
than actual combat.

Suddenly Joe Miskoski's voice came over the LASH
from the rear of the column. "Choppers coming in on our
six!"

Everyone immediately took cover by going into the shadows along the slopes of the valley. Within moments the noise
of helicopter engines could be heard drawing closer. But instead of flying overhead, they suddenly eased back.

Chief Matt Gunnarson's hoarse voice sounded through
the headsets. "The son of a bitches is hovering!" A moment
later he spoke again, saying, "Hovering my Aunt Tillie's tits!
They're landing!"

Everyone listened as the engines quieted down further,
until they made the slow "chop-chop" sound of the rotor
gears being disengaged. Within fifteen minutes they revved
up again and could be heard climbing back into the sky.
Then they turned away, the sound diminishing as the aircraft
flew rearward out of the area.

"Two-I-C and senior chief report to me," Brannigan ordered through the LASH.

Jim Cruiser and Buford Dawkins rushed from their respective places in the column and joined Brannigan just to
the rear of Alpha Fire Team. The Skipper waited as they settled down beside him. "It's obvious the chopper lift has
brought an enemy unit to our direct rear," Brannigan said.
"And they've already landed people to the front."

Dawkins's voice was somewhat distorted by the pebble in
his mouth. "That means they know where we are."

"Yeah," Brannigan agreed.

"How the hell did they figure that out?" Cruiser asked in
irritation.

"Prob'ly recon patrols, sir," Dawkins suggested. "We're so godamn tired they just snuck up on us."

"It doesn't matter," Brannigan said, irritated. "But there is also the unpleasant prospect that the enemy ahead of us marched to that location rather than use helicopters. And that means we can't accurately estimate how many they are."

"I hadn't considered that," Cruiser said.

"Even if they did put a small force ahead of us, they'll be bringing a much larger one eventually. They may be close to linking up even as we sit here. The ones behind us will want to drive us forward."

"Well," Cruiser said, "that makes it easy to figure out what to do."

"Right," Brannigan said. "We're going to attack the small group to the rear for a breakout. And I haven't got a clue what we'll do or where we'll go once we've cleared our way to open country."

"Out of the frying pan and into the fire," the senior chief remarked, spitting out the pebble.

"Whatever," Brannigan said, shrugging. "Get your teams ready." He watched as Cruiser and Dawkins returned to their men, and he spoke over the LASH to Mike Assad and Dave Leibowitz up on point. "Get your asses back here."

"Aye, sir!" came Mike's reply.

THE MUJAHIDEEN
1500 HOURS LOCAL

THE former mujahideen chief Ayyub Durtami stood off to the side alone as he watched his men gather into a mob to his direct front. Durtami's former faithful assistant Ahmet Kharani was no longer a part of his entourage. Kharani had found favor with Warlord Hassan Khamami and had been made a lieutenant in the garrison guard. This was an undeniable indication to Durtami that he was now an outcast. His best hope was to martyr himself in battle and seek redemption and reward in Allah's Paradise. There would be nothing for him in Khamami's fiefdom unless a miracle occurred.

Durtami's men each had a single canteen on a strap around the shoulder, and this small amount of water gave evidence that their chances in the coming battle were considered minimal at best. The Lee-Metford Mark II rifles they carried were in sorry condition. All were dirty, and at least a dozen of them could not be loaded because the bolts were rusted shut. The magazines were designed to hold ten rounds in a double column, but the men had been issued only three. However, those who could not load their rifles gave their three to close friends, so a few had six to fire at the infidels.

Durtami whistled and clapped his hands for attention. When the crowd of sacrificial fighters quieted down, he spoke to them in as firm a voice as he could muster. Even a true believer was nervous when facing certain death.

"Listen, brothers! At this moment Allah looks down on you with great love and appreciation. He is aware that you are ready to martyr yourselves for Islam without hesitation. He also knows which ones of you will sacrifice your mortal lives for His immortal glory. Already there are places in Paradise set aside for you. Your families will weep with great joy, knowing you have honored them and all true believers!" He paused, looking at the fierce pride shining in their eyes. "Are you ready?"

"*Allah! Allah akbar!* God is great!"

The cries and chanting rose in volume as the mujahideen encouraged one another for the ordeal ahead. Durtami did his best to take heart from their morbid celebration. He knew that his karma offered only two possibilities after the battle. He would either come out of it alive to return to the unlikely good graces of his brother-in-law Warlord Khamami or he would find his reward in Paradise. Either way required that he put himself in the front of his men and lead by example.

"Brothers!" he cried, pointing toward the enemy. "That is the direction to everlasting glory! Follow me!"

He held his prized pearl-handled Beretta 9-millimeter automatic pistol in his hand, raising it high above his head. Then he turned to trot toward the objective at a steady pace, raising his knees high to emphasize his fervor and passion. Durtami did not look back as his men cheered and fell into a disorganized crowd to his direct rear.

THE SEALS
1615 HOURS LOCAL

BRAVO Fire Team, with Senior Chief Petty Officer Buford Dawkins in charge, moved slowly down the valley, leading Brannigan's Brigands. The team, like the rest of the platoon, felt like they were simply spinning their wheels, since the outfit was now moving back in the direction from where they had come. The men held their weapons ready, their eyes scanning the tops of the valley as well as the area to the direct front.

For once Mike Assad and Dave Leibowitz were not on the point. Lieutenant Brannigan had kept them back with him and Frank Gomez as part of Alpha Fire Team. Charlie Fire Team was directly to their rear, led by Lieutenant (J.G.) Jim Cruiser. Chief Matt Gunnarson's Delta Fire Team brought up the rear with Bruno Puglisi being the tail-end Charlie.

Suddenly the sound of shouting men could be heard. Brannigan quickly ordered a halt via his LASH headset so they could determine who was raising so much hell. The disturbance grew steadily louder until it was accompanied by the pounding of running feet. A moment later a mob of mujahideen appeared around a bend some one hundred meters away.

The senior chief, Connie Concord and Chad Murchison immediately opened fire. Four men in the front of the crowd toppled to the ground, but dozens more now came into view. The Bravos fell back to join the four Alphas. Now a total of

seven weapons poured 5.56-millimeter rounds into the attackers. But they continued advancing, leaping over their
fallen comrades as if they sought death more than victory.

The Alphas and Bravos retreated back to join the seven
men of the Second Squad. The mujahideen fired hardly at
all, and those shots were aimed straight up into the air. The
SEALs didn't bother to take cover as they continued sending
salvos to rake the front ranks of the enemy. There was no
choice but to back up, even though they were inflicting
heavy casualties. Any hesitation or slowness would mean the
SEALs would be physically overwhelmed by the suicidal
maniacs stampeding toward them.

Brannigan wanted to break contact to get enough time to
organize some sort of defense, but the assault suddenly halted.
It was Chad Murchison who first noted what had brought the
short, sharp battle to a halt.

"There are no more of them," he said into the LASH.
"We've killed every single one."

Now everyone moved forward and could see that all the
attackers were down. Connie Concord walked forward and
picked up a rifle from one of the dead mujahideen. He ex-
amined it carefully. "This thing is a fucking antique," he announced as the others gathered around. "And it's as rusted as
a garbage scow's keel."

Milly Mills was confused. "What the hell was this all
about?"

Brannigan noticed they were all shoving fresh magazines
into their weapons. "These poor dumb bastards were sent to
draw fire. That means the force ahead of us is probably
stronger than we thought."

"Right," Dawkins said. "And it also means that another
group of these ragheads is coming behind these crazy sons
of bitches. And they'll be one of their better fighting outfits."

James Bradley happily pointed to the corpses. "They
have canteens!"

"One man from each fire team get over there and gather up

as many as you can," Brannigan shouted. "Make it snappy. We've got to get ready for some more visitors."

Dave Leibowitz, Chad Murchison, Joe Miskoski and Bruno Puglisi rushed out to collect the water containers. As Joe went from corpse to corpse, he came across a particularly bloody one. The man, his dead face locked into a fierce scowl with the mouth opened in a silent scream of fury, appeared to have been hit at least a half dozen times. A pearl-handled Beretta automatic was still grasped in his hand.

Joe grinned. The pistol would make a nice souvenir.

THE MUJAHIDEEN
1630 HOURS LOCAL

THE two Mi-24 helicopters came in and landed. Major Karim Malari and his radio operator jumped from the first, then turned to watch other mujahideen quickly disembark. The choppers immediately took off to pick up more fighters.

Malari took the handset from the radio and raised Warlord Khamami back at his CP. "*Amir,* Durtami and his men have made their attack. It did not take long, but from the sound of firing, the infidels expended many bullets to stop them."

"Very well," Khamami came back. The tone of his voice revealed his exultation. "Order Tanizai to move forward. Make sure he has troops up on the high ground as well as in the valley. The enemy will be forced to flee across open country by morning."

"I have already issued the order," Malari said. "The helicopters continue to bring us more troops. Within an hour there will be more than four hundred men in our two units. The unbelievers will be caught between us. Even now they are unable to break out." He handed the handset back to the RTO, and looked over at his sub-commanders. "Get your men formed up! As soon as the next lift arrives, we shall be ready to move out and destroy the Infidels once and forever."

THE SEALS
31 AUGUST
0100 HOURS LOCAL

THE problem of thirst was solved at least temporarily. That was the good news. The bad news was that by the time a shortage of water became a problem again, there was a strong chance that none of the platoon would be alive to be aware of it. Brannigan had pulled the Brigands back to an area where the slopes on both sides of the valley were not so steep. First Squad took one side while Second Squad took the other. They had situated themselves as best they could without digging fighting positions, using the brush and top of the valley for cover. When everyone had settled down, the Skipper sent Mike Assad and Dave Leibowitz out to do a reconnaissance.

0230 HOURS LOCAL

THE Odd Couple eased themselves off the high ground onto the slope of the valley. They moved slowly down the firm terrain, making a slow descent. Although they were no longer thirsty, each was nearing the end of his physical endurance. They walked through the OP manned by Senior Chief Buford Dawkins and Chad Murchison. Dawkins stood up as they approached. He spat, reaching for the liberated canteen to treat himself to a drink. "Y'all bringing good news?"

"Not hardly, Senior Chief," Dave Leibowitz replied as he and Mike walked past. "To put it politely: we're in deep yogurt."

Dawkins watched them walk way, and took a swallow of the water. It was tepid, but delicious after the long dry days. The only thing that could improve it would be some Jack Daniel's for flavoring.

The Odd Couple continued down to the valley floor, crossed it, then went up to the spot where Lieutenant Bill Brannigan's CP had been set up. It was no more than a patch of open area between a couple of thick stands of thorn bushes. Brannigan's greeting was only a tired nod as the two scouts settled down beside him.

Mike Assad shrugged almost apologetically. "Sir, we're ringed in tight here. They got us heavily outnumbered on all sides."

"Yes, sir," Dave agreed. "We couldn't make an exact count o'course, but I'd be willing to say they got us at about twenty or thirty to one."

"The ragheads have at least a battalion out there," Mike added.

Brannigan was silent for a moment before he spoke. "Okay, guys. Take a break. Try to get some sleep."

He watched the Odd Couple move off into the darkness, then turned his thoughts to the situation at hand: (1) There was no way in hell they would be able to fight their way through the enemy. Even if they broke through on one side, the mujahideen could quickly rally other fighters on their perimeter to go after them. (2) No doubt the enemy had brought along their mortars, and that meant they could leisurely bombard the platoon to pieces if an attempt was made to set up defense positions. (3) The SEALs were low on ammo after expending so much to kill the loonies who had made the suicide charge against them. (4) Surrendering would be as sure death as would be fighting to the end. The only alternative was to go through the open country in a wild attempt to break through. Chances of that succeeding were slim to none.

Brannigan reached in his vest and pulled out an energy bar. He bit into it and chewed slowly. He really regretted that he and Lisa had parted while angry with each other. It all seemed so trivial now in the light of what tomorrow would bring. He wished he could leave a note or some sort of last words to let her know he died thinking of her and loving her now more than he ever did.

Brannigan folded the wrapper over the remnants of the energy bar and shoved it back into his pocket. He touched the throat mike of the LASH headset and spoke in a whisper. "Two-I-C and chiefs report to me at the CP."

CHAPTER 19

ALTHOUGH Brannigan's Brigands were a platoon in U.S. Navy terminology, the organizational charts of the U.S. Army and U.S. Marine Corps would have identified the group as a section or a reinforced squad. A normal platoon consists of forty-plus individuals broken down into four squads led by a platoon leader who is assisted by a platoon sergeant and four sergeants as squad leaders. Thus, when the Brigands moved out that morning to ascend the slopes of the valley and begin their escape attempt across the flatlands, the combat formation they assumed was called a *squad diamond* in military parlance.

The name of the configuration, used when all-around security is needed, signifies a point on all four sides. In the case of the Brigands, the front was led as usual by the Odd Couple Mike Assad and Dave Leibowitz, while the rear was brought up by Bruno Puglisi. Chad Murchison was on the left flank and Joe Miskoski manned the right. Lieutenant

Wild Bill Brannigan stayed in the center for command and control, while the other eight SEALs filled in between the points to balance out the firepower.

Now properly aligned, they moved through the darkness aided by their night vision goggles, taking slow, deliberate steps in an effort to maintain noise discipline. The morale of the platoon had sunk so low that a sort of emotional numbness dominated the collective mood of the men. The mission, originally laid on as a simple link-up, had gone completely to hell, to the point that they now faced imminent death. Military life consisted of many upsets and setbacks, but this particular mission was so far down the tubes nobody could spot even the dimmest of lights at the end of the tunnel.

Things had reached such a state of hopelessness that the SEALs drank liberally from the canteens they had recovered from the dead mujahideen the day before. No one said it aloud, but all knew that there was no reason to conserve water when they would more than likely not be alive to see the noonday sun overhead.

Suddenly muzzle flashes blinked rapidly from the left flank and were immediately followed by the sound of numerous shots. Bullets split the air with wicked cracking noises as they whipped by. The SEALs on that side of the diamond immediately returned fire. Then a flare was shot upward from the mujahideen lines a short distance away. The illumination, hanging on the bottom of a small parachute, gave the scene an eerie daylight quality.

"Double time!" Brannigan commanded through the LASH.

The intensity of incoming rounds increased as the platoon rushed through what appeared to be a single-sided line-formation ambush. But this misconception was recognized when fresh salvos of incoming rounds came in from the opposite side, on the right. In less than a heartbeat, the Brigands began receiving more fire from the front and rear. Additional flares came up to add to the unwanted artificial glare over the scene. The platoon was surrounded, with nothing left to do but tough it out by continuing to charge straight ahead in a desperate attempt to break through the well-concealed enemy positions.

Dave Leibowitz's voice came over the LASH, broken by heavy panting from running. "There's a . . . depression in the . . . ground at one o'clock . . . not much cover . . . but better than open ground!"

"Take us there!" came back Brannigan's gruff voice.

The direction of movement took a slight turn to the right front, and they reached the terrain feature some ten seconds later, frantically throwing themselves into it. In spite of the calamitous confusion of the moment, they maintained fire team integrity as they manned all sides of the earthen indentation. The sunken area was only fifteen meters across, but that made it easier to defend.

Suddenly all firing stopped and the flares burned out one by one until darkness settled over the scene. Brannigan spat as he shoved a fresh magazine into his CAR-15. The mujahideen now knew they had the upper hand. The SEALs were pinned down, surrounded and trapped. If they fought, they would all die; if they surrendered, they would all die; and if they tried making a desperate breakthrough, they would all die. Bruno Puglisi on the perimeter spoke out in a hoarse whisper, summing up the mood.

"Shit happens."

DAWN

THE two old Soviet Mi-24 helicopters flew a circuitous route around the battle site. Warlord Hassan Khamami was in the lead aircraft, staring down through the gap of the open fuselage door. He could easily discern the enemy's defensive position, looking pitifully small in the midst of his surrounding forces. He grinned and rubbed his hands together. This victory would confirm his rule over an enlarged fiefdom. The next visit he received from the government in Kabul would be for negotiating a peace treaty with him. He

would be able to realistically demand numerous concessions.

The choppers made a slight turn then went into a hover,
slowly settling down in the vicinity of Major Karim Malari's
CP. When the wheels touched the ground, Khamami leaped
out, closely followed by his radio operator and a small entourage of bodyguards. Major Malari was waiting, and
snapped a salute as the warlord walked up.

"*Amir!*" Malari said happily. "We have the infidels surrounded. A reconnaissance patrol discovered them trying to
skulk away in the darkness. But they quickly fired on them
and shot flares into the air. My men were in position to immediately surround them. They cannot escape."

"I spotted the dogs of the West in their little crater as I flew
over," Khamami said. "What are your tactical plans, Major?"

"I have ordered Captain Tanizai to rush his company
here," Malari said. "As soon as he arrives and is in position,
we will launch a final attack."

Khamami looked around. "What about Durtami and his
men?"

"They are all martyred, *Amir*," Malari replied. "They did
not last long when they attacked the infidels. They accomplished their mission by forcing the nonbelievers to expend
much ammunition."

"I had only a brief glance at the enemy," Khamami remarked, "but it appeared from the air that there are no more
than a dozen or so of them."

"That is true, *Amir*. And when Tanizai arrives, we will be
more than four hundred to go against them. The final attack
will be quick and decisive."

"I am pleased with your decision to wait for Tanizai,"
Khamami said. "I want to keep our casualties down. We cannot replace our losses by recruitment or conscription as can
regular armies."

"Tanizai has a mortar section with him," Malari said.
"We could use that to blast the infidels to bits without
spilling a single drop of Muslim blood."

Khamami shook his head. "I want the men to attack and destroy the enemy by fire and maneuver. Thus, they will see that these overfed Westerners are not supermen."

"As you command, I obey, *Amir!*"

"And another thing," Khamami added. "Take no prisoners."

THE DEPRESSION

THE sun was now bright in the cloudless sky, sending down waves of radiating heat on the SEALs. Everyone had eaten an energy bar and popped one of James Bradley's pep pills. There was no shortage of water and they continued to drink unlimited quantities from the mujahideen canteens. The pills were also a sort of mood elevator that took at least a little of the edge off the gloomy mind-set of the platoon. They stayed at their positions, not conversing among themselves, as a constant vigil was maintained on the bleak horizon surrounding the position. Now and then a sporadic shot could be heard that either whined overhead or sent up spurts of dirt when the bullet struck the ground. The mujahideen were letting them know there was danger all around.

Bruno Puglisi, brooding with a dark anger, finally left his position to crawl to a small stand of thorn brush a few meters out in the open. Although he had no scope on his M-16 rifle, he was determined to nail one of the ragheads who were firing at the depression. Fifteen minutes passed before a couple of mujahideen heads bobbed up into view from what seemed to be an OP. Bruno aimed carefully at the one on the right, then gently squeezed the trigger. The man was jolted out of sight by the bullet's strike. The SEAL quickly shifted the barrel and fired again. The second man's skull exploded and he too was knocked out from view.

"Ha! Whacked the rat bastards!" Bruno said, grinning in grim satisfaction as he scooted back to his place in the depression.

0630 HOURS LOCAL

THE platoon had sunk into emotional doldrums. There were no exchanges of words or gestures as they sat in the heavy silence of the hopeless situation they faced.

When chanting abruptly sounded in the distance, the Brigands raised their heads slightly to gaze out toward the enemy who surrounded them. They could not make out the words of the foreign language except for the repetitious call to Allah. The mujahideen were psyching themselves up for a massacre, using their religion to build up all the hate and mercilessness in their souls. The SEALs instinctively gripped their weapons, making silent vows to sell their lives dearly and kill as many of the enemy as possible before they drew their last breaths.

Frank Gomez, with his commo gear beside him, felt the awful pressure of a heavy, pressing grief. Thoughts of his wife and child had been with him constantly since they climbed out of that valley the day before. There was a chance that Linda was pregnant again, and he wondered if he would leave two orphan children behind. He'd always known he might be killed in action and, like most military professionals, had learned to face up squarely to the unhappy potential. But he never thought he would be sitting around in some distant foreign land waiting for death to come to him, at the whim of a half-civilized enemy. He reached in his pocket and retrieved the photo of his family that he had taken from his wallet. The radio operator kissed it lightly, then looked up when his PRC-112 unexpectedly came to life. Frank, puzzled, spoke into the transmitter, answering the call that had come in.

"This is Brigand One, over."

"Brigand One, this is Ears Three," came back a voice. "We've picked up your beacon and are following it to you. What's your problem? Over."

Frank's mind spun like a kid's top, and he stared stupidly at the small radio in his hand.

The voice spoke once more. "I say again. What's your problem? Over."

Frank recovered from the shock. "Who the hell are you? Over."

"U.S. Navy aircraft," came back the answer. "We're on a routine patrol. Now, what's your problem? Over."

"Wait!" Frank said. He gestured over to Brannigan. "Sir! We've been raised by a Navy aircraft. He picked up our homing beacon."

Brannigan leaped up and ran over to grab the handheld commo set. "This is Brigand One," he said. "We need air support fast. We're surrounded in a valley at—" He stopped. "I got to get out my GPS. Wait."

"We know where you are," came back the aircraft. "In fact we're closing in now according to the signal." A moment passed. "We see some sort of military force arranged in a circle. Is that you? Over."

"Negative! Negative!" Brannigan said. "We're the poor dumb bastards in the middle. Those others are about to attack. I say again. We need air support *fast*! Over."

"We work with an F-16 squadron outside of Kabul," the pilot said. "Hang on. They have a patrol in the air not far from here. Out!"

Brannigan stood up and yelled so loud the mujahideen in their front lines faintly heard him even if they didn't understand his words. "Air support coming in! Hang in there, you guys!"

A combined spirit of optimism and relief swept through the Brigands. They leaped to their feet and cheered hysterically, waving their weapons over their heads. Senior Chief Buford Dawkins was the only one who kept his head besides Brannigan. He bellowed, "Shut up! There's about a million ragheads about to charge in here whether we got air support or not. Get back down in your positions and keep your eyes peeled on your fields of fire! *Now!*"

0650 HOURS LOCAL

THE shouting from the mujahideen positions had grown steadily louder. To the SEALs it sounded like every Muslim in the entire Middle East was out there ready to charge across the flat land to the depression. Then a skirmish line appeared from the north, running straight at the American positions facing that direction.

Senior Chief Dawkins and Chad Murchison responded to the threat with carefully aimed three-round automatic fire bursts. A couple of the mujahideen crumpled under the salvos before the rest made a quick withdrawal out of range. The next attack came out of the west. It was up to Chief Matt Gunnarson, Bruno Puglisi and James Bradley to deal with that threat. Once more, after a couple of casualties, the ragheads pulled back. Almost immediately the next assault was launched by the enemy. This one came in from the south with Lieutenant Jim Cruiser, Milly Mills, Joe Miskoski and Gutsy Olson answering the threat. It also faded away, as did the next one, from the east, which was handled by Brannigan, Frank Gomez and the Odd Couple.

"Stay alert, guys," Brannigan said. "They were just probing us to satisfy their curiosity about our exact positions and strength on the different sides of the perimeter. The next assault will be carried out by their varsity."

The PRC-112 in the commander's hand came to life. "Brigand One, this is Falcon Four. We're fully briefed by the Navy aircraft. Get your heads down! Over."

A trio of F-16s came in low, speeding toward the enemy on the east side. MK-83 GP bombs were loosed and fell in gentle arcs to the ground. The resultant explosions swept down that part of the mujahideen lines in orange and black flashes of fire and smoke. The Air Force flight made a steep turn and came back to begin a series of strafing runs that spewed 20-millimeter rounds from the M-61 guns mounted on each aircraft. They continued the attack for fifteen minutes, until their ammunition was expended. Then they formed up and made a wide circle around the area.

"Brigand One, this is Falcon Four," came over the radio. "Our view of the target area indicates it is destroyed. Over."

"This is Brigand One," Brannigan replied. "From where we sit that is great news. Over."

"Anything else we can do for you? Over."

Brannigan grinned. "Are they all dead? Over."

"I'd say them that wasn't wished they was," the pilot replied. "We think a helicopter may have gotten away but we destroyed the other. Anyhow, we'll turn you back to that Navy guy. Good luck. Out."

The next voice was from the aircraft that had followed the beacon signal to the site. "This is Ears Three. It looks like that part of the world belongs to you now. We've passed on your location and situation. Orders have been sent for us to relay to you. You are to remain where you are until contacted. Some choppers will be dispatched to your location. They should arrive tomorrow. Understand? Over."

"Affirmative," Brannigan said. "Who are you, Ears Three? Over."

"We're an EA-6B off the *Jefferson*," came back the answer.

Brannigan stood in humble silence. His wife and her friends flew EA-6Bs. Those were the same people he had shown so much contempt to back at the Officers' Club at North Island NAS.

0800 HOURS LOCAL

THE SEALs were in a line of skirmishers as they moved along the lines that now consisted of nothing more than dead, dying and wounded mujahideen. The weaponry of the F-16s had turned most of them into hunks of raw meat. None of the living offered resistance, only staring in fearful confusion at the men who had somehow destroyed them at a time when they had been assured of Allah's blessing and a quick victory. Most thought the airplanes belonged to the infidels who now walked so confidently among them. The Brigands dropped the canteens they had been using to pick up fresh ones from the conquered foe.

Brannigan noticed that the ragheads had state-of-the-art infantry weaponry and equipment. One platoon seemed to be fitted out in modern American webbing gear. They even had the letters "U.S." stenciled on them. A gift from the CIA back in the 1980s no doubt.

Lieutenant Jim Cruiser joined Brannigan as the tour of the enemy lines continued. Cruiser sighed and shrugged. "It's impossible to make an accurate prediction in regards to the fortunes of war, huh, sir?"

"Yeah," Brannigan agreed. "Did you notice the damaged chopper sitting over there? There was another one that flew out of here after the air support boys left."

"Yes, sir," Cruiser said. "They must have had it stashed out of harm's way. I suppose that means the big chief escaped."

"I hope what happened today is enough to defeat him," Brannigan said. "I sure as hell don't want to see another battalion of those sons of bitches charging over the hill."

"Amen to that!"

"I'm also wondering if we're finally going to be relieved when those choppers arrive tomorrow."

Mike Assad yelled at them from a hundred meters off to the left. "Sir!"

"What'd you find?" Brannigan shouted back.

Mike bent over and stood up, dragging an uninjured man to his feet. "It's a European, sir."

"Bring him over here."

Mike pushed the survivor along in front of him, up to where the two officers waited. When the stranger arrived, he seemed to be dazed by the aerial attack that had pounded the enemy positions. He recovered slightly by shaking his head, then assumed the position of attention. He raised his hand in the Russian version of a salute, introducing himself in a thick accent. "I am Warrant Officer Gregori Ivanovich Parkolov. Soviet Army."

"There isn't any more Soviet Army," Brannigan said.

"I am prisoner of war," Parkolov, aka Mohammed Shari-wal, said. "Warlord Khamami forcing me to be helicopter pilot. When American airplane attack, I run and hide. I want for to go home. I am here for many years." He pulled a faded red I.D. book from his pocket and opened to the front page, showing the Cyrillic writing to Brannigan. "Is my name and is my rank," he explained. An old photograph of a young, rather sad Russian soldier was beneath the printed words:

$$\text{гРигоРий пАРколоВ}$$
$$\text{пРАпоРщик}$$

Brannigan could see that the younger man in the photo and the older man standing in front of him were one and the same. "All right," he said. "What do you want from me?"

"I tell you I want go home," Parkolov said.

"I'll see what can be done for you," Brannigan said. "But right now consider yourself a prisoner of war."

"Of course," Parkolov said. He grinned. "I know how to be prisoner. I got lots of experience."

"I'll bet you do," Brannigan said. "And I have a few questions to ask about your former captors. The first is: will they be back here with reinforcements?"

The Russian shook his head. "*Nyet*—no. You have defeated them. The leader and his staff have run to hide."

"All right," Brannigan said. He gestured to Senior Chief Dawkins. "I'll let you do the rest of the interrogation."

"Aye, sir," Dawkins said. He took the prisoner by the arm. "Let's go, Russki."

Parkolov was deliriously happy. "May I have American cigarette please? Maybe you are having Lucky Strike, *nyet*?"

CHAPTER 20

THE platoon stood in the midst of the shrapnel-slashed-and-burned corpses that were dismembered and scattered around the area in grotesque positions. Many were naked, their clothing blown off by the violence of the aerial bombardment.

The "chop-chop" sounds of a half dozen UH-60 Blackhawk helicopters approaching in trail could be heard in the distance. When the aircraft were within a kilometer, four of them broke off from the formation, while two came straight in. All six settled down to gentle landings, and when the four that had separated from the flight touched the ground, a squad of 101st Airborne Division troopers came out of each one. The soldiers formed up in two columns, then marched out to take up security positions around the area.

The other two choppers had settled down close to where the fourteen SEALs awaited them. Two figures disembarked from the nearest, walking rapidly toward the spot where Lieutenants

Bill Brannigan and Jim Cruiser waited. Lieutenant Colonel Harry Latrelle, the Army civil affairs officer, and Afghanistan government envoy Zaid Aburrani came to a sudden stop when they finally noted they had walked into the midst of charred and mutilated human carnage.

"Holy Mother of God!" Latrelle exclaimed. "Did you guys do all this?"

"Well, part of it," Brannigan said, offering his hand. "The F-16s did most of the killing. How are you, sir? It's nice to see you again."

"Same here," Latrelle said. "You remember Mr. Aburrani, do you not?"

"Certainly," Brannigan said.

The Afghan shook hands with the two SEAL officers. "Your victory is complete, gentlemen. You have every reason to be proud of yourselves."

"Not exactly," Brannigan said. "The big chief got away. All we've got is a prisoner of war, and he's a Russian who claims to have been held by the mujahideen and forced to fly a helicopter for them. He told me the warlord escaped in the one surviving chopper. His two field commanders are evidently among the dead." Brannigan turned and waved at Senior Chief Buford Dawkins and Chad Murchison. The two had a man between them, and they brought him over.

Gregori Parkalov saluted the colonel and nodded to Aburrani. "I am asking for asylum and for return to Soviet—er, that is—Russia."

"It would seem repatriation to your country could be arranged," Latrelle said. "How long have you been here in Afghanistan?"

"Twenty years," Parkalov answered. "I am taken prisoner when my helicopter is shot down by partisan enemy." He looked over at Aburrani and started to say something, but the Afghan frowned at him as a silent signal he mustn't reveal that they knew each other. The Russian turned his attention back to Latrelle. "I am most happy to answer what questions you have for me to ask."

"You can return to Kabul with Mr. Aburrani and me when we go back," Latrelle said. "Our intelligence people will want to have a friendly visit with you. Afterward, if things work out, I'm certain you will be turned over to the Russian embassy there."

"Thank you," Parkalov said.

"Meanwhile," Latrelle said, speaking to Brannigan, "we are going to fly over to the warlord's stronghold. I can tell you confidently that he is defeated and most of his army is wiped out. However, he has great influence in this area and Mr. Aburrani has assured me that he will be most cooperative with us due to the drubbing he suffered here yesterday."

"That is most true," Aburrani added. "He will be useful in the pacification program of the government. Our contacts have assured me that he is ready to practice the Pashtun custom that is called *nanawatey*. He has admitted defeat and is willing to humble himself before us in total surrender, as well as beg for forgiveness."

Brannigan's voice was cold when he said, "I'd like to put a bullet in the son of a bitch's skull."

"Now, Lieutenant," Latrelle said, "this is just one of many atypical situations that arise in our work in Afghanistan. Believe me, *nanawatey* is a very serious custom. You are to be congratulated for your efforts in bringing this about. It is the best kind of victory as far as the local people are concerned."

"I'd still like to put a bullet in the son of a bitch's skull," Brannigan insisted.

"I need to see a very quick change in your attitude," Latrelle said seriously. "You will be going with us to Khamami's fortress. The fact that there are only fourteen of you will serve to impress him and his people of the fighting qualities of the American armed forces. The rifle platoon over there is also for show, but they are fully armed in case of trouble."

"That's fine, sir," Brannigan said. "By the way, I have two KIA buried on West Ridge where we had our base camp. I would appreciate it if arrangements can be made to have them disinterred and returned home." He reached in his pocket and pulled out a slip of paper. "These are the GPS coordinates of the graves. We also cached a lot of equipment. Some of it is personal property of platoon members. They would like to get it back."

"Of course, Lieutenant," Latrelle said. "I'll have this information radioed to Kabul. That can be taken care of today. Your equipment and possessions will be put into the Navy's administrative and logistic channels." He nodded to Aburrani. "Are we ready to go?"

"Indeed," Aburrani replied.

"You and your executive officer can fly in the first chopper with Mr. Aburrani and me," Latrelle said to Brannigan. "The rest of your men can take the second."

Dawkins took Parkalov by the arm. "I'll get everyone aboard."

OUTSIDE WARLORD KHAMAMI'S FORTRESS
1000 HOURS LOCAL

HASSAN Khamami had set up a large tent some fifty meters from the entrance to his fortress. A carpet had been put on the floor and cushions provided for seating. The warlord and his new chief lieutenant, Amet Kharani, sat inside. With the deaths of Major Malari and Captain Tanijai, Durtami's former assistant had been promoted to this new prestigious post. Now he and the warlord hardly spoke a word as they unhappily waited for the arrival of their expected visitors.

"Amir!" a guard at the entrance called out. "We can see helicopters flying in this direction."

"Very well," Khamami replied in a resigned tone of voice. Although he hid it well, the loss of his field commanders grieved him deeply. They were old comrades who had shared many episodes of danger with him. Their loyalty and friendship went far beyond mere professional relationships. Khamami took a deep breath of resignation, glancing over at Kharani. "Please go to welcome my guests."

Kharani got to his feet and walked from the tent in time to see six helicopters settling down to a landing. Their rotor blades blew up clouds of fine dust along with small pebbles that peppered the tent behind Kharani and the guards. When the engines were cut, Kharani spotted Aburrani getting out of one of the aircraft, with three American officers. One was in a starched, press BDU while the others appeared as if they had been rolling in the dirt. The Pashtun walked over and bowed low.

"Pakhair," Kharani said, making a Pashto welcome that only Aburrani understood. "It is good to see you again, Brother Aburrani."

"Likewise," Aburrani said. "Does the warlord await us?"

"He is in the tent," Kharani said. "Follow me, please."

He led the four visitors to where the pair of guards on duty salaamed respectfully to them as they entered. Khamami was on his feet, but immediately dropped to his knees, leaning over until his forehead touched the carpet. He began speaking in Pashto, in a low, mournful voice.

Aburrani whispered to the Americans. "He is performing *nanawatey.*"

The warlord spoke unceasingly for almost a quarter of an hour before stopping. He remained in the subservient position as Aburrani spoke to him, indicating that all his past transgressions were forgiven. When the government envoy finished his speech, Khamami stood up. He motioned to the pillows arranged in front of the one he used.

"He is inviting us to take seats," Aburrani said to his companions. He continued as they settled on the pillows, with Jim Cruiser choosing one in the rear. "The warlord has expressed his sorrow for his past conduct and asks for forgiveness. He also says he is more than willing to atone for any indignity or discomfort he might have caused us."

Brannigan's teeth were clenched in anger. "Can he speak English?"

"Alas, no," Aburrani said. "I must act as translator."

"It's probably better that way," Latrelle said, glad that any outburst from Brannigan would not be understood by the warlord. Cruiser, thinking the same thing, showed a wide grin.

"At any rate," Aburrani continued, "I will now introduce you." He spoke in Pashto again, pointing to Brannigan, Cruiser and Latrelle. Khamami said something, then Aburrani looked at Brannigan. "He is now aware of who you are and knows you were the leader who opposed him in battle. He also stated that now he knows for sure you had no more than fourteen men. But he wishes to remind you that it was the airplanes that defeated his army. The warlord is most positive he would have destroyed your command otherwise."

Brannigan knew the man was right, but he wasn't going to give him any satisfaction. "Tell him my second in command and I were just about to demand that he surrender when the planes showed up."

Khamami's eyes opened wide when the statement was translated, then he laughed aloud.

"I'm glad the son of a bitch is amused," Brannigan said sourly.

"He merely stated that audacity is in the war chest of every great commander," Aburrani said.

Brannigan shrugged. "Well, he's right about that."

"Now I must have a long conversation with the warlord," Aburrani said. "Please excuse me, my friends." He looked at Khamami, the expression on his face serious as he began speaking in Pashto. "Listen to me, Khamami. You are at the mercy of the government in Kabul now. You have lost your army, and any misbehavior on your part will bring American warplanes that will bomb this fortress into rubble and kill all your people. Understand?"

"I understand," Khamami said. "And I hope *you* understand why I did not choose to fight to the death as I normally would have."

"Of course," Aburrani said. "You realize that if you submit to Kabul's authority, you will be under government, thus American, protection. And your activities in the opium trade will be able to continue unabated without us having to find a replacement for you."

"If I cannot have glory in war, then I will console myself by becoming a wealthy man."

"That is most wise of you," Aburrani said. "By the way, the helicopter pilot Mohammed Sheriwal has surrendered to the Americans. He used his Russian name, saying nothing about converting to Islam. The fellow has asked them to help him get home to Russia."

"He wants to go to Switzerland to get his money out of the bank," Khamami said. "He will leave behind his women and never come back."

"It doesn't matter," Aburrani said. "You must let him go. If he is forced to stay, he will betray you, me and many others who make money from the poppies."

"Very well."

"There is an American rifle platoon here along with Brannigan's men," Aburrani explained. "They will be watching you and your surviving mujahideen most carefully. The infidels know you cannot defeat them in battle, and any bad conduct by you or your people will be severely punished."

"I am serious about *nanawatey*," Khamami said. "So let us get back to business. Will there be any problem smuggling out the next opium crop?"

"None at all," Aburrani said. "Now that everything is settled, I will inform my companions that you have formally surrendered and agreed to serve the causes of the new Afghan government." The envoy turned to Brannigan, Cruiser and Latrelle.

Both Khamami and Kharani sat in silence as their friend spoke in the strange language of the infidels.

1330 HOURS LOCAL

THE 101st Airborne troopers began setting up a tent camp for the stay at the fortress. When the SEALs offered to help, their commander, an African-American lieutenant by the name of Lawton, told the Navy men they had been through enough. The air assault troopers were more than happy to do the work.

As the camp was erected, Colonel Latrelle had some more important information for Lieutenant Brannigan. And the SEAL skipper was not pleased by most of it.

"There'll be a UN aid team coming in here tomorrow," Latrelle explained. "They're coming for the purpose of giving help and instruction to the people living in the fortress and the villages around it."

"What the hell is that all about?" Brannigan asked.

"The usual stuff," Latrelle said. "There'll be two medical clinics. One for men and the other for women and children so as not to offend any Islamic sensitivities. The UN people will also present a special program for the women about female things, and other lessons that will pertain to everybody. They use posters and leaflets as well as videotapes to explain nutrition, hygiene and sanitation in their presentations. It's actually quite beneficial to the indigenous personnel."

"Does this have anything to do with me and my men?"

"You are to remain here with the rifle platoon for security reasons," Latrelle said. "When SOCOM deems it is time to end your mission, you will return to Kabul. The UN aircraft will be provided to you for the flight."

"Godamn it!" Brannigan cursed. "We came over to this fucking place to pick up a defector on a quick in-and-out operation. So far we've been on this mission almost a month, fought several major battles, lost two damn good men, and now we're supposed to stand around a fucking dilapidated fort with our thumbs up our asses."

"Hey, Lieutenant," Latrelle said testily. "I'm only the messenger. SOCOM wanted you to hang around here because they feel the Pashtuns have a great deal of respect for you." He shrugged. "Actually, they're scared of you."

"They have good reason to be," Brannigan snapped.

2 SEPTEMBER
0945 HOUR LOCAL

ALL the SEALs felt stabs of homesickness when the white United Nations C-130 touched down and taxied across the hard-packed terrain toward the tent camp. They knew this was the aircraft that would carry them out on the first leg of the long trip home. The sight of the big plane made them anxious to get aboard and haul ass away from Afghanistan as fast as possible.

The rear door slowly opened under the hydraulic drive, then a loading ramp was pushed out by the crew. The first thing to appear was a Mitsubishi truck that was driven off the plane. Another followed, then a couple of dozen people pulling roll-out luggage walked down the ramp to the ground. The SEALs' collective interest rose when they noticed that among the disembarking passengers were a number of females. A man led the group, and he paused to look around as if searching for someone to greet him. Brannigan and the leader of the rifle platoon, Lieutenant Lawton, picked him out to be the head man. They walked up and introduced themselves.

"How do you do?" he said. "I am Dr. Bouchier. I have some tents and other accommodations to set up. There is a crew of laborers still aboard the aircraft to do the work. Where do you recommend that we establish ourselves?"

Brannigan pointed to the south side of the warlord's fortress. "The wind is cut off there. You'll be more comfortable."

Lieutenant Lawton made an offer. "I have a platoon of men here if you need any help."

"No, thank you," Dr. Bouchier said. "We have plenty of hands to tend to the task. The sight of soldiers putting up our camp gives a bad impression."

"All right, Doctor," Lieutenant Lawton said. "I don't suppose good impressions mean much if it turns out you need any protection, so we'll be close by."

The doctor ignored the remark that bordered on sarcasm. "Our laborers will go back with the plane tomorrow, but will return to repack us when it's time to leave." Then he added, "By the way, I am Belgian not French."

I almost give a shit, Brannigan thought, but he said. "Really?"

"Yes," Bouchier said. "Really." He turned and yelled out some orders in French. The effort produced a dozen Afghan laborers who cheerfully trotted down the ramps over to the trucks. An impatient gesture from the doctor set the vehicles off in the right direction.

Chad Murchison stood with his CAR-15 over his shoulder, with Senior Chief Dawkins and Connie Concord, watching the activity. He had started to turn to go back to the platoon tents when a female voice caught his attention.

"Chad! Chad Murchison!"

He turned to see who had hailed him. A young woman wearing white coveralls walked rapidly toward him, and the sight caused a deep feeling of sweet sadness to sweep over the young SEAL. It was Penny Brubaker, the girl who had dumped him for a varsity jock back in their college days. He managed an awkward grin, not really happy to see her.

"Hello, Penny."

She embraced him tightly around the neck and kissed his cheek. "Chad! Oh m'God! I never expected to see you. I mean here. Y'know, in Afghanistan." She laughed nervously. "Oh m'God! I am so flustered."

"I'm a bit surprised to see you too," Chad said.

"Oh m'God! I hardly recognized you," she said. "I had to stare a minute to make sure it was you."

He noted that she wore a name tag on her coveralls with her last name as BRUBAKER instead of ARMBREWSTER. The big man on campus she'd gotten engaged to was Cliff Armbrewster. She suddenly realized what he was looking at. "Oh! Cliff and I never married. He was such a shallow buffoon." She gave Chad a bold gaze. "You look so rugged! And you've filled out! But then you're a SEAL, aren't you? I heard about it from Pauline Dillingham. She said you had gone into the Navy and became a SEAL. How exciting. I thought that was so brave and mature of you."

Suddenly his feelings of awkwardness disappeared and he felt manly and macho. "Yeah. It was tough sledding, but I made it."

She saw her companions following after the trucks. "I have to get over there with my people. Oh m'God! We have to get together for a long, long talk, Chad. Really!" She kissed his cheek again and hurried after the other UN workers.

Senior Chief Dawkins and Connie walked up to him, grinning. Dawkins chuckled. "Man, Murchison, you work fast, don't you?"

Connie laughed. "She hadn't been off the plane a full minute before you made your moves. Way to go, guy!"

"Yeah," he said sadly. "I'm a regular Don Juan."

He walked away, wanting more than anything to be by himself. Seeing Penny again had stirred up old feelings of hurt and humiliation, of being rejected and unwanted. He was both sad and angry at the same time. He had pushed the girl into the far distant recesses of his heart, but now here she was back, all beautiful and desirable as she had always been.

Evidently the old maxim about women all being the same when they stood on their heads did not apply to Penelope Brubaker.

CHAPTER 21

DR. Pierre Bouchier's medical and advisory teams were now into their second day of ministering to the Pashtuns living in and around Warlord Hassan Khamami's fortress. Even the people who belonged to the now defunct band of the late Ayyub Durtami were included in the program. Khamami had generously allowed them to take advantage of the UN offerings because of the martyrdom of their men in the final battles with the American SEALs. Another very important aspect he considered was the fact that their sons would reach adulthood someday to serve as his mujahideen. They would come in handy when he renounced the recent surrender to launch a campaign to renew his former glory. This future coup d'etat would be more than amply financed through opium poppy cultivation.

The UN's initial efforts in the fiefdom were a bit chaotic on the first day. The relief workers had not expected the five hundred people to show up all at once. But most of the staff had faced similar situations in Africa during civil wars that produced hordes of refugees. In only a short hour, using interpreters from the UN center in Kabul, the people were lined up in groups and pointed in the direction they should go.

The Pashtuns accepted the help offered them with a silent, dignified gratitude. Most of the attendees were women who brought their children in for treatment of such things as rashes, diarrhea and other conditions that would be considered minor in the more advanced areas of the world. The relief workers were aware that there must have been scores of little graves in the area that held babies who had quickly succumbed to more serious illnesses in the past. It was a pathetic situation, but there were no pharmacies out in the hinterlands of Afghanistan, and most remedies were homemade or derived from faulty folklore. The arid terrain offered little in the way of the healing herbs that were available in the jungles and forests of the globe's temperate and torrid zones.

Dr. Bouchier's plate was also full. Many surviving mujahideen had suffered debilitating wounds during their service. Without proper medical treatment and convalescence, a great majority of these fighters were either crippled up or suffered chronic pain from old injuries. The doctor employed his skills as an orthopedic surgeon to bring comfort and mobility to the suffering veterans.

One of the busiest places was the dental tent. It seemed that the majority of the people suffered from toothaches, diseased gums and other problems of the mouth. They would have been more than willing to accept the pulling, drilling and filling of teeth without anesthetic, but were happy to find out that the learned Western dentist and his hygienists had a magic needle that, although it pricked hotly when stuck into the gums, quickly produced a welcome numbness. Even the noisiest of their whirring instruments could be endured in great comfort. The whole program was turning out to be a pleasant experience for Khamami's people.

Then Khatib the Oracle made an appearance.

The wizened scarecrow, wearing a tattered and soiled chador as a serape, stalked into the area. "What are you miserable sinners doing?" he shrieked in his reedy voice at the Pashtuns. "Have you lost your minds? You are letting infidels examine your bodies and give you strange medicines and treatments that go against the holiest of Islamic laws! Their serums and elixirs are impure and unblessed."

The people, still fearful of the old faker, recoiled physically, causing their carefully formed lines to curl and buckle.

Khatib strode among them, waving his arms, his face contorted into a righteous rage. "Allah the merciful and beneficent will cure your ills in His own way! If you die, it is His will! Suppose your mortal life slips away while you are under the care of these unbelievers? Do you want to show up at the gates of Paradise bearing the curse of unholy therapy given to you by infidels? You will be turned away to join the heretics of the faith who have been doomed to hellfire forever!"

Warlord Khamami had anticipated an appearance by the old man, and sent Ahmet Kharani with a half dozen guards to put an end to his haranguing. The preaching of religious fervor no longer benefited Khamami and he was more than ready to get rid of Khatib the Oracle. He had become a source of great disturbance in the fiefdom.

The guards, under Kharani's supervision, simply grabbed the skinny oldster and hauled him out of the area, frogmarching him away. They were under orders to take him back to the mountains to renew the hermitage he had foisted upon himself for fifteen long years.

Kharani watched the old man's forced departure, then turned back to the crowd, raising his hands for attention. "Pay no attention to what the insane ancient has told you. *Amir* Khamami blesses the efforts of these good people who have come to help us. You may continue to receive their healings and medicines."

The lines quickly reformed.

UN CLASS TENT
1015 HOURS LOCAL

PENNY Brubaker's assignment in her relief team was
the position of instructor in the diet, sanitation and hygiene
program. Her training aids were posters, videotapes, pamphlets and one translator fluent in the Pashto language. No
matter where she had gone in her short UN career, her
classes were made up wholly of women who eagerly sought
her counsel. Their knowledge of even the most rudimentary
sanitation practices was severely limited, and the first lesson
Penny imparted was the benefits of boiling water before use.
From there she progressed through cooking, cleaning and
the proper placement, construction and uses of latrines. When
those basic subjects were mastered, she moved on to more
complicated matters such as proper diet. This latter could be
extremely difficult to teach in areas suffering from shortages
of food due to famine, war or extreme poverty.

Penny and her interpreter had just finished the second
lecture of the series, and had put a tape in the VCR. While
the women in her class sat enthralled by this method of pre-
senting instruction on maintaining healthful diets, she went
outside the tent for some fresh air and some time to collect
her thoughts.

The unexpected meeting with Chad Murchison had
shaken Penny more than she realized. He was always a cute
guy in a sort of awkward way, and his physical ineptness
was charming. But he'd seemed so immature, even though
he was a brilliant student who was always on the Dean's
List. The rugged physical strength and manly handsomeness
of Cliff Armbrewster had attracted her in a way that Chad
never could.

But seeing him here in Afghanistan had shocked her to
the point of giddiness. It wasn't so much from finding him in
this isolated place, but seeing how much he had changed. He
had been armed, wearing a battle vest complete with military equipment, and a camouflage-pattern uniform; but most

of all, his once scrawny physique had blossomed into a sharp muscularity. His shoulders and chest filled the jacket, and his arms were corded with muscle. He still had long slender fingers, and they were a charming contrast to his ruggedness.

Additionally, Chad's face, once long and sort of girlish, was square-jawed now, with a masculine maturity that made it hard to realize he was that same sweet boy she had known through their preppy years and into college.

"Oh m'God!" she whispered to herself. "He's so handsome! So Brad Pitt!"

The tent flap opened and her assistant instructor stepped out. "Penny, the video is over. It's time to continue the instruction."

Penny nodded. "All right. I'm ready."

The two women went back inside the tent.

1700 HOURS LOCAL

THE day's work had ended for the UN team, and their evening meal would soon be ready, but Penny Brubaker was too excited to eat. The one thing she wanted more than anything else at that moment was to see Chad Murchison again.

When she walked into the SEAL bivouac, she noted that they had situated themselves in a sort of circle arrangement of tents. They sat in front of their canvas shelters in twos and threes, speaking quietly with one another. After a quick glance around, she saw Chad seated on a camp stool with two other men. As she approached them, the oldest noticed her and gave her a smile and a wave.

Chad turned, and stood up when he saw her. He smiled a greeting. "Hello, Penny."

"Hi, Chad," she said. She looked at the others. "Hello."

"Penny," Chad said, "these are a couple of my platoon mates. Guys, this is a friend from my hometown. Penny Brubaker. Senior Chief Dawkins here is our fire team leader."

"How're you doing?" the senior chief said politely.

"And I'm Guttorm Olson," the other man said, introducing himself. "It's nice to meet you, Penny."

"Thank you," Penny said. "It's very nice to meet you too. Are you Norwegian?"

"Only by ancestry," Gutsy said. "I'm from Minnesota."

"Can we fix you a cup of coffee?" Chad asked. "All we have are MREs, but it'll be hot and invigorating."

"No, thank you," Penny said. "I just dropped by so we could bring each other up to date."

"That's a great idea," Chad said. "How about a stroll? We're actually safer out here than we'd be in a large American city."

"I can believe that," Penny said. She smiled at the senior chief and Gutsy. "It was nice meeting you."

The two young people walked out of the bivouac and began strolling along a route that would take them around the SEAL bivouac, the UN camp and the area occupied by the troops from the 101st Airborne Division. Everyone seemed tired from the day's activities, except for a half dozen air assault soldiers playing flies and grounders with a bat and softball.

Chad only took short glances at Penny during the impromptu promenade. Even without much makeup and wearing coveralls, she was still alluring. He cleared his throat to speak. "So how're things going with the United Nations?"

"Pretty good," she said. "The people here gave us an enthusiastic welcome. All of our facilities are going at full speed. I teach diet and sanitation, and just started some groups this morning."

"We're not doing a thing but keeping an eye on the warlord in the wooden castle over there," Chad said. "Between standing watch and patrolling, we're starting to get bored."

"I don't quite know what to think of that chief or whatever he is," Penny said. "My interpreter told me she learned that he and his people have slaves."

"I haven't heard anything about that," Chad said.

"They were evidently conquered by the warlord in some battle or war a long time ago," Penny said.

"You say they're slaves?"

"Yes," Penny replied. "And they are not allowed to take advantage of our services."

"Can't your boss do anything about that?"

Penny shook her head. "He can't do a thing to ease the situation because of a UN mandate that forbids aid teams to interfere with certain local customs and practices. We try to keep friction between us and the people's leaders to a minimum."

Chad stopped walking, turning to look at her. "I'll bet the Skipper can help out those slaves in the winking of an eye."

"Who is the Skipper?"

"My commanding officer," Chad said. "Lieutenant Wild Bill Brannigan. He'll go over there and give that warlord an attitude adjustment."

"Oh m'God!" Penny exclaimed. "They told us he was a powerful man! A warlord! He has an army, Chad!"

"He *had* an army," Chad said. "We just kicked his and his troops' asses but good. If that son of a bitch as much as blinks the wrong way, he'll find his butt right between the rock and a hard place."

Penny was stunned. Here was this tough guy she had once known as an awkward boyfriend, who in reality was now a stranger. That proverbial ninety-eight-pound weakling of those long ago days had disappeared forever. Instead, here he was as muscular as a football player, and talking about defeating entire armies in the company of somebody he called Wild Bill.

Chad took her hand. "Let's go talk with the Skipper. C'mon!"

BRANNIGAN'S CP
1720 HOURS LOCAL

LIEUTENANT Wild Bill Brannigan lay on his mattress pad inside the tent he used as an office. With very little paperwork to do, he had no furniture. Frank Lopez had organized a commo center with the newly acquired Shadowfire radio and the platoon's PRC-112s in another tent.

The Skipper had almost drifted to sleep when he perceived the sound of footsteps approaching. He opened his eyes and waited. A moment later he heard Chad Murchison's voice.

"Sir! I need to have a word with you. It's me, Murchison."

"Well, c'mon in then," Brannigan said irritably.

"Are you decent, sir? I have a young lady with me."

Brannigan laughed. "I'm having my way with two of the skankiest whores this side of Baghdad. So maybe I better join you out there if you're with a fucking lady." He got up and went to the flap, stepping outside. He stopped, his eyes opened wide. "Jesus, Murchison! You *do* have a young lady with you." He grinned as his face reddened with embarrassment. "Excuse me. Please. I thought Petty Officer Murchison was joking with me."

Penny smiled. She had run into all sorts of situations since going to work for the UN. "That's perfectly all right. I just hope those skanky whores can spare you for a moment or two."

Brannigan, liking her right away, laughed. "I truly apologize. And Murchison should have said he was with a *charming* young lady."

"You're most gallant," Penny said, smiling at the compliment.

"Sir," Murchison said, suppressing a chuckle. "This is Penny Brubaker, who works with the UN relief group. We're old friends from way back. She has some information she'd like to pass on to you."

"I just mentioned a situation to Chad," Penny said. "My boss, Dr. Bouchier, can do nothing about it. Chad said you could help."

"What's going on?"

"We've learned through our interpreters that this warlord, or whatever he is, has slaves," Penny explained. "He is not allowing them the benefits we are giving the other people."

"I'll get my cover," Brannigan said. "Take me to the doctor."

DR. BOUCHIER'S TENT
1730 HOURS LOCAL

THE doctor sat in the folding chair across from Brannigan. They sipped brandy from a couple of goblets that Bouchier kept in a special trunk along with other luxury items he allowed himself. He not only had Italian brandy, but could also boast of French champagne, Danish vodka and other expensive liquor. Additionally, he possessed bartending implements and an assortment of glasses in which to mix his favorite libations.

Brannigan had come over expecting an argument when it came to the matter of the slaves owned by the warlord. But he found that Bouchier not only had no objections if the SEAL officer chose to deal with the problem of the captive laborers, but encouraged him to take action.

"I am tightly bound by regulations," Bouchier explained, swirling his brandy around in his glass. "We in the UN must be exceedingly careful that we do not trespass into specific areas that deal with matters that are rather sensitive. Do you understand what I am saying?"

"Of course," Brannigan said. "It's a lot like what I have to put up with. There are times when I feel very strong about blowing certain people or places off the face of the earth. I realize that the world would be better off without them, but I can't do a thing because of orders or regulations."

"But you say you can deal with this warlord?"

"I defeated him in battle," Brannigan said. "I've been assured this gives me a certain leverage with the man. He evidently feels he has something to lose if any big trouble occurs around here."

"That is correct," Bouchier said. "It would interfere with the opium trade. It would be exceedingly costly to him if that enterprise was taken away."

"I'm not concerned with that," Brannigan said. "All I want to deal with are those poor bastards he thinks he owns. Will you be able to help them?"

"I'll see that they are given priority over the others when they appear at our camp," Bouchier assured him.

Brannigan finished his brandy. "It may take a day or two, but I'll have them here." He stood up and offered his hand. "Nice to do business with you, Doctor."

"Likewise, *monsieur le lieutenant*."

**UN RELIEF CAMP
4 SEPTEMBER
0845 HOURS LOCAL**

ACTING under Lieutenant Wild Bill Brannigan's extremely stern orders, Warlord Hassan Khamami smothered both his pride and his anger to send his chief lieutenant, Ahmet Kharani, with a party of guards, over to the Dharyan camp to gather up the slaves.

The UN relief workers had seen much human suffering in their experiences with bringing aid to victimized peoples, and the Dharyans weren't the worse by far. They were not walking skeletons covered with sores, but it was obvious they had been badly used by their masters. The clan was malnourished, dressed in rags and suffered from various ailments brought on by the mistreatment.

As soon as they arrived at the relief camp, the slaves were quickly and efficiently split up by sex and age. After the proper grouping was accomplished, they were further divided according to their physical conditions. Many of the men, though in need of sustenance, had a natural strength that served them well. The women, on the other hand, were all in terrible shape. Giving birth had sapped their strength, and their men had kept them pregnant as if it were a divine command sent down to them from Allah. The children they brought into the world showed the effects of suckling at the breasts of malnourished mothers. On two occasions, UN workers gently but firmly pried dead infants from the arms of delirious young women who had been carrying them around several days after death.

At that point, Dr. Bouchier decided to forgo any medical treatment for the moment. That was just as well because all the Dharyans had any interest in was getting something to eat. When the first packets were passed out, the hungry people quickly tore them open to scarf down whatever victuals needed no cooking.

Even as they consumed the packages of dried fruit, energy bars and candy, they were herded over to a spot where tents had been erected for them by mujahideen who had survived the battle with the SEALs. This camp also included blankets, along with cooking pots and utensils. The clan leader took over from the UN at that point. His name was Bashar Dahrain, and he was a young man aged far beyond his years. He quickly prodded and hollered at his people until the various family groups were properly installed in individual tents.

Within a quarter of an hour pots of rice were hanging over fires while wheat flour was being molded into dough for bread. Penny Brubaker and her small team went from family to family, passing out powdered milk and nursing formula. The interpreters gave quick and adequate instruction on how to use the plastic bottles and nipples to feed the babies. The mothers, ecstatic with the knowledge that they could now give nourishment to their infants, turned their attention from the cooking tasks to see to the feeding of the little ones. Older daughters and nieces took over the other chores.

Dr. Bouchier gazed at the tents with his assistant surgeon. "We'll take care of the medical examinations tomorrow." He looked over at the edge of the camp, noting the arrival of a half dozen SEALs. *"C'est bon!* Lieutenant Brannigan has sent some of his men to make sure these poor people are not molested."

The assistant surgeon, a pacifist Canadian, shook his head in dismay. "If only we could accomplish our goals without help from the military."

BRANNIGAN'S CP
1400 HOURS LOCAL

THE Dharyan clan chief Bashar Dahrain and the UN interpreter entered Brannigan's tent. He offered them seats on a couple of camp stools. He remained standing, his arms across his chest. "What can I do for you?"

The interpreter was a Kabul city youth dressed in Western clothing. He spoke English with a combination of American and British inflexions. "Mr. Dahrain wishes to express his most sincere gratitude for the help you have given his people. They now have their freedom and are being helped back to their former lives. He wishes for Allah to bestow countless blessings on you."

"All right," Brannigan said. "Tell him that he's welcome."

The interpreter spoke to the Dharyan for a few moments, then turned back to the American. "Mr. Dahrain begs your pardon, but he must ask you for more help. He says that his people have not all been freed by the warlord. He says there are eighteen young women who are still held in the fortress. He humbly pleads for you to see that they are rejoined with their families." The interpreter paused for a moment. "Dr. Bouchier is aware of this situation and also requests your help. He has dealt with similar cases in the past. He feels the women will need medical attention even more than the ones he has already seen."

Brannigan was puzzled. "Why is the warlord holding these females?"

"I fear he has forced them to become inmates of a brothel, sir," the interpreter said. "They have been outraged now for many months by the mujahideen."

"Tell this gentleman that those unfortunate women will be taken to the UN clinic before this day is out," Brannigan said. "And I will need your services as an interpreter to put this crappy situation right."

"I will be only too glad to serve you, sir."

AL-SABAYA CASTLE
1420 HOURS LOCAL

WHEN Warlord Hassan Khamami took in the late Ayyub Durtami's people, he also became the master of the farming village Heranbe in the dead warlord's fiefdom. This added several more fields to his opium poppy enterprise.

Now Khamami and Ahmet Kharani were holding an important meeting in the throne room. The two men were deep into the process of planning out the next harvest program of the valuable crop. Production estimates had to be made, schedules designed for transport to the clandestine shipping center, and the next year's prices established. All this was done without paperwork. In an environment where most of the people were illiterate, it would have been impractical to establish complicated administrative procedures. The centuries-old custom of handshakes and committing to memory all arrangements of how the business would be conducted worked out fine in those Afghanistan mountains. A side benefit of the primitive system was that it was impossible for the authorities to trace these clandestine goings-on. A computer system had yet to be devised that could penetrate men's minds to read their thoughts and intentions.

The work was interrupted when the captain of the guard rapped on the door and stepped into the throne room. He bowed deeply to the warlord. "*Amir,* please forgive this interruption. The American commander and a UN man are outside. The American insists on seeing you now."

"Send them in," Khamami said. He looked over at Kharani. "I wonder what demands he has now."

"Let us remember what his honor Aburrani cautioned us about, *Amir*," Kharani said. "We must keep the opium farming a secret at all costs."

Lieutenant Wild Bill Brannigan strode in boldly with the interpreter behind him. When he stopped, the interpreter stepped to the front and made the expected polite greetings and inquiries into the warlord's health.

Khamami was impatient. "What does this foreigner want with me?"

The interpreter turned to Brannigan and spoke. Brannigan uttered a discourse in English, his voice stern and authoritative. When he finished, the interpreter spoke again to the warlord, diplomatically leaving out certain expletives and impolite references as he had learned to do in his UN training. *"Amir,"* he began, "this gentleman has heard that there are Dharyan women still being held under your authority. This grieves the gentleman much and he wishes for them to be returned to their kinsmen."

"What women is he talking about?" Khamami asked.

"The ones in the brothel, *Amir*."

"Them? Why does he bother with those harlots?" Khamami asked. "They are disgraced and soiled beyond redemption. Many men have known them. They have no future but to remain as they are until the day they die. It would be kinder for them."

The interpreter had expected that response. "Nevertheless, *Amir*, the gentleman begs for their release."

Khamami looked up into Brannigan's angry face, then swung his eyes back to the interpreter. "It doesn't sound to me like he's begging." Then he shrugged. "Certainly! If he wants them sent to their families, so be it."

"They are to go to the UN doctor first," the interpreter said.

"Tell the American his request will be granted within the hour," Khamami said.

The interpreter bowed and spoke aside to Brannigan. "He obeys your command, sir. The women will be taken to Dr. Bouchier immediately."

Brannigan gave the warlord a curt nod, then turned and strode out, with the UN man scurrying after him.

UN CLINIC
2000 HOURS LOCAL

TWELVE of the sex slaves, rather than eighteen, were delivered to Dr. Pierre Bouchier. The explanation was that six of the eighteen had died during the time they served the lusts of the mujahideen.

Even the first cursory examinations the doctor gave the women indicated they were in poor health. They had all been in their teens when taken into captivity and had endured a long period of cruelty. Although they were fed reasonably well to keep their physical appearances acceptable, the repeated rapes had caused them all serious internal medical problems. The human vagina was not designed for repeated entrances on a nightly basis. It was impossible to gauge their exact psychological conditions, but it was obvious most of the women were candidates for long periods of treatment in mental health centers.

Dr. Bouchier sent a note over to Lieutenant Brannigan informing him that the women were in no shape to be returned to their families yet. They would have to first be airlifted to the UN medical facilities in Kabul for badly needed hospitalization.

CHAPTER 22

IT was almost time for the forenoon watch to relieve the morning watch, and Mike Assad glanced anxiously over at the tent area to see if his relief, Dave Leibowitz, was in sight. After a few minutes Mike could see the figure of his buddy ambling toward the sentry post.

Mike checked his watch as Dave walked up. "It's about time."

"I'm early," Mike said, shifting the CAR-15 on his shoulder. "If I wasn't such a good friend, I'd have waited until right at oh-eight-hundred to take over the watch." He grinned and thought a moment. "Maybe I'll do exactly that." He stepped backward several paces.

"Have mercy!" Mike jokingly beseeched him. "I'm exhausted from long hours of keeping my shipmates from harm."

"Oh, all right, you poor bastard," Dave said with a wink. "You're relieved."

"What's been going on since I came out here?"

"Not much," Dave said. "They found out that the warlord had put a bunch of them slave women in a whorehouse somewhere in that wooden castle."

"No shit?"

"No shit," Dave responded. "They weren't volunteer whores either. The poor girls were in their teens and had been forced to work there. I guess they were raped every night. They're gonna send them back to their families after the doctor is done treating them."

"They can't do that!" Mike exclaimed, suddenly serious.

"Sure they can," Dave said.

"I got to go see the Skipper." Mike took off running toward the CP.

"What the hell's the matter with you?" Dave yelled after him.

Mike didn't answer as he rushed back to the platoon bivouac. When he reached the Skipper's tent, he went directly inside. Lieutenant Wild Bill Brannigan, drinking a cup of coffee, looked up at the interruption to his morning routine. "What are you all worked up about?"

"Dave told me that a bunch of those slave girls had been sent over to the UN doctor for treatment," Mike said.

"Yeah," Brannigan said. "They'd been forced into prostitution. As soon as they're fixed up, they'll go back to their families."

"They'll kill 'em, sir!"

"*Who* will kill them?" Brannigan asked.

"The men in their families," Mike exclaimed. "They disgraced their kin by what they did. Their dads and brothers are obligated to murder them. It's called honor killing."

"Are you sure about that?"

"Yes, sir," Mike said. "There was this family from Syria living in my neighborhood back in Michigan that had just immigrated to America. One of their daughters fell in love with a Christian kid in our school. The two ran off and eloped. The family had already arranged for her to marry some guy back in Syria. It was bad enough she disobeyed them about the marriage, but she'd also fallen love with a non-Muslim, and that was a double dishonor for the family. So her father and his oldest son were going to murder the girl when she and her husband came back. I guess the girl figured the old rules didn't apply in America."

"Well, godamn it, they don't!" Brannigan said angrily.

"It doesn't make any difference to people from the old country," Mike said. "I even know of a girl who was taken out of my high school and sent back to Jordan against her will to get married." He took a deep breath. "Anyhow, a warning was sent to the Syrian girl by her younger sister. The boy's family came unglued and made arrangements for them to stay with relatives in Texas. They're still out there as far as I know."

"Well," Brannigan said, "I don't think those cases apply here. These local girls were *forced* into prostitution. They weren't seduced by pimps or anything. Hell, they were prisoners."

Mike violently shook his head. "That don't make any difference, sir!"

Brannigan could see how serious Mike was. He stood up. "Let's go see that doctor."

They left the tent and walked toward the UN camp in long strides. "Say, sir," Mike said. "Have you seen Murchison's girlfriend?"

"Yeah," Brannigan replied as they hurried along. "She seems like a nice young lady."

"She's hot," Mike said in genuine admiration. "He's a lucky guy."

"Let's keep our minds on the lives of those poor girls," Brannigan snapped.

"Aye, aye, sir!"

When they reached the medical tents, Brannigan went straight to the doctor's quarters. Dr. Pierre Bouchier was sitting at his desk filling out forms to be inserted into the UN's administration mill regarding the data on the treatment programs they were using with the Pashtun population. He looked up from the work. "What can I do for you, Lieutenant?"

"This is Petty Officer Mike Assad," Brannigan said. "He's an American of Arab descent, and he tells me that the women taken from the brothel will be killed if they're returned to their families."

"That's true," Bouchier said. "Honor killings, they're called."

"But it's not the women's fault what happened to them," Brannigan protested.

"That doesn't matter," Bouchier said. "It wasn't too long ago that an Islamic court in Mauritania sentenced a married rape victim to be stoned to death for adultery. Only strong pressure from the UN got her sentence commuted."

"We can't let these women be murdered," Brannigan said.

"I haven't the slightest intention of letting that happen, Lieutenant," Bouchier replied. "It's not widely known, but the UN maintains an area for abused Muslim women in Cyprus. If I can get these young women to Kabul, they can be easily transported to safety there."

"Do you need any help?"

"It wouldn't hurt to have some armed men handy if necessary," Bouchier admitted. "I plan on calling in our C-130. It can be here this afternoon. Meanwhile, I'll have these unfortunate victims put in the back of our vans. They can make a quick trip out to the airplane and *voila*! They will be flown to our compound in Kabul."

"I'll post some of my men here," Brannigan offered.

"That is not a good idea, Lieutenant," Bouchier said. "We must make things appear as if nothing extraordinary is happening. If the Dharyans get suspicious, I fear it would engender a deadly confrontation. It would be best if you had your men located nearby where they can keep an eye on things."

"I'll alert my platoon," Brannigan said. He grabbed Mike by the sleeve. "C'mon, let's get Senior Chief Dawkins in on this."

The two SEALs left the tent.

BRANNIGAN'S CP TENT
0930 HOURS LOCAL

BRANNIGAN'S Brigands kept their personal weapons, along with extra bandoleers of ammunition, close at hand. Senior Chief Petty Officer Buford Dawkins had placed them on standby in case the situation with the Dharyan women got out of hand.

Brannigan had taken his camp chair out in front of the CP after buckling on his pistol belt with the Sig Sauer 9-millimeter automatic in its drop holster. He also had binoculars in his lap, and he raised them every once in a while to gaze over at the UN camp. He had noticed a small group of indigenous Afghanistan males approaching the tents. He waited for a few minutes, then they reappeared and begin walking toward the CP. He took another look and noted that the young interpreter was with them. The Skipper let out a shrill whistle to alert the platoon.

It took five minutes for the small crowd to reach him, and the Skipper maintained his seat to show he was the boss man. The interpreter spoke in a somewhat forced cordial way. "Dr. Bouchier has asked me to bring these six gentlemen to see you, Lieutenant. They are inquiring about the women rescued from the brothel, and wish to have them returned to their families. The doctor explained that you were the senior military commander present, and they must speak to you."

"Sure," Brannigan said, maintaining a haughty air.

The interpreter turned and spoke to the visitors in Pashto, then gave his attention back to the American. "This gentleman is Bashar Dahrain, the chief of the Dharya Clan. He is the one making the request."

Dahrain salaamed politely to the American.

"Tell him that the unfortunate women are receiving medical treatment for a number of ailments and injuries," Brannigan said. "When they are deemed to be fit, they will be returned to their families."

The interpreter translated and Dahrain then spoke at length. When he finished, the interpreter gave Brannigan an apologetic look. "The clan chief asks you to return them now, sir."

Brannigan mustered a frown of anger. "Tell him that would not please me! So I'm not gonna do it, godamn it!"

The message was delivered, though in a more courteous manner than Brannigan had spoken it. The visitors salaamed once more, then abruptly whirled around and stalked angrily away. The interpreter watched them depart. "I think that will hold them for the time being, sir."

"Those women will not—I say again—*will not* be returned to their families to be murdered," Brannigan said. "Tell Dr. Bouchier I will give him all the help possible to keep that from happening."

"He will be happy to hear that, sir."

1430 HOURS LOCAL

THE white C-130 appeared in the distance, the deep hum of its four engines barely discernible. Senior Chief Buford Dawkins quickly alerted the SEALs and formed them up in front of the CP. The whole platoon was present, with the exception of Milly Mills and Gutsy Olson, who were on the afternoon watch.

Lieutenant (J.G.) Jim Cruiser walked up from the Second Squad area just as Brannigan came out to see what the hell was going on. He quickly noticed the approaching aircraft, and he called over to Dawkins. "Take the guys over to the UN medical tent, Senior Chief. Lieutenant Cruiser and I'll tag along."

By the time the SEALs arrived at the UN camp, the C-130 had landed and was taxiing up toward the tents. Dr. Bouchier appeared, and a look of relief flooded his features when he saw Brannigan's Brigands. *"Mon Dieu!"* he exclaimed. "I am so happy to see you. We have been under constant surveillance by the Dharyans." He signaled off to the side, and the vans immediately drove up and stopped. The drivers got out and opened the side doors.

"Maintenant!" Dr. Bouchier said toward the tent flap. "Now!"

The flap was brushed aside by an emerging nurse who held it open. The first of the Dharyan girls appeared, quickly followed by the others. They were pathetic looking young women, their eyes wide with fear as they nervously glanced around. Brannigan felt a surge of anger as he imagined these teenagers forced to endure the sexual cruelty of lusting, laughing mujahideen.

"Vite!" Dr. Bouchier said, urging them to hurry.

As the last girl emerged, another nurse followed. She counted off six for the first van and another six for the second. Suddenly a dozen men and boys of the Dharya Clan appeared around the tent. When they perceived what was going on, they let out a collective howl and surged forward to pull the girls from the vehicles.

The SEALs went into action.

The Dharyans were unarmed, so the Brigands left their CAR-15s slung over their backs. But they charged forward, and punched their way into the crowd of men. The smaller Dharyans were quickly overwhelmed, but their rage gave them enough strength to fight back savagely. Several tried to go around or through the SEALs to grab at the women. Consequently, the SEALs got rougher and delivered sharp kicks to punctuate the pummeling.

After a minute the Dharyans' fury subsided under the relentless pounding. They were eventually pushed back far enough that the vans could be started and driven out toward the aircraft. The C-130 sat with idling engines, ready to receive the panicky passengers.

Several of the less injured Dharyans attempted to follow, running out toward the aircraft. But the swifter Americans caught up with them and gave them additional attitude adjustments via their fists. Within short moments the clansmen were down on the ground, getting some more kicking to make sure they stayed there. By then the first of the girls were out of the van and climbing into the interior of the fuselage.

A minute or so later, when the aircraft engines roared to life, everyone—American and Dharyan alike—watched the C-130 roll along the ground, then begin a slow climb into the air. Brannigan spotted the clan chief, who was on his hands and knees. The Skipper grabbed him and hauled him to his feet, shaking the man violently in his rage.

Bashar Dharain, knowing he'd been outsmarted, dropped back to the ground, touching his head to the earth. He began muttering in Pashto. Dr. Bouchier walked up, smiling. "He is giving up. The Pashtos call it *nanawatey*."

"Yeah," Brannigan said. "I've heard of it. It's a kind of apology ceremony or some fucking thing."

Warlord Hassan Khamami and Ahmet Kharani walked up with their entourage of bodyguards. Khamami smiled at Brannigan and spoke in his native tongue.

The interpreter, who had been watching the melee, quickly translated. "The warlord asked if you now understand why he was so harsh with the Dharyans."

Brannigan asked, "How do you say yes in Pashto?"

The interpreter told him, and Brannigan looked over at Khamami. *"Au!"*

Both Khamami and Kharani laughed aloud.

UN AID TEAM MESS TENT
1900 HOURS LOCAL

CHAD Murchison sat next to Penny Brubaker at the long table. A total of eighteen diners occupied the other places on the benches, waiting for the food to be served. It took the SEAL several moments to figure out that the picnic table was actually three separate ones, pushed together and covered by a large cloth. He felt strangely out of place

among the civilians. They were of various nationalities, and
he picked up snippets of conversation in French, German,
Italian and Spanish. As a linguistic scholar, he was fluent in
all four, so was able to eavesdrop with little trouble. Most of
the talk involved their day-to-day work with the indigenous
women and children. Evidently the UN people were enjoying a good reception from their patients and students, while
making excellent progress in their work.

The recently hired waiters, all teenage boys from the
nearby village, suddenly appeared and began placing the
dishes of food on the table. The menu for the evening was
green tossed salad with Roquefort dressing, roast beef,
fried potatoes, green beans and rolls. This was Chad's first
chance in a long time to have a real meal of Western-style
dishes, and he found the fare delicious beyond description.
The chef was a Senegalese who had left a prestigious job in
a four-star Paris restaurant to serve in the UN's humanitar-
ian efforts.

Penny had invited Chad to eat with her colleagues after
learning that he and the SEALs were living on MREs. She
would have liked to have invited the entire platoon over, but
Dr. Bouchier rightfully figured it would be too big a strain
on their food supply. He was absolutely correct. If the Brigands had come to eat, they would have easily left the UN
personnel on half rations.

The relief workers were polite but reserved toward the
SEAL. These were hard-core, experienced people who were
already anti-militaristic before leaving their native lands to
serve humanity abroad. After enduring countless experiences of seeing people in the depths of absolute misery and
despair, it was not surprising that their pacifist tendencies
had been reinforced. This was mainly because much of this
misery had been caused by military actions. Consequently,
they had developed an animosity toward the soldiery of even
democratic nations.

The dining experience was a pleasant one for Chad and
Penny, who found it a good opportunity to swap some more

news about their old haunts. Although both had been away from home for a long time, they had garnered snippets of information through exchanges of letters with family and friends.

THE COUNTRYSIDE
2010 HOURS LOCAL

CHAD Murchison and Penny Brubaker walked side by side but did not make any attempts to hold hands. Although there was no real danger, Chad had strapped on his pistol belt with the 9-millimeter weapon, loaded with fifteen rounds and one in the chamber. There was always the chance that some disgruntled Dharyan still held a grudge about the young sex slaves. Chad's latest experiences in Afghanistan had taught him that Pashtuns were an unpredictable, wildly emotional people.

Neither young person talked much during the initial minutes of the stroll, and Penny would glance at Chad with fond nervousness from time to time. Finally she blurted out, "It was a big mistake of me to take up with Cliff."

Chad shrugged. "What the hell? He was a lot better looking than I. I couldn't blame you at the time."

"There are different types of handsomeness," Penny said. "You were a cute boy, Chad." She sighed. "Oh m'God, I was such a stupid girl."

"Pardon my cliché," Chad said, "but it's all water under the bridge. He was a varsity football hero and an older fellow. I accepted it and got on with my life."

"He was a self-centered egotist," Penny said. "The fact he came from a wealthy family was the only thing that kept him from becoming a complete loser when his days of athletic glory came to an end."

"What happened to him?" Chad asked, not really giving a damn.

"His parents stuck him in a do-nothing job in the insurance

company where his dad was the CEO. They completely dominated his life, and I knew that was what would happen to me. His mother actually began planning the wedding without allowing any input from my own mom or me. After three months of that, I broke the engagement."

"I guess you knew what was best," Chad remarked.

"I went back to Boston to find you," she said. "I . . . I really wanted to see you, Chad. But I learned you'd joined the Navy and had become a SEAL. I was going to write you, but it occurred to me that you might not want me to."

Once more a surge of the old romantic feelings flooded into Chad's heart. The emotions were triggered by the revelation that she had come back to Boston to find him. It was as if he had taken a giant leap back in time. His mind and passions removed him from the present.

He stopped, then turned toward her. Penny looked at him expectantly. Chad took her in his arms and kissed her. This wasn't like the affectionate pecks he used to give; it was a full kiss with his arms tightening, drawing her closer. When he gently and reluctantly loosened the lip lock, she pressed her face into his chest. Chad noticed she was weeping.

"What's the matter, Penny?"

"I'm not a virgin," she sobbed. "Cliff was so insistent one night, and—"

Chad, whose first time had been in a Tijuana whorehouse, gently placed his hand under her chin and raised her face. He kissed her again. "Water under the bridge."

Then the hormones really kicked in.

CHAPTER 23

BOREDOM and frustration weighed heavily on the Brigands. The rifle platoon from the 101st Airborne Division was taking care of overall security as well as maintaining defensive patrols around the area. The SEALs' watch bill shrunk to having only one man on duty at the CP except for Frank Gomez's commo watch. Unless an emergency situation flared up, the SEALs had nothing to do.

This was bad enough under normal circumstances, but Brannigan's Brigands had just come through that series of harrowing experiences that included the battle near the Wadi Khesta Valley when they were certain their deaths were imminent. Their subconscious minds still reeled from those incidents.

Bad episodes of flashbacks come out of such ordeals.

Consequently, Brannigan knew the platoon had to be kept busy at vigorous, demanding tasks to challenge them both physically and mentally. He quickly established a ball-busting PT program that consisted of endless repetitions of calisthenics that left the men breathing hard and sweating profusely. They were given time to get a gulp or two of water, then the day's workout culminated in a fast-paced five-mile gallop complete with chants done in cadence. An activity like that could relieve stress better than any of James Bradley's pills.

After getting the men good and tired, the two chief petty officers conducted a series of classes on basic military subjects. It was not unlike preseason camp in the NFL, when the fundamentals were reviewed to keep old skills sharp and ready for the coming season's struggle on the gridiron.

The only guys exempted from the programs were the ones who stood CP and commo watch.

BRANNIGAN'S CP
0930 HOURS LOCAL

LIEUTENANT Wild Bill Brannigan had been alerted via LASH by Bruno Puglisi, who was on duty at the CP. "You got some visitors coming, sir. One of 'em is the UN interpreter guy and the others is them ragheads whose asses we kicked yesterday. There ain't but three of 'em."

"How does their mood seem, Puglisi?"

"They ain't carrying any sticks or nothing," Puglisi replied. "I'll alert the senior chief and have the guys standing by."

"Carry on," Brannigan said. He buckled his pistol belt around his waist and stepped through the tent flap. He could see the four men walking toward him. The interpreter gave a friendly wave as they approached.

"What can I do for you?" Brannigan asked when they had arrived. He recognized the clan leader Bashar Dahrain.

"Dr. Bouchier has asked me to escort these gentlemen to you," the interpreter said. "They wish to inquire as to the status of their women who were flown away."

"Tell 'em the women are gone forever," Brannigan said. "They should have understood that already."

This led to a murmured exchange between the interpreter and Dahrain. The interpreter spoke to Brannigan. "Mr. Dahrain says his people are very sad because the women are gone."

"Ask him why," Brannigan said. "We know they planned on killing 'em."

"This is a sensitive situation, Lieutenant," the interpreter cautioned. "We mustn't insult these Dharyans."

"All right," Brannigan said. "Tell him that they were all sick as hell and had to be taken away. They're all probably going to die from being repeatedly raped over the better part of a year. Maybe that'll satisfy the rotten bastards."

The interpreter smiled. "I shall be more diplomatic, Lieutenant. I shall tell them that the women are not expected to live long because their ill treatment. With your permission, I will quote you as saying you believe it is God's will."

"Sure," Brannigan said. "You tell 'em that."

The interpreter turned to Dahrain, speaking in a formal, solemn manner. The clan chief exchanged a few words with his companions. All nodded to indicate acceptance of the American's pronouncement. Then they faced Brannigan and salaamed. The Dharyan group walked away.

"They have acknowledged the situation," the interpreter said. "Their honor is satisfied."

"Piss on their honor."

"At any rate," the interpreter said, "you will happy to know that the young women are now in a place of safety."

"What will happen to them?" Brannigan asked.

"They are more than likely illiterate," the interpreter said. "The UN will provide schooling and see that they are settled somewhere in the refugee system. With any luck, some of them may find nice boys to marry." Then he added, "But not Muslim lads, hey?"

"No," Brannigan said. "Not Muslim lads."

COMMO TENT
1500 HOURS LOCAL

FRANK Gomez's commo duties were not too demanding. After the morning PT, he had nothing to do but monitor the receiver of the Shadowfire AN/PSC-5 radio for the rest of the day. So far there had been nothing but the hissing of empty air.

Now, as he sat beside the equipment reading, Frank's head began to nod. He looked forward to the afternoon naps, deciding that when he retired from the Navy he would sleep no less than twenty hours a day to make up for all the slumber he lost while in the service. Suddenly the platoon's call sign came through, breaking into his dozing, and he came instantly awake. As usual the message came in encoded five-letter word groups. Frank took them down rapidly, wondering what the hell he would be reading when he decoded the rather lengthy missive. After SOCOM signed off, it took him another twenty minutes to change the word groups into intelligible English. When he finished, he grinned to himself.

The mission was officially ended.

Brannigan's Brigands would be exfiltrated and returned to the amphibious base in Coronado within seventy-two hours. There was also some data about the cached equipment that had been uncovered on West Ridge, along with the melancholy news that the bodies of Petty Officer First Class Adam Clifford and Petty Officer Third Class Kevin Albee had been disinterred. After a stop at the U.S. Army mortuary unit in Kuwait, the remains had been shipped to the two dead SEALs' hometowns.

Frank hurried from the commo tent to the CP.

UN CAMP
1630 HOURS LOCAL

CHAD Murchison walked through the camp, looking for Penny Brubaker. The tents were white, with the big blue letters "UN" stenciled across the tops, and the brightness of the canvas structures gave him an instinctive feeling of uneasiness. They attracted the eye too much for a young man who had been trained to always use camouflage when he was in an OA.

He saw a young blond woman hurrying past with a stack of VCR tapes under her arm. Chad called out, "Excuse me, please."

The woman stopped and looked at him with a slight smile. *"Wie bitte?"*

"Entschuldigen Sie," he said, noting she had spoken to him in German. *"Ich bin ein Freund von Penny Brubaker. Und—"*

She interrupted him by turning and pointing at a tent and speaking English. "She is over there."

"Thank you," Chad said.

He hurried to the canvas structure and stopped, not sure if he should enter or not. He decided to call out. "Penny!"

He heard a rustle inside, then she appeared. "Chad! What a nice surprise."

"Can I talk to you? It won't take long."

"Of course, darling," she said, taking his arm.

They walked past the clinic and out into the area between the compound and the SEAL bivouac. "We're going back Stateside," Chad said. "SOCOM has scheduled us to leave in three days."

"Well," Penny said in a resigned tone. "Well, we knew we were going to have to face up to that sooner or later. Our UN team will be here for a while. They're talking about setting up a semi-permanent mission here. They have to make a study first to make sure it is a safe enough area."

"That's a good idea," Chad said. "The Al Qaeda might be lurking nearby waiting for the American military to leave."

"Anyway, Chad," Penny said, "we never had a serious discussion about where we stood."

"I guess we didn't," Chad said. "The other evening we obviously took up where we left off back in college."

Penny smiled. "We didn't leave off making love. That was something new. Our relationship is a lot more grown-up now, Chad." She looked at him to make sure he sensed the seriousness in her words. "What are your future plans?"

Chad shrugged. "At the moment I want to stay in the SEALs. The idea of going back to the civilian world isn't that appealing at this particular juncture of my life. I don't think I'd fit in back there."

"The last time I visited your parents," she said, "they were expecting you to return to school and get your degree. Then they would find you a position in the family banking system."

"I don't think I could handle that," Chad said. "Not now. Not after everything I've been through."

"Maybe if you became an officer, your family would be more accepting of your naval career."

"I don't want to be a fucking officer—whoops. We enlisted men just naturally say that," Chad said. "Anyhow, if I got a commission I'd have to leave the SEALs to follow the Officer Career Program. That would mean I would eventually become a headquarters puke. If I can't be a SEAL, I don't want to stay in the Navy."

"Chad, I'll go wherever you go," Penny said seriously. "Even if you remain an enlisted man, we would have our trusts to augment your Navy pay. We'd live in the best parts of town in a really nice house. It wouldn't be difficult for us to afford a housekeeper and cook."

Chad thought of how that would segregate him from his buddies. He would become the "rich guy" in the platoon. Right now none of the Brigands gave his former privileged civilian existence much thought or consideration. "I'd be gone a lot."

"I don't care," Penny said. "I could be a good Navy wife."

Suddenly Chad felt she was intruding into his life, putting

his friendships in jeopardy and threatening a lifestyle he had learned to love. And she seemed girlish and immature to him now. This sudden flash of negativity surprised him, especially when it was directed toward a girl he once worshipped and dreamed of as his wife.

Penny frowned. "Why aren't you saying anything, Chad?"

"I think we should stay in touch and keep all this under consideration," he said. "We're still young and have the luxury of time on our side." He checked his watch. "I've got to go. I'm on the second dog watch at the CP."

"What in the world is a dog watch?" she asked.

"The dog watches are two hours each between sixteen- and twenty-hundred hours," Chad explained. "It keeps you from having watch at the same time every day. It's also when the evening meal is served aboard ship."

"But you're not on a ship," Penny pointed out.

"But we're in the Navy, so we follow naval tradition." He looked at his watch again. "I have to go, but I'll come off watch at twenty-hundred. Can we go for another walk tonight?"

"All right."

"Let's make love again, Penny," he urged, with more feelings of horniness than romantic affection.

She nodded yes and smiled at him, yet she felt a sudden nagging uneasiness. She had always been able to manipulate boys, especially Chad. But somehow she sensed things had changed where the SEAL was concerned.

C-130 AIRCRAFT
OVER THE MID-ATLANTIC OCEAN
12 SEPTEMBER
0930 HOURS LOCAL

THE debriefing at Station Bravo in Bahrain had taken more time than expected. The Army's Special Forces were planning some operations in the area of the ravines, and their A-Teams scheduled for the mission had a plethora of questions. All this had to be taken care of in Isolation, where the platoon performed the functions of assets. The SEALs were sympathetic to their brothers-in-arms and presented a thorough briefing along with sketch maps to help out the soldiers. They gave dire warning of the shortage of water in the OA. None of Brannigan's Brigands envied the Green Berets for the ordeal they faced.

Now sitting in his usual spot in the aircraft, next to the cockpit, Brannigan relaxed back into the roar of the four engines, his mind turning off the sound as he reflected on this, the platoon's first mission. The results were excellent. Even though they were unable to link up with the defector as in the original OPORD, they destroyed two unruly warlords who had the potential of aiding Al Qaeda operatives in Afghanistan. It was a damn shame that Kevin Albee and Adam Clifford were KIA.

The Skipper glanced over to where Senior Chief Buford Dawkins and Chief Matt Gunnarson sat napping. They were the best chiefs in the Navy as far as Lieutenant Wild Bill Brannigan was concerned. The two had the uncanny ability to anticipate just about everything that happened. At no time were they stumbling around in confusion; instead, they reacted quickly to unexpected incidents in a timely manner. Lieutenant Jim Cruiser had been a laid back 2IC, but that was nothing against him. Some guys just aren't real emotional or verbose, but he was always effective and quick-thinking.

Chad Murchison seemed withdrawn where he sat by himself in the midst of the webbed seating. The whole platoon knew he'd taken up with a girl who had once dumped him for another guy. From the way Chad was talking, it was evident to everyone that there was an aura of uncertainty about their romance. No doubt some lingering anger over the old romance still troubled the SEAL. That was something the two kids would have to work out.

The Odd Couple were both napping; Puglisi, Connie Concord, Guttorm Olson, Milly Mills and Joe Miskoski were playing poker at the rear of the fuselage, and the clever Puglisi seemed to be pulling in the most pots. James Bradley was inventorying his medical kit while Frank Gomez, like Chad, was lost in deep thought. He was thinking about his wife and child, no doubt.

Brannigan knew that later on the whole bunch would either be napping or reading some of the paperback books left over from the package sent up to them from Kabul. Brannigan laughed without sound in the pounding of the engines when he remembered that most of the novels were adventure books. It was hard to conceive guys who had plenty of excitement and danger in their lives wanting to read fictional accounts of made-up characters and their escapades.

Brannigan checked his watch, then turned his reverie to his wife Lisa. He wondered if it was all over between them. He couldn't blame her if she wanted a divorce, especially after the incident of flinging that pilot over the hors d'oeuvre table. But he'd like to give things another try. Of course she might have already found another guy. She was in daily contact with plenty of eligible bachelors who would appreciate her sexiness and beauty. The thought of her being with someone else stung Brannigan emotionally enough to cause a wave of sadness and regret to sweep over him. If Lisa now preferred someone else, the guy would probably be a pilot. It was better that way for her. Brannigan loved Lisa enough to want her happiness to come first. And she sure as hell couldn't be on cloud nine married to Wild Bill of the U.S. Navy SEALs.

The Skipper yawned, and his eyes slowly closed. Within moments he was fast asleep.

CHAPTER 24

BRANNIGAN entered the club at the front door, cutting across the foyer to go directly to the bar. He slid onto a stool, ordered a vodka tonic and sat tapping his fingers impatiently until it was served. He downed the libation in three quick swallows. "Another, please."

"Yes, sir," the bartender said indifferently. The young sailor was used to pissed-off or stressed-out people quickly knocking back the first drink even that early in the afternoon. He mixed another vodka tonic, this time a little bit stronger, and served it.

Brannigan took a sip, then set the glass down, checking his watch.

He'd called Lisa the day before from McConnell Air Force Base in Wichita, Kansas, during a refueling stop. She'd told him that her squadron would be finishing up their training operation on 15 September, and they should return to North Island by 1400 hours that same day. She said it would be more convenient if she met him at the officers' club between 1700 and 1800. He'd shown up a half hour early to get a little extra lubrication of vodka for their get-together. It occurred to him that instead of their driving home together, she might inform him that the locks on the house had been changed and he wouldn't be able to get in. He would have to find a place to stay in the BOQ.

They had really been on the outs when he went into Isolation back in early August, and he had been unable to speak to her since that time. He knew his confrontation with the mouthy pilot at the squadron party had pretty much demonstrated that their professional rapport had gone to hell along with their marital relationship. Things were bad and showed every potential of getting worse. He dreaded the words he would hear from her. No doubt the announcement of a separation followed by divorce was in the works. When everything was finalized, the BOQ would be his permanent home.

Brannigan shrugged. What the hell? That was where he was living when he first met her. He took another swallow of the cocktail, feeling strange in civilian clothing after the long weeks in the OA. He wore a polo shirt, jeans and loafers. There was not an item of equipment or weaponry either strapped on or hanging off him. The atmosphere of the club was also alien to this man who had only recently been prepared to make a last stand against an overwhelming enemy force. Now he was back in this other world where people existed in a peaceful, ordered environment.

He glanced over at the bartender, who had begun preparing his workstation for the busy hours to come that evening. Brannigan considered the fact that this serviceman worked behind a bar during his duty hours, never stood watch, never went on combat or reconnaissance patrols and never became involved in firefights with crazy-ass mujahideen. He wondered why such a guy would even think about enlisting in the armed forces. He'd be better off at a resort hotel or maybe an upscale bar in a big city somewhere serving wealthy clients while pulling in big tips. The kid wasn't bad looking either. Maybe he'd find some rich old lady who would keep him in fine style.

Brannigan finished his drink and pushed the glass forward to signal for yet another refill. He glanced up in the mirror behind the bar and saw the reflection of Lisa as she walked into the room dressed in her flight suit. He turned on the stool and smiled. "Hey."

"Hey," Lisa replied. She walked up and kissed him on the mouth. "Welcome home."

"Same to you," Brannigan replied. He studied her face, noting that she displayed no animosity. She even seemed glad to see him. "Care for a drink before we leave?"

She smiled. "What's the matter, sailor? Not horny after a long absence? I'm suspicious."

Brannigan grinned. "I just wanted the honor of having a cocktail with the prettiest pilot in the United States Navy."

"I think that would be a guy named Brucie I know of in an F-14 squadron."

"Oh yeah?" Brannigan said. "How about introducing me to him?"

"You haven't been gone *that* long," Lisa said, laughing. "Now shut up and order me a Black Label on the rocks."

Brannigan signaled to the bartender.

BRANNIGAN RESIDENCE
CORONADO, CALIFORNIA
1900 HOURS LOCAL

THE couple's lovemaking had been intense and passionate, but with a touch of tenderness too. Neither spoke a romantic word as they took pleasure in the act, letting their physical actions express the love they felt for each other.

Now, following their custom of having a beer during the post-physical period of sexual intercourse, Brannigan and Lisa sat up in bed, leaning back on pillows propped against the headboard. Neither one spoke as they enjoyed the somatic comfort brought on by a combination of the lovemaking and the beer. It was Brannigan who broke the silence.

"The platoon was in a sort of hairy situation out there a couple of weeks ago."

Lisa looked over at him. This was how Bill always began when he wanted to relate one of his combat experiences that had been particularly dangerous. The man was a master of the understatement. She asked, "What happened?"

"We had our backs to the wall and all of a sudden we got this call over the radio," he said. "It was a Navy aircraft wanting to know if we could use a hand." He tipped up his bottle and drained it, then reached over to the six-pack on the bed stand for another. "It was a Prowler."

"No kidding?"

"No kidding. Just like what you and your squadron fly. He called in some Air Force F-16s to give us some support," Brannigan said. "They saved our asses."

Lisa knew her fright about the incident was belated, but she still felt a stab of nervousness, even though everything had obviously turned out fine. "Well! That was lucky, huh?"

"When the dust settled, I had to admit to myself I felt like the quintessential asshole for being such a shit heel toward your friends."

"They admire you, Bill," she said. "They really do."

"I find that hard to believe."

"My colleagues aren't idiots," Lisa said. "They know you lead a tough life, and they cut you slack. We do it for each other too when one of us is on edge."

"What about that guy I threw over the hors d'oeuvre table?"

She grinned. "I'll admit I was upset about that when it happened. So was everybody else. But we talked about it the next day and everyone agreed he had it coming. The guy's an asshole, Bill. He's an egotistical son of a bitch with a big mouth who's full of himself. You taught him a pretty good lesson." Now she laughed out loud. "God! He looked so fucking stupid with that food all over him."

"I can't remember what he said, but it really pissed me off," Brannigan said. He stretched contentedly. "Anyhow, I'm a lot wiser after those fly guys gave us a hand. My sophomoric attitude toward other branches of the service is fading away. Hell! Everyone does his bit, as our friends the British say. Without each part the whole would fail."

"That's quite a statement coming from a SEAL," Lisa remarked.

"I'll make you a promise," he said. "I'm going to make an extra special effort to be nice to your friends at the squadron functions."

"I'm going to hold you to that," Lisa said, nudging him. "But the next time I'm at a SEAL party, I'm going to throw one of your guys over the hors d'oeuvre table to get even."

Brannigan chuckled. "Do it to Senior Chief Dawkins, okay?"

**BASE CHAPEL
NAVAL AMPHIBIOUS BASE
CORONADO, CALIFORNIA
17 SEPTEMBER
1030 HOURS LOCAL**

A table draped with bunting had been placed in front of the altar. Photographs of Petty Officer First Class Adam Clifford and Petty Officer Third Class Kevin Albee had been set up on it along with two display boards. Each bore the awards, decorations and qualification badges the two SEALs had earned in training and combat.

The pews in the small building were completely filled. The survivors of Brannigan's Brigands sat along the front. The wives of Lieutenant Bill Brannigan, Petty Officer Michael Concord, Petty Officer Frank Gomez, and Petty Officer Gutsy Olson were among the group. Salty and Dixie Donovan; Commander Thomas Carey, N3 operations officer; Lieutenant Commander Ernest Berringer, N2 intelligence officer; and other personnel and families of the base SEAL teams filled the rest of the seats. The chaplain had just finished his invocation and opening prayers, and now Brannigan walked to the front of the small room. He turned to face the audience.

"We're here this morning to say farewell to our shipmates Adam Clifford and Kevin Albee. They have given their lives in the service of their country, making that most unselfish of all sacrifices that so many fine men and women of the United States Navy have done over countless wars and conflicts in American history. Petty Officer Clifford, as many of you know, spent his boyhood in the nation's capital, where his father served in the Justice Department as a federal attorney. Cliff was a career Navy man, having shipped over for the second time just before his last mission. He was a good man, quiet and steady, who was always at the forefront of the action. He'll be sorely missed by the platoon, and the world is a little poorer now without his presence.

"Petty Officer Kevin Albee demonstrated the unlimited devotion he had for the service when he died risking his life to save his comrades. Without any regard for his own personal safety, he exposed himself to shoot down an enemy helicopter gunship that was strafing our positions on West Ridge. He was killed in this effort that was truly beyond and above the call of duty. I submitted his name for an award of the Silver Star, and I'm happy to report that earlier this morning I received word that this posthumous award has been approved by the Department of the Navy.

"I, as their commanding officer, am saddened by the loss of those brave men. My grief is eased somewhat by the pride I have from serving with them and other fine men of the United States Navy's SEALs. For that honor I shall be eternally grateful."

Brannigan ended his discourse and went back to his place beside Lisa. Lisa, wearing the service dress blue uniform of her rank, reached over and took her husband's hand.

Next, Cliff and Kevin's two fire team leaders, Lieutenant James Cruiser and Chief Matthew Gunnarson, came

up together, and each made additional remarks in regards
to two fine shipmates who gave their lives so far away from
their native land while serving and protecting their people.

The memorial ceremony continued with further eulogies
from members of the platoon. When everyone had had a
chance to express his sense of loss, the chaplain brought the
event to a close with a final prayer and a blessing to the con-
gregation.

Now, with the final honors having been bestowed on
fallen comrades, it was time for Brannigan's Brigands to return to duty.

FOULED ANCHOR TAVERN
CORONADO, CALIFORNIA
2145 HOURS LOCAL

A few of Brannigan's Brigands gathered at the tavern for
what they termed an After Action Wrap-Up, not realizing
they were establishing a tradition that would continue as
long as the platoon was carried on the active rolls of the
United States Navy.

They pushed a couple of tables together at the rear of the
place, and the Odd Couple, Milly Mills, Joe Miskoski,
Bruno Puglisi, James Bradley and Chad Murchison were
joined by Salty Donovan for an evening of beer drinking.
The absent members of the Brigands were all the married
men who were home with their wives and children.

The exceptions were bachelors Senior Chief Buford
Dawkins and Chief Matt Gunnarson, who were hotly pursuing a couple of middle-aged cuties they had met in a Chula
Vista bar. Lieutenant Jim Cruiser was living up to his sur-
name by cruising the North Island officers' club for available single women.

Dixie, holding two pitchers by the handles in each of her
hands, set the four servings on the table. She had already
cried herself out over Kevin and Cliff, and was ready to get

on with her life, as were the members of the platoon. She stepped back and gazed down at them. "It looks like Brannigan's Brigands have worked their way into a shipshape outfit."

"Yes, ma'am!" Mike Assad said. "I think we were functioning really good together from the moment our boots touched down on the DZ over there in Afghanistan."

"Yeah," his buddy Dave Leibowitz agreed. "We're ready to take on whatever the Navy throws at us."

James Bradley raised his glass. "Here's to what the future holds for Brannigan's Brigands."

Chad Murchison stood up a bit drunkenly, holding his beer up for a toast. "Allow me to quote some lines written by the poet George Banks. He wrote it a long time ago, but it pertains to us in every way:

> *For the cause that lacks assistance,*
> *For the wrong that needs resistance,*
> *For the future in the distance,*
> *And the good that I can do.*

"That was most profound, Chad," James said.

"Yeah," Bruno agreed. "What was that guy's name again?"

"George Banks," Chad replied.

"No shit?" Joe Miskoski said. "What platoon is he in?"

EPILOGUE

THE three South American diplomats sat in sullen silence at one end of the large conference table. Arturo Sanchez of Bolivia, Patricio Ludendorff of Chile and Luis Bonicelli of Argentina were special envoys from their respective governments. Their mission to the American State Department was one of extreme sensitivity and confidentiality. It was of the utmost importance that the subject to be discussed that day not be revealed to the outside world, particularly to the populations of the emissaries' home countries. Revelations of the conference would cause untold embarrassment to all concerned, not to mention instigating a trio of the bloodiest revolutions in the history of Latin America.

The door to the room opened, and the trio of South Americans snapped their eyes over in that direction. Carl Joplin, PhD, an American undersecretary of state, joined them, taking a seat at the head of the table. "Good morning, gentlemen. Or should I say, *'Buenos días, caballeros'*?"

The three visitors smiled slightly in a subdued manner of greeting.

"I was most surprised to hear from all three of you at the same time," Joplin said. "It is hard to imagine what situation would have brought Argentina, Chile and Bolivia together in what appears to be a common cause."

"Then you realize that only the gravest of circumstances would have brought about this event that you find so electrifying," Ludendorff said.

"Frankly," Joplin said, "I must admit that at this moment I am more than just a little apprehensive. Your grim demeanors do nothing to allay my uneasiness." He leaned back in his chair. "I believe it is obvious that since I know nothing of your mission, I am unable to officially open this diplomatic session in which no agenda has been introduced." He smiled. "Would one of you gentleman kindly do the honors?"

Bonicelli spoke up in the realization that he and his two companions would have to start the ball rolling. "It begins with a fascist Spaniard by the name of Jose Maria de Castillo y Plato."

"Ah!" Joplin exclaimed. "The Far Right enters the picture, hey? I am very familiar with Don Jose Maria and his political background. It appears you are having problems with neo-Nazis in your particular necks of the woods. Is this the case?"

"Not neo-Nazis in the strictest interpretation of the term," Sanchez said. "In this case it is Falangistas, Dr. Joplin. *El señor* Castillo y Plato is a wealthy Spanish officer who had always dreamed of reestablishing a right wing dictatorship in his country. We believe his regime would be even more draconian than that of *el Generalísimo* Francisco Franco."

"A moment please," Joplin said. "As I recall the Falangists were the political party that ran Spain under Franco."

"The same," Ludendorff said. "And since Castillo cannot realize his dream in Spain, he has chosen to establish a new fascist country he is calling Falangía. He has chosen South America for this dubious honor. To be more precise, he wishes to do this in an area where Argentina, Chile and Bolivia come together."

Joplin shrugged. "This is pretty far-fetched, is it not? The whole concept is preposterous."

Sanchez shook his head. "I beg to strongly disagree, sir! Castillo has taken dissident officers and noncommissioned officers of the armed forces of the three countries into his movement. They have looted entire garrisons to get the material and weaponry they need. They are now well equipped, armed and have begun making raids against isolated military posts in the area. These *Falangistas* have hidden camps in the jungles and river country of the territories they occupy. The populations living there are under their command and control."

"I would think," Joplin said, "that if you sent the armies of your nations against these rebels, you could easily crush them."

Ludendorff looked at his two companions, then turned a sad expression on Joplin. "The Latin-American military has always been fond of political adventuring. Consequently, we do not know who to trust in our armed forces. We require outsiders to rid us of this problem."

"To be more precise," Bonicelli said, "the situation requires *fuerzas especiales*—special forces—to defeat the *Falangistas*."

"Let's speak plainly, gentlemen," Joplin said. "You are requesting American military assistance in battling and destroying these fascist revolutionaries, are you not?"

"Precisely," Ludendorff said.

"Then we should get to the specifics and requirements of the situation," Joplin insisted. "Without a detailed analysis of our adversaries, I cannot forward your request to my government."

"As of the moment," Ludendorff said, "they are no more than a detachment."

"A detachment is an ambiguous military term," Joplin said. "It is impossible to determine the makeup of such an organization."

Sanchez sighed. "We do not know their exact numbers, Dr. Joplin. But they have the potential of growing stronger—*mucho más fuerte!*"

"I see," Joplin said. "In that case, I must insist that you pass on to me all the intelligence you have on these fascists. I cannot possibly bring this matter up with my government with no more than sketchy details."

All three South Americans reached under the table for their briefcases crammed with data. Now they could get down to business.

GLOSSARY

2IC: Second in Command
AA: Anti-Aircraft
AFSOC: Air Force Special Operations Command
AGL: Above Ground Level
AKA: Also Known As
ARG: Amphibious Ready Group
ASAP: As Soon As Possible
ASL: Above Sea Level
AT-4: Anti-armor rocket launchers
Attack Board (also Compass Board): A board with a compass, watch and depth gauge used by sub-surface swimmers
BOQ: Bachelor Officers' Quarters
Briefback: A briefing given to staff by a SEAL platoon regarding their assigned mission. This must be approved before it is implemented.
BDU: Battle Dress Uniform
BUD/S: Basic Underwater Demolition SEAL training course
C4: Plastic explosive
CAR-15: Compact model of the M-16 rifle

CATF: Commander, Amphibious Task Force
CNO: Chief of Naval Operations
CO: Commanding Officer
Cover: Hat, headgear
CP: Command Post
CPU: Computer Processing Unit
CPX: Command Post Exercise
CRRC: Combat Rubber Raiding Craft
CS: Tear gas
CSAR: Combat Search and Rescue
CVBG: Carrier Battle Group
DPV: Desert Patrol Vehicle
Det Cord: Detonating cord
Draeger Mk V: Underwater air supply equipment
DZ: Drop Zone
E&E: Escape and Evasion
FLIR: Forward Looking Infrared Radar
FTX: Field Training Exercise
GPS: Global Positioning System
H&K MP-5: Heckler & Koch MP-5 submachine gun
HAHO: High Altitude High Opening parachute jump
HALO: High Altitude Low Opening parachute jump
HE: High Explosive
Head: Navy and Marine Corps term for toilet; called a latrine in the Army
HSB: High Speed Boat
JSOC: Joint Special Operation Command
K-Bar: A brand of knives manufactured for military and camping purposes
KIA: Killed In Action
LBE: Load Bearing Equipment
LSSC: Light SEAL Support Craft
Light Sticks: Flexible plastic tubes that illuminate
Limpet Mine: An explosive mine that is attached to the hulls of vessels
LZ: Landing Zone

M-18 Claymore Mine: A mine fired electrically with a blasting cap

M-60 E3: A compact model of the M-60 machine gun

M-67: An anti-personnel grenade

M-203: A single-shot 40-millimeter grenade launcher

MATC: A fast river support craft

MCPO: Master Chief Petty Officer

Medevac: Medical Evacuation

Mk-138 Satchel Charge: Canvas container filled with explosive

MRE: Meal, Ready to Eat

MSSC: Medium SEAL Support Craft

NAS: Naval Air Station

N2: Intelligence staff

N3: Operations staff

NAVSPECWAR: Naval Special Warfare

NCP: Navy College Program

NFL: National Football League

NVG: Night Vision Goggles

OA: Operational Area

OER: Officer's Efficiency Report

OP: Observation Post

OPLAN: Operations Plan. This is the preliminary form of an OPORD.

OPORD: Operations Order. This is the directive derived from the OPLAN of how an operation is to be carried out. It's pretty much etched in stone.

PBL: Patrol Boat, Light

PC: Patrol Coastal vessel

PDQ: Pretty Damn Quick

PLF: Parachute Landing Fall

PO: Petty Officer (e.g., PO1C is Petty Officer First Class)

PT: Physical Training

RIB: Rigid Inflatable Boat

RPG: Rocket Propelled Grenade

RPM: Revolutions Per Minute

RTO: Radio Telephone Operator
SCPO: Senior Chief Petty Officer
SDV: Seal Delivery Vehicle
SERE: Survival, Escape, Resistance and Evasion
SITREP: Situation Report
SOCOM: Special Operations Command
SOF: Special Operations Force
SOLS: Special Operations Liaison Staff
SOP: Standard Operating Procedures
SPECOPS: Special Operations
Special Boat Squadrons: Units that participate in SEAL
   missions
SPECWARCOM: Special Warfare Command
UN: United Nations
Watch Bill: a list of personnel and stations for the watch
WIA: Wounded in Action

Armored Corps

by
Pete Callahan

West Point graduate Lieutenant Jack Hansen is
stationed near the 38th Parallel in South Korea with the
1st Tank Battalion. They haven't seen any action yet,
but that's about to change.

On Christmas day, North Korea's power-mad dictator
launches a surprise attack, and Hansen and his
battalion of untested warriors must charge into
battle to halt the invasion.

0-515-13932-7

Available wherever books are sold or at
penguin.com

Where the best of the best take to the skies

Dale Brown's
Dreamland

The *New York Times* betselling series
written by
Dale Brown and Jim DeFelice

Dreamland
0–425–18120–0

Dreamland (II): Never Center
0–425–18772–1

Dreamland (III): Piranha
0–515–13581–X

Dreamland (IV): Armageddon
0–515–13791–X

**Available wherever books are sold or at
penguin.com**

J934

Penguin Group (USA) Online

What will you be reading tomorrow?

Tom Clancy, Patricia Cornwell, W.E.B. Griffin,
Nora Roberts, William Gibson, Robin Cook,
Brian Jacques, Catherine Coulter, Stephen King,
Dean Koontz, Ken Follett, Clive Cussler,
Eric Jerome Dickey, John Sandford,
Terry McMillan...

You'll find them all at
penguin.com

*Read excerpts and newsletters,
find tour schedules and reading group guides,
and enter contests.*

Subscribe to Penguin Group (USA) newsletters
and get an exclusive inside look
at exciting new titles and the authors you love
long before everyone else does.

PENGUIN GROUP (USA)
penguin.com/news